# *Love* UNDER QUARANTINE

*NEW YORK TIMES* BESTSELLING AUTHOR
## KYLIE SCOTT

#1 *NEW YORK TIMES* BESTSELLING AUTHOR
## AUDREY CARLAN

Cover Design: Jena Brignola

Cover Image: Brian Kaminski

Editor: Jeanne De Vita

ISBN: 978-1-943340-14-9

We dedicate this book to our readers all over the world.

You matter. We hear your fear. We have it too.

May this love story provide a healing escape,
if only for a little while.

All our love and well wishes,

Kylie & Audrey

# Note to Readers

Hello friends,

First and foremost, we hope this message finds you in good spirits and feeling healthy. As with any book we write, *Love Under Quarantine* will have a lot of real-to-life experiences and some things that are straight up fiction. We took some liberties as every single person has a different experience during their time sheltering in place. However, we did our best to have Evan and Sadie share some of our personal experiences and things we heard, did, said, and lived in order to flatten the curve during the COVID-19 pandemic.

This story is purely fiction. Every city, state, and country will have their own ways of handling a pandemic. We are not experts in this field but did our best to portray a story that's filled with hope, love, and survival during a world tragedy.

We hope you enjoy it.
Thank you.
Kylie & Audrey

# Love UNDER QUARANTINE

# Chapter
## ONE

### QUARANTINE: DAY 1

EVAN

"**T**HEY LOCKED DOWN THE FUCKING CITY, MAN!" I RAGE into my cell phone while pacing my best friend Jake's apartment.

"Ev, bro, relax. I can hear your blood pressure skyrocketing all the way from Africa. And I sincerely doubt that they're locking down San Francisco. It's one of the biggest cities in the world. There's no way the government can close off a city of six million people, not to mention the commuters. You need to..."

"Jake...I swear on my mother's life. The Department of Public Health laid it out, and the governor agreed. There's a stay-at-home order for the entire Bay Area. Rumor's in the press that it's going to go statewide."

"Okay, I understand you're freaked out. You have a lot on your plate." His patronizing tone makes my blood heat.

I fist the hand that's not holding the phone to my ear in a vice-like grip until my fingers turn white. "Freaked out? I'm a sitting duck! If the media finds out where I am, it's over for me. My side of the story hasn't come out and I'm still working with my publicist on the best way to handle the shitshow that is my life right now."

A heavy sigh comes through the line. "Evan, don't be a douche. I'm in Africa fighting HIV/AIDS, malaria, and meningitis—to name a few—from killing hundreds of thousands of people. You will survive a minor inconvenience in the largest free country in the world."

*Shit.* Now I do feel like a douche. I rub my forehead and push my fingers through the dirty blond waves of hair at my crown. "They're calling it coronavirus. I guess it's similar to the flu."

In the background I can hear my friend sifting through some papers. "Yeah, we received the reports from our liaisons about the concerns. It originated in China in a small town called Wuhan. It looks like the World Health Organization received information about it in or around December. Much more serious and contagious than the flu. Seems as though the reports, data, and specifics are emerging daily."

"It's March, man. Why the heck are we just hearing about it now?" I grind out, irritation coating every word.

Another sigh trails through the line. "It's simply not that easy. They can't announce something *could* end up being a pandemic. We'll just have to ride this out and see what's happening. Word is China and Italy are devastated. Most of the world is still figuring out how bad this could get."

"And while all of this is going down, I'm stuck in San Francisco," I offer dryly.

"Stuck? Evan, you play for the Oakland Marauders. Your house is a twenty-minute drive away. It's not like you're stuck in bum-fuck Egypt. Besides, you could do worse than my apartment. It's safe, you're on the twentieth floor, and you've got company. Thanks for watching Gloria, by the way." My best friend chuckles, instantly pissing me off more.

"You mean devil-kitty?" I glare at the orange cat hissing at me from her perch on top of the media center. I swear if that cat jumps off and attacks me, it will lose all nine of its lives taking a swan dive over the balcony.

"That's not nice. She's my pretty-pretty ginger princess. She just misses me, but eventually she'll warm up to you. Give her some of the treats in the top right cabinet near the coffee pot. That will help win her over."

Stomping into the kitchen, I open the cabinet and pull out the cat treats. The second I shake the bag, devil-kitty races into the kitchen and leaps onto the counter like a parkour ninja.

"Jesus Christ! What the fuck, cat?" I jump back while the feline stares me down as if she's demanding that if I give her the treats now and walk away, no one will get hurt. Psycho cat.

Jake's deep laughter fills my ear. Instead of feeding her the treats from my hand, I shake some directly onto the counter a good two feet away from the animal. I'll be keeping my fingers today, thank you very much!

"She's excitable. Wouldn't you be if you were getting a treat?"

"If the treat was a tall blonde with big tits and a bubble butt, yeah. Though that won't be happening any time soon since I'm in lockdown in my best friend's apartment."

"Okay, I'll be right there." Jake murmurs, his voice sounding far away from the phone, as though he's talking to someone else. "Look Ev, I gotta go. I'm sure you'll be fine. I'll check in with you in a couple days. Just lay low. Eventually the truth will come out and your name will be cleared, yeah? Have a little faith."

"Faith?" I huff. "In the press? In my team? Or maybe mankind at large?"

"All of the above. And wash your hands before and after you go out. They're saying this thing has a two-week incubation time frame which means symptoms might not present themselves for up to fourteen days."

"Two weeks! I'll be stuck here for two weeks!" I holler, but he ignores my complaint.

"Be safe. And be nice to my cat! Bye!" He hangs up the phone before I can respond.

Two weeks.

What the hell am I supposed to do for two weeks? I scan the apartment. It has two bedrooms and two baths with an open layout for the kitchen and living room. The kitchen has a small L-shaped bar counter with four stools beneath it. The area where most people would have a kitchen table is set up as Jake's office. A tall, wooden, hutch-style desk stands against the wall, complete with a computer, giant monitor, and an ergonomic chair.

The living room is bachelor chic. Two black leather couches—one a three-seater, the other a loveseat. A few soft throw pillows in a light gray tone are scattered along the surface. An afghan with a pattern in shades of black, gray, white, and light blue that looks like a Native American design rests across the back of the large couch. There's a glass end table with chrome edges between the couches. A matching rectangular table sits in the center. A bright blue lamp with a white shade sits on the end table. A cigarette lamp stands tall and proud in the corner near a single large potted plant—though I'm not sure the plant is real. Will definitely have to check that out or that sucker will die a slow death during my two-week stay. Across from the couches is a state of the art media center. Fifty-five-inch TV, Xbox, stereo, DVD player...the whole nine.

Fuck. I hope it's only two weeks that I need to be here. I mean how long can it take for doctors to figure this type of thing out? Jake said it landed in China last year and it's now mid-March. Another thing to look into while I'm waiting to see if my entire career flushes right down the toilet.

Everything I've worked for—gone.

All it took was a well-timed photo delivered to the media and the subsequent search of my locker, and my head ended up on the chopping block.

Drugs and doping. After everything I've put into my career. All the blood, sweat, and tears tossed out the door like yesterday's garbage. Worst part, I had no business being in that room or at that party in the first place. I don't even know who took the picture and sold me out. Not really. The media refuses to release their source, but it sure as hell looks really bad.

Half the team believes the lies. And why wouldn't they? I'm a player and partier in every sense of the word. At least I had been in the past. More recently, after turning twenty-nine, I started to re-evaluate my life. Made some long-needed changes. The first of which was to quit boozing and partying it up with women barely of age. The second, focus solely on the game.

I was in prime shape. Treated my body like a temple and I worshipped it in the gym six days a week, two hours a day, if not more. I'm in the best shape of my life. And career-wise, I'm the best and highest paid running back there is. My last contract was for a cool fourteen mil and until this broke I expected to make even more next year.

Who knows where I'll be now?

One of the only rules in the brotherhood of football is you do not chemically enhance your body. We get there on sheer will and our own grit. Being suspected of not only doing drugs at a party, but doping before games? Sacrilege.

Being the fastest running back in the league last season was my claim to fame. Now it's worthless. Even if I can prove my innocence, I may always be under the microscope. This is a guilty until proven innocent situation, not the other way around.

Not that I had any say in the matter. I remember drinking heavily that night. Sharing some laughs with the guys. The coach snuck off to get a little side action with one of the cheerleaders and I was trying to be the cool one, Levi and I hanging out with the other chicks he brought. We all partied hard together. Drank like fishes, played pool and cards, danced with some of the groupies. Nothing out of the ordinary. Eventually I was led to a bedroom by a hot chick. I don't even remember her name. The last thing I remember was her straddling me on the bed. She offered me a glass filled with what I assumed was whiskey. I drank from it. Then it was lights out.

When I woke the next day, I found myself in a strange bed with a gnarly hangover. Unfortunately, that was not an uncommon occurrence in the past, even though I'd been staying pretty straightlaced most of the past year.

At the time I went home, crashed, and slept it off. Woke up to a media shit storm—my half-naked body passed out on a bed with booze and drug paraphernalia all around me on the front page of the newspaper and the leading story on every media source from here to Timbuktu.

Coach called me into his office the next day. Ripped me a new one before taking the team risk assessment manager and security to search my locker. At the time I thought nothing of it. I didn't have anything to hide. Until the security team pulled out a kit with syringes and some bottles filled with liquid I'd never seen before. The words anabolic-androgenic steroids caught my attention though. Not to mention Coach's.

I promised that I wasn't doing drugs and definitely not doping. The team doctor took tons of my blood to do his own tests. Though he did mention that steroids usually leave the system within twenty-four hours. However, he also took hair and urine. Those tests would prove more conclusive, but took some time. Didn't matter.

The press was waiting for me when I left the arena.

And now here I am, sitting in my lifelong best friend's apartment licking my wounds and staying out of sight.

The world is falling apart with the threat of a pandemic and

I'm under quarantine in a city I'm not that familiar with. In a building I only visited when Jake was in town. With a neighbor on one side that plays their TV so loud I don't even need to watch the daytime soaps to know what's happening. And the other neighbor is currently doing…what the fuck is that? Yoga maybe? I look out the glass window to see a tall and curvy blonde facing the view, standing with one bare foot on the knee of the opposite leg with her hands in a prayer position over her head—all while balancing on one leg.

I can't see her face at all, but her body is bangin'. Curves for days, in all the right places.

No, no, no, no! The last thing I need is another freakin' blonde ruining my life. The girl I took to bed that night at the party was blonde too. Jesus, I sure have a type.

I grind my teeth as my phone rings. I glance down and find it's my publicist. Thank God!

"Yeah, tell me you've got a plan," I clip into the phone.

Polly aka Pauline Frederickson is the leading spin doctor for sports celebrities. When I started running the ball into the endzone multiple times a game and my pay kept increasing, she sought me out. Now she's my ace in the hole.

"Well hello to you too, Evan."

"Polly, cut to the chase, will ya? I'm stuck in San Francisco and the city just went on lockdown. I'm in no mood for niceties." I open the sliding door to let in some fresh air and press my forehead to the cool glass. The breeze chills my overheated skin instantly.

"Well, I've got mostly bad news. Coach says it's going to take some time to clear you of any wrongdoing. You'll have to be willing to share the blood, urine, and hair analysis results with the media. The picture says a thousand words, but the steroids…"

"Excuse me!" All the Bay Area ocean winds in the world couldn't cool down the blazing ire firing through my system.

"He says this makes the team and him look really bad. And they can't afford these types of risks."

"Are you kidding me! I make the team look bad? The coach is a cheating bastard! Parties like a rockstar. And yet he has an iron-clad contract! What about mine?"

"I understand you're upset, but we're going to figure this out. I promise."

"This is insane! And half the team believes this shit?" I run my hands through my hair. "Those men are like brothers to me!"

"I'm sorry, Evan. These things happen. And unfortunately, with your recent past and the pictures of you sprawled on a bed with booze and drugs clearly visible, there's not a lot we can say without proof."

"Jesus, I don't know what to do. Someone is setting me up! What do you think?" I suck in a huge breath, trying my damndest to calm my racing heart and ease the dread filling my mind.

"Right now? Lay low. Let a little bit of this blow over. This coronavirus thing everyone is talking about is taking center stage in the media. It's going crazy here in New York. You know how these things go. Wait a bit and let another jacked-up story take the front page. Then if we're lucky and you stay out of the press, this will all fade, and we can work it out directly with your agent and team."

"I'll do whatever you say. Maybe you're right. A little time away from it all will do some good. Though I'm not sure what the hell I'm going to do all day in a small apartment in downtown San Francisco with a stay-in-home order from the governor."

"Do what everyone else is doing," she offers unhelpfully.

"And that would be?" I chuckle and watch as the blonde stretches her arms out in a T, legs in a wide stance, and bends over giving me an incredible view of her rounded ass. I bite down on my lip and squint to get a better look.

"Take up reading, lifts weights, do a puzzle, surf the net, and the best and most consistent way to burn time…Netflix and chill."

"Netflix and chill?"

"Yep! I recommend *Point of Interest* or *Lucifer* or maybe *True Blood* if you're into vampires."

"Vampires?" I shake my head and rub my palm over my tired face. "I'm gonna let you go."

"Call you in a few days unless something else comes up."

"Great, thanks."

"And Evan?"

"Yeah?"

"You haven't been taking steroids. Have you?" Her voice is direct and devoid of emotion.

My stomach sinks. Even my own publicist is questioning the truth. What the hell does that say about me?

"No, I didn't."

"Then what's in the past is in the past. Now, we move forward." Her tone is chipper and upbeat. The exact opposite of everything I'm currently feeling.

"Great. Thanks, Polly. We'll be in touch."

"Take care of yourself, Evan. Remember, Netflix and chill. No media sightings."

"Aye aye, captain!" I salute the air even though she can't see it.

Clicking off the phone, I stare out over the view. My eyes scan the tall buildings and the lack of cars driving up and down the streets. I'd rather look at the beautiful woman next door.

Taking a gander at the balcony to my immediate left I'm sad to see the blonde with the spectacular ass is no longer there.

Guess Netflix and chill it is.

♡

## SADIE

Okay, reposition feet hip-distance apart and centered on the mat. Inhale and let it all go on the exhale. I look over the balcony across the barren city and try to find perspective. What did the teacher say? Set your intention? My intention is to maintain a modicum of good health and to not go insane during self-isolation. Fingers crossed on both fronts. Getting some work done wouldn't be a bad idea either.

"They locked down the fucking city, man!" The voice blocks me from finding my zen spot. Some big blond dude is pacing back and forth in the neighboring apartment. Guess we've all got to get our exercise one way or another. A nice quiet doctor owns the place, but he's overseas right now. No idea who this guy is. The new cat sitter, maybe? If so, I hope Gloria housetrains him quickly because all of this shouty behavior is not okay. Not if I have to share a wall with him for the next few weeks.

My new neighbor's voice lowers to a more tolerable level and I take a deep, calming breath before moving into my next pose. Much better. Despite having questionable balance and being new to this whole yoga thing, I'm not doing too badly. It's weird how quiet the city is with everything on lockdown. Peaceful, almost.

"Two weeks! I'll be stuck here for two weeks!" he rants once more.

Ugh.

Due to the architect's penchant for floor to ceiling windows—perfect for letting in the light—I have quite the view of my new neighbor's performance. Much angst. Such woe. Like we're not all going to go stir crazy during lock in. Even if it has only just started. I for one can't wait to see how many divorces and break-ups this causes. Call it morbid curiosity. Though, being a romance writer, my mind would be better served dwelling on the possibilities for true love in this situation.

A random casual hook-up turning into so much more due to weeks of forced interaction? Roommates bonding over newly revealed shared interests? Nuh. Roommates entering into a sex pact to stave off boredom! Now that could work. Broken beds and broken hearts. That's how to get things done. With the requisite happy ever after at the end, of course.

"Excuse me!" he shouts, shoving a frustrated hand through his head of thick, wavy, dark blond hair. New phone call, I think. After all, you can't yell at the same person *all* day long. How tedious would that be?

Call me distractible, but watching him is actually a hell of a lot more interesting than perfecting my Downward Dog or doing yet another inventory of my pantry. Damn Oreos. I could have sworn I had another package. Day one and I'm already out of my favorite snack. Just bring on the apocalypse already. Without Oreos my life is already functionally over.

"Are you kidding me!" The man sure has a set of lungs on him. Unfortunately, at this point, he about-faces and strides back into the apartment. Still yelling, of course, though I can't quite make out what he's saying.

On the plus side, in those blue jeans, his ass is a thing of wonder. Honest to God. In less pandemic-y times, I'd charge my friends a bottle of wine to come over and witness the beauty of that thing. So tight. So nice. I lick my lips. Impressively broad shoulders beneath his T-shirt too. When he paces back to the front of the apartment, I'm presented with a strong jawline, high forehead, and a nose that could be slightly crooked. At least, it will be in the book. Readers dig that shit. The hint of a complicated past with a dash of violence thrown in for good measure. Ideally, he'd have broken it defending a small child or rescuing puppies. A combination of the two, perhaps?

Yes, it's a definite. Apart from the anger management issues, this guy is officially hot stuff. Not that I'm after an actual love interest. Just inspiration for the hero of my next book.

Which is when it hits me…big buff dude reveals surprisingly sensitive side to sexy single introverted neighbor during quarantine. Hmm. It has possibilities. I stop procrastinating and move onto the next pose, arms out in a T, legs wide, and a slow bend at the waist. I exhale, pondering the plot idea along with the thickness of his thighs. The way the denim lovingly embraces every inch of his musculature. It's like it's on a loop playing over and over in my head. Okay, maybe I'm a little sex starved. He can feature in my masturbatory fantasies as well. After all, he's that kind of can-do, helpful guy. Or at least, he is in my mind. And that's where the man will stay. At a safe and appropriate distance. For both the virus and my heart.

Back to building my hero. What color should his eyes be? Blue as the sky on a cloudless summer day? Green as the first leaves of spring. Brown as…I don't know, something that's brown. Obviously, my brain is sugar starved due to insufficient snacks. A situation that needs to be remedied ASAP. The Reece's Pieces were meant to be for tomorrow, but oh well. These are trying times and sacrifices must be made. I also have notes to make. Lots and lots of them.

With a little pep in my step, I roll up my mat, tuck it under my arm, and sneak one last glance at my neighbor. His forehead is resting against the glass window, cell phone plastered to his ear. He seems defeated, sorrowful. Now I'm wondering if something happened to him. Could it be related to the virus? Silently I wish the dude well, along with hoping he keeps his volume down. I've got a great first chapter to write, and Mama needs a snack.

# Chapter
## TWO

## QUARANTINE: DAY 2

SADIE

"No, Mom, you can't do that. You need to stay home." I hold my cell in one hand while rubbing at the tension building in my temples with the other. "The idea is to only go out once a week for groceries, and even then you need to wash your hands before and after as though you were a doctor getting ready for surgery. Why don't you stress-bake cookies instead? I know your German coffee cake is great, but you've got plenty of other supplies to perfect a new masterpiece of epic baking proportions."

"But it's your father's favorite," she whines.

"Pretty sure you're also his favorite, so having you alive and well is kind of important. You can't expect me to listen to him go on and on about golf after you die, leaving me his auditory victim. That's just cruel, Mom."

She sighs heavily, probably weighing the pros and cons of her daughter's advice and finding something lacking in my lecture.

When did parents become so high maintenance? And apparently bulletproof. Just yesterday Dad went out for new gardening gloves despite the repeated warnings from the government and every medical professional and scientist under the sun. They were bored, and fair enough—I'm bored too—but holy cow. I was terrified one of them would catch the virus over something as stupid as needing an emergency Snickers bar.

"At least you have a house and yard. I'm stuck in an apartment." So I'm not above doing a little whining myself. Such is life. It's been raining on and off all day. The sky is gray and miserable overhead. Perfect weather for hunkering down and living in sweats. Pity about the small bout of cabin fever. "I know you're a grown adult and I don't mean to lecture you—"

"Yes, you do," she retorts immediately.

She's not wrong. I want to scare her. Them. They need to heed the warnings. "Mom, you're in the most at-risk age group. It's so important you and Dad be careful."

"Have you heard from Sean lately?"

I look to heaven. It's entirely possible my parents love my ex-boyfriend more than I ever did. They certainly aren't above using him to stop me from lecturing them about the dangers of the pandemic. Sean plays golf and made partner at his accountancy firm. Sporty in a way that appealed to Dad and solvent in a way my mother could admire. Too bad he is boring as all hell out of the sack. Also, since he went through an ugly divorce prior to us dating, his views on relationships are tainted to say the least. I'm surprised the man didn't insist on me signing a pre-nup on the first date.

"No," I said. "So much no, Mom. The no is everywhere, spilling onto the floor, climbing up the walls…"

She huffs. "There's no need to get dramatic, Sadie. Sean is a very nice man."

"Sorry." I am not sorry. That is a blatant lie. "*Sean and Sadie.* That sounds bad anyway. For all future relationships I'm going to set a definite anti-alliteration rule. It's just too confusing. Imagine if we'd moved in together and gotten monogrammed towels. We'd never know which one belonged to whom."

"Now you're just being silly. Are you sure you don't want to come home to Texas for this self-isolation thing?"

Good Lord. She truly does not get it. "We're not supposed to travel and I'm fine here. Really."

"Fine. Go do some work. And don't forget to eat properly!"

"Yes, Mother. I love you, Mother." I glance at my snack cabinet planning my next treat. I'm thinking M&M's this time.

At this, she laughs and hangs up on me. Just about sums up our family dynamic. A dash of humor, a pinch of obligation, a spoonful of interference, and a whole heap of love.

The rain stops and the air grows cool. I step out onto the balcony and look out over the city. Still preternaturally still with everyone on lockdown. Only the occasional vehicle in the street. People walking the recommended six feet apart carrying what I assume are grocery bags. Somewhere in the distance, laughter echoes. I hear the faint murmur of a truck a couple blocks away.

And then *he* had to go and make his presence known. The new neighbor.

Despite the average weather, he sits attempting to sun himself on a deck chair, sunglasses on and T-shirt off. You'd think he was at the beach or something. Boy, does he have some pecs on him. With a bottle of beer in hand, he sings the words to Kenny Rogers's "The Gambler." Loud. And given his limited vocal talents, way too proudly.

"Oh God, you're getting the words all wrong." I wrinkle my nose. Not that he could hear my constructive criticism with his earbuds in. Probably a good thing. "And you definitely missed that note. Do not give up your day job, buddy."

"Harsh," he comments, looking at me over the top of his sunglasses.

Oops.

He takes out the earbuds and places them in his lap. For a long moment he just studies me, as if he were waiting for something. Who knows what? Finally, he asks, "I take it you're familiar with the tune?"

"It's one of my father's favorite songs." I shrug one shoulder.

Again, he watches me in silence. Not even a hint of an expression on his handsome face. Dude could definitely beat me at poker.

"Sorry. I didn't mean to disturb your party for one," I mumble dryly.

At this, he chuckles, raising his beer to his lips. His neck is disturbingly alluringly, thick and strong. And the way his throat works up and down, moving with each swallow of his beer… Hmm. I lick my lips.

"You sing it then," he dares.

"Hell no! Unlike you, I know my vocal limitations."

Another chuckle. "What's your name, neighbor?"

"Sadie."

"Hello, Sadie. I'm Evan." He actually has a nice voice when he isn't singing or yelling. Deep and a little rough. The man definitely doesn't lack for confidence, what with the way he tosses aside his sunglasses and blatantly sizes me up. Given I was ogling his bare chest a minute ago, I shouldn't really complain.

"Hi." I raise a hand in welcome. Nope. This isn't awkward at all.

"Want to join me in day drinking, Sadie?"

"Uh, no. Thanks. It's barely midday and I have work to do." A whole book to write in fact, with him as the muse. But there is no need to go into details with him about that. Ever.

"Aw, I see. You're a good girl." He snorts knowingly. Sneers, even. Asshat. As if he knows a damn thing about me. And…his words aren't slurred, but who knows how many brewskis he's imbibed so far.

"And you're kind of obnoxious," I fire off, no longer enjoying our little *tête-à-tête*.

This only makes him laugh harder, his head falling back and arm going over his abs as he lets it fly. Definitely tipsy, if not actually drunk. This kind of shit I do not need. If I wanted to be judged, I'd have continued the call with my mother.

"Nice to meet you, Evan." On that note, I head for the door.

"Wait! Please. I'm sorry." He rises out of the chair and walks to the railing closest to my side. "I didn't mean to make you uncomfortable."

I turn back to him, arms crossed. Waiting.

"If anything, I'm a little lonely with this whole lockdown thing. It's sort of doing my head in, having to stay indoors all the time." He rubs at his golden chest.

I can't help but watch the movement. His chest is massive. A smattering of blond chest hair sprinkled evenly across the expanse in just the right amount. Not too furry or caveman-like, but definitely manly. I bet it's soft. Farther down are eight—yes, eight—visible abs. Who on earth has an eight-pack nowadays? Maybe he's a personal trainer. Hmm… Personal trainer gets locked in an apartment during quarantine, ends up "training" the housekeeper, and they fall in love. I scrunch up my nose again. Too cliché and porn-like. Nah, I'm going back to hot jock.

"You're usually out and about, huh?" I ask.

"Yeah. Training, work, catching up with friends…different things. You know." His smile is small, but seems sincere. "How about you?"

"I normally work from home so it's not quite as big a difference for me. And I love my apartment and the view." It is one of the reasons I didn't move back to Texas after finishing my English degree at Berkeley. I fell for San Francisco. The bay and the bridge and the nightlife and everything. The hills and the trams and the little restaurants down by the water. I adore it all. "Annoying not to be able to just go out and do whatever you want, though."

"It sure is," he agrees.

"I talked to my family and FaceTimed one of my friends earlier, but just going to grab a decent coffee and a pastry or going for a walk or hitting the gym…"

"Tell me about it." When he leans on the railing, the muscles in his shoulders and upper arms flex in a fascinating manner. "I'm usually there a couple of hours a day. Push-ups and sit-ups in the living room don't really have the same effect. There's a treadmill and a bike in the spare room, but it's not the same."

"And we're only on day two."

"Shit. Don't remind me." He runs a hand through the dark blond waves at the top of his head. The layers scatter and fall back in place, like he intended it that way.

"So, you're apartment-sitting for Jake?" I ask. Because I'm nosy. Most of us writers are.

Evan looks away for a moment, taking in the overcast sky and empty city. "Yeah. I, ah…I'm just looking after the place for him while he's overseas working."

"Okay."

His response sounds off somehow, but I'll let it go for now.

A fluffy ginger feline appears and winds herself around his legs. Evan glares down at the animal, his brow deeply furrowed. The man is seriously perturbed.

"Gloria," I coo. "How's the little fur baby?"

He raises a brow. "You like the cat? You want it?" His words are flat and emotionless. He's serious and something about that has me chuckling.

"Give Jake's cat away and he might not be so interested in letting you use his apartment again."

"Hopefully I'm not going to need it again anytime soon." His

18

big shoulders drop as if he's suddenly carrying the weight of the world. "She doesn't even like me. She's just putting on a display for you. Evil little devil-kitty."

"Oh, poor Gloria. She probably misses her daddy." I smile. "You're not a cat person, huh?"

"Apparently not." He grimaces at the cat.

I laugh. The expression of disgust on his face is hilarious. And Gloria just went right on rubbing her sweet little head against his calf muscle without a care in the world. Cats are awesome. All of the attitude in the world and then some. Such champion nappers, too. "I'm allergic or I'd happily have Gloria over for a holiday."

"Why don't you have a dog? You seem like an animal lover."

"Too high maintenance. They need walks and sometimes I'll go ages without going out. If I'm working on something, really in the right headspace for it, then I don't want to have to stop just to take a pooch for a walk."

"They're loyal and fun." He is trying to make it sound more appealing.

"They do dog biscuit farts, Evan."

He throws his head back and laughs. My God, he's pretty. Somewhere low in my belly tenses in the most pleasurable way watching him laugh. Those muscles flexing and moving deliciously. So, apparently my loins still work. Nice to know. Flirting with my new and temporary neighbor, however, would be bad. Unwise. For reasons my lusty brain will figure out any time now.

How the man goes from being a drunken ass to prime eye candy within the space of a few minutes is disconcerting, to say the least. Though, to be fair, I was eyeing up his impressive body before we even exchanged words. All of those hours he spent in the gym showed just fine, thank you very much. Not that I'd ever be interested in a gym rat. Nope. Not me. Not after Sean with his

19

KYLIE SCOTT & AUDREY CARLAN

ironclad routine and high expectations. Constantly working over-time and on call around-the-clock.

Next time I'm going to go for a more free and easy man. Someone I can just relax with who makes me laugh. Someone who doesn't grill me about my 401k. I bet my new neighbor never even eats ice cream. Sure as hell, there isn't an inch of body fat on him. Meanwhile, my ass owes a debt to cookies that can never be repaid.

"Come on, have a drink with me." He smiles boyishly and I can't help but return the grin.

"I have to work." I really need to get more words on the page. My editor and publisher have been hounding me for my next manuscript for months. Only for some reason, my muse has gone kaput. She's been extremely persnickety as of late. Quiet as a mouse. Until this isolation hit and I laid eyes on my new neighbor yesterday while he hollered at assorted people on the phone. Apparently I'm a peeping tom. Who knew? Just last night I completed the entire first chapter of a new novel. Four thousand glorious words on the page. And now, I'm thinking maybe Chapter 2 will entail hot jock having a workout or a shower. I bite down on my lip imagining all that is Evan naked, wet, and in the shower.

My skin heats and I wave a hand in front of my face to help cool me down.

"You just said you work from home. Doesn't that give you the perfect excuse to play hooky? You're under quarantine. Come on, live a little." He waggles his brows before chugging the rest of his bottle.

I purse my lips. "I don't have any beer."

This has him grinning wildly and I swear my heart stops. The man is gorgeous when he's smiling. Bright white teeth. Blue-green eyes. From this distance I still can't tell exactly what color they are. There's a good eight feet between our balconies.

"Well it's a good thing I stocked up. I have plenty of beer. I'll leave a sixer in front of your door."

Before I can say no, he disappears through his glass slider.

"Why do I feel like I'm going to regret this?"

♡

## EVAN

Not even worrying about putting on a shirt, I hit the kitchen and pull out a six-pack for my gorgeous neighbor and an extra bag of Doritos. She's an interesting one. Doesn't give away much. Definitely has opinions about Kenny Rogers's music. I laugh under my breath and tread barefoot to the door. Quickly I set the six pack and Doritos down on the carpet in front of her door and then knock twice before heading back to my current hideout. I'd love nothing more than to stand there with the beer and have her invite me in, but she seems way too smart to let in a stranger, especially when everything on TV and online right now says to avoid all people as best you can.

The city is only allowing its citizens to get food and necessities. Beer is a necessity for me, so I bought two twenty-four packs when I went to the store before I moved in. I had to ensure I had enough to drown my sorrows.

I still haven't heard anything from the team doctor, or my coach, but it's only been a couple days. I could call some of my teammates, get the low down on what the word is about me, but frankly, I don't want to know what people are guessing. I'd rather get the hard-core facts and move on. I just hope to Christ that moving on means going back to my team—and not moving on to an entire new career.

My dad would be crushed. He lives and breathes his son

playing the game professionally. Tells all his buddies back home in Indiana about my career. He even roots for the Oakland Marauders while everyone in Indiana bleeds blue and silver for the Mustangs. Still, my dad takes all the heat from his brethren with a smile on his face and his chest puffed up in pride.

Visiting the fridge once again I pull out two cold ones and grab the other bag of Doritos. I gave her the Nacho Cheese variety because it's the safer choice. Everyone likes the nacho cheese blend, but not everyone loves the Cool Ranch. I'm an equal opportunity Dorito lover myself so I can go either way.

Cradling my loot, I head back onto the patio and set the beers on the side table. Then I rearrange my chair so I'm facing Sadie's balcony. I ease into my seat and wait.

And wait.

A full ten minutes and one full beer down the hatchet before she finagles her body out the slider, ass-first, dragging something along with her. Aw, a folding chair. It didn't dawn on me that she didn't have any seats on her balcony.

"Whatcha doin' over there?" I stand and lean on the edge of my railing while watching her push and pull a chair, the six pack, and the bag of Doritos all out at once.

And she's changed her top. She was wearing a hoodie before. Now she's got on a long-sleeve V-neck purple top that clings to her ample bosom. They're not huge tits, but definitely a small handful. Just right if the lush expanse of cleavage I'm seeing is anything to go by. My dick stirs in my jeans and I palm it once, then shift it a bit to give the sucker a bit more room. While she's busy, I unbutton the top button and sigh at the slight centimeter more of space.

Her hair is now pulled into a high messy bun when before she'd had it down, the golden waves falling all over her shoulders. I prefer it down, but beggars can't be choosers.

Eventually she spins around, sets her beer on the ground, and flops into the chair. "Whew! Okay. And thanks for the Doritos."

"And the beer," I add good naturedly because who forgets about free beer?

"Oh yeah, and that. I'm more of a snack type of gal so you win extra neighbor-in-quarantine-points for the chips."

"So, the way to your heart is through your stomach? Good to know."

She rips open the bag, pulls out an orange square, and puts the entire thing into her mouth. Damn! Wonder what else she can put whole into her mouth.

Once again, my cock takes notice but this time it goes full-out, hardening painfully against the denim of my jeans. For a full minute I think of Gloria scratching my eyes out and killing me in my sleep. Instantly, Mr. Happy takes a breather and settles more comfortably to half-mast.

I sit down, rip open my bag, and suck down a huge swallow of beer. The sun is starting to peek its way through the gray of the morning and my mood is lifting. Having a drink and a snack with a beautiful woman, a little sunshine, a great view... Maybe this quarantine thing will be all right.

At least for today.

"Okay then. Tell me something about yourself that nobody knows." I crunch on another ranch-coated chip.

"Wow. You go straight for the gusto."

I shrug. "Only way to play. Live out loud. It's my motto." Though fuck if that motto's done me well this past year.

"Hmm, okay, sparky. I'll play."

"Sparky? How do you know my name? Did you hear something about me?" Dread coats my throat as I narrow my gaze on my neighbor who's sitting cross-legged in her folding chair facing me with a strange expression marring her pretty face.

"Uh, no, dude. Calm down. Why? Should I recognize you?"

"Shit, I'm sorry. That came out wrong. My last name is Sparks. Uh, just figured maybe Jake talked some shit about me." I attempt to redirect the conversation.

"No way! I'm a freakin' genius." She smiles wide and gulps down some beer. "Wonder if I've turned psychic overnight? That would be cool."

I pay close attention to see if she is lying through her teeth, but she seems genuine.

"Honestly, that was completely coincidental, but now you're never gonna live it down."

"Back to you. Something no one knows about you. Go." I sip my beer and lean back while crossing an ankle over my knee.

She chomps on her chips heartily. I'm kind of surprised. The women I've dated aren't so real. They never eat much. Drink prissy fifteen-dollar drinks and never dress comfortably. I can't remember the last time I saw a beautiful woman in a pair of sweatpants and a simple, albeit sexy as hell, long-sleeve shirt.

"I once had to parachute out of a plane that was about to crash." She deadpans.

"Shut the fuck up? Seriously?" I'm beyond impressed.

Her eyes widen and she bursts out laughing. "No. That's Mission Impossible-level theatrics. I just wanted to see if you'd bite. And it's safe to say, Sparky, you bit. Hard. I got you so good with that one!" She dances in her chair and drinks more of her beer.

"Practical joker, I see. Well you realize this means I'm going to have to get you back when you least expect it."

She smiles and winks. "I'd like to see you try, buddy."

For the next couple of hours and three more beers for me—I count two for her—we shoot the shit. Never actually talking about anything of value, just being friendly and taking jabs at one another whenever we can.

As the sun is cresting over the horizon, she stands up and stretches her body. I watch in fascination as her tits rise and I catch a slip of skin at her small, rounded abdomen. The woman isn't a hard body, but she's soft in all the right places. Chest. Ass. Hips. Thighs.

My normal type is statuesque—fake tits, lips, and skin tone. This girl, she's real. Everywhere.

And I fucking like what I see more than I should.

"Take a picture. It'll last longer," she teases, smiling. "I've had fun but I really do need to get back to work."

"Okay. Good luck. And Sadie?" I call out while she's pushing her chair back into her home.

"Yes, Evan?"

"I had a good time. Thanks for keeping me company."

"You're welcome." Her cheeks turn pink as she pushes a lock of hair behind her ear.

"Sadie?" I call out again.

She chuckles and looks my way. "Yes, *Evan*." She enunciates my name.

"Same time tomorrow?" I suggest with my own laughter but in reality, I'd like nothing more than having a standing balcony date with the intriguing neighbor.

"We'll see. Have a good night. Be safe."

"You too."

I watch her until I'm left with the sunset, the nice breeze, and my thoughts. I smile out at the view. For the first time since I stepped into Jake's apartment and this city, I no longer feel quite so alone.

# Chapter THREE

## QUARANTINE: DAY 3

EVAN

I AWKWARDLY MANEUVER THE WEIGHT BENCH ONTO THE open space on the balcony. Luckily the sun is out and it's a fine sixty-degree morning in the Bay. I glance over at Sadie's balcony and see the sheer c[urtains firmly closed. Then I head back inside to get the six weights that go with the bench.

It was dumb luck finding a brand new, still-in-the-box weight bench in the spare room closet. I went in there to ride the bike this morning, but I didn't want to miss a potential sighting—or *date* as I've taken to calling them in my mind—with Sadie, the hot, mysterious, and hilariously funny neighbor. When I was scanning the space, I found an entire set of weights stacked in the corner with a blanket tossed over them.

I shake my head, lift two forty-five pounders, and bring them outside. "Poor Jake," I mumble, thinking of my friend working abroad.

Bastard is always working his ass off. Going from saving one human to the next. Part of me thinks he does it so he doesn't have to save himself. Losing his sister the way he did—in a water rafting trip when we were just teenagers—changed him. After her death, he set his mind to becoming a doctor and saving the world. Only who was saving Jake? Definitely not a beautiful woman who could warm his bed, support his career, and love him for the great guy he is.

Maybe Sadie has a friend?

Shit, maybe Sadie has already seen my good-looking friend Jake naked?

Fucking hell. Maybe they've dated!

Once I set down the weights and head inside for the others, I pull my cell phone from my loose workout shorts and bring up the text messages. Not being one for math, I don't attempt to figure out what time it is in Africa. If I knew the time difference, I would have called his ass immediately.

From: Evan
To: Jake
*You ever date your neighbor Sadie?*

I read the short message over and over before hitting send, praying they've never dated and most certainly have never seen one another naked. I grind my teeth at the mere thought of another man seeing her bare flesh.

He better not have. Bro-code means I can't go there if he has, and after yesterday, I'm definitely interested in going there. Repeatedly.

Lifting the rest of the weights, I head outside. Once I'm on the balcony and the gear is set up, I remove my white T-shirt and work out. I start off with the dumbbells and do a series of arm curls before switching to a crossbody hammer curl. Next, I stretch my arms out to the sides and lift the weights in a dumbbell dead-lift maneuver. Once those are complete, I lunge holding the fifteen pounders in each hand. Then it's all about the squats.

By this time, I'm sweating profusely. It's a good forty minutes into my workout and still no sighting of Sadie. A wave of sadness has me sitting on the bench which I strategically placed so I'd face her home, so I'd see her the moment she came out. Since when do I get emotional about a girl I barely know? Since they put us in lockdown, I guess. The TV only offers a little comfort and companionship. But even porn gets boring after a while. Not that I've been in the mood for it lately. Too much shit on my mind.

Lying down, I lift the dumbbells and do my standard bench press with smaller weights before taking a break to jog in place. I need mindless activity, focusing on my breath and the view. Getting antsy for Sadie, I jog around the weight bench in a circle and then reverse it, checking her balcony every lap.

Nothing.

I know she's there. Why isn't she coming out? She could wave, say hello…something. Maybe she didn't have as much fun drinking and shooting the shit as I did yesterday. I thought we hit it off. But perhaps I'm imagining things. *Damn.*

Grinding to a halt, I suck in large breaths of clean, crisp, ocean air until my heart calms down.

Why do I care anyway if she comes out? It's not like I need her to be entertained. I've done this workout a thousand times before. Granted it's usually in a huge workout space with my buddies around me. Speaking of which… None of them have even attempted to call me.

What the fuck kind of brotherhood is that?

My mood hits the pits. I pull my phone back out and rest my ass on the bench.

First call I make is to Robby, the happiest guy on the team. Wouldn't hurt a fly. Always smiling, never down. He's the guy on the team everyone uses as their personal therapist because he's so even-keeled.

He answers on the first ring. "What?" He answers with fire in his tone, something I've never heard in the few years I've known him.

"Hey, Robby. It's Sparks. Just wanted to check in on the team, man. Take the temperature, you know?"

A solid twenty seconds of silence fills my ears before he eventually says, "I can't fucking believe you. 'Roids? What were you thinking?"

"Excuse me? No, Robby, I didn't do—"

"I saw the pictures, man. We *all* saw them. Then we found out you had steroids in your locker. How dare you make a mockery of the sport. Making our team look bad. All those kids that look up to you. I expected more from you. So much more from the team's—hell, the *NFL's*—best running back. Now we find out your stellar record and performance were because you were juicing!"

"You've got it all wrong!" I attempt, but he's undeterred.

"Fuck you, man. Fuck you. I hope you lose it all." He blasts me before hanging up.

I let the phone drop from my hand. It hits the concrete, but thankfully doesn't break.

Robby. One of the only guys I expected to give me the benefit of the doubt—hates my guts. Believes I took the easy way out.

"Fuck me!" I roar, spearing my fingers into my hair and tugging at the roots. The bite of pain hits and I wince. "How could this happen. I didn't fucking do it! Jesus!"

My phone buzzes against the concrete. With hope in my heart, I grab the phone and answer it without seeing who it is.

"Robby?"

"Nah, man, it's Levi. How the hell are you?" His voice is a much-needed brotherly balm coating my frantic mind and heart. Levi is my best friend on the team and also a running back. Second for my position. Though probably first right now. At least it's him and not some other schmuck that's filling in. I trust him implicitly.

"Brother, everything is so jacked up. I didn't juice and I know I didn't do any of those drugs at that party. I was set up. I swear to God!"

"Shit, man. I don't know what to say… But I believe you. You work damn hard. This is crazy. Add in the quarantine and everything is tits-up."

I rub my forehead, slicking off the remaining drops of drying sweat, and look up to see if Sadie has made an appearance.

No dice.

Sighing, I lie back on the bench with the phone pressed to my ear. "Levi, I'm scared."

"I can imagine, brother. This situation is no joke. Who do you think is setting you up?"

I shake my head and close my eyes against the sun's bright rays. "I don't know. Most of the team are like brothers to me. Maybe it's someone on another team. Another player wanting to win against us? Or maybe another running back in the league who wants to take me out and have his record rise above mine? Fuck! You have no idea how frustrating this is. I can't even clear my name."

"Where are you anyway? Before the quarantine I tried to stop by your place. It was packed with paparazzi."

"At a friend's place. Laying low like Polly demanded."

"Aw, Polly. Such a hellcat, that one. What I wouldn't give to dip my wick in that piece of sweet cherry pie."

I chuckle. Polly is beautiful. A redhead with clear blue eyes and a stellar rack. A petite spitfire who would just as soon cut off your balls and feed them to the wolves, all the while buttering you up for a press conference.

"You couldn't handle Polly," I say. "She'd eat you alive."

He laughs and it lifts me up a little.

"But what a way to go." His voice drips with innuendo.

That has me laughing. "Hey, thanks for calling. You've made

me feel a bit better. At least not everyone hates me. I just got done chatting with Robby and he basically shoved a stake through my heart. The guy believes I did it. Which kills, man, fucking kills."

"I know, brother. Just stay strong. I'm sure it will all come out all right. Are you being safe, staying inside with the virus?"

I inhale fully and let it out in a long slow breath. "Yeah, but it's boring as hell being alone all day. Though I've got a few distractions keeping me sane." I glance at Sadie's apartment. The curtains haven't moved.

Where the hell is she?

"All right. Well call me when you need a breather. Keep your chin up," he offers.

"Thanks, Levi. Means a lot you believe in me and that you called to check in. You're a true friend."

"Of course. We're brothers."

Brothers.

I guess I have one on the team when I thought I had fifty.

"Catch ya on the flip, Sparks."

"You too. Bye."

"Later."

I press the off button and look up at the sky. Out of nowhere a light sprinkling starts. Fucking San Francisco weather. It can't ever decide what it wants to be. One minute sunny and breezy. The next wet and windy. Then back to the sun or overcast, but warm.

I head inside and make myself a sandwich, grab a bottle of water, and put on a gray hoodie, then take the entire lot back onto the balcony.

It's drizzling, but I don't want to miss it if Sadie eventually comes out. I flip up my hood and hunker over my sandwich, sitting in the rain for a fucking woman I've known for three days. This has to be the epitome of pathetic. Then again, it's not like I have other plans. A little water never hurt anyone.

While waiting, I scan sports news on the Internet.

Unfortunately, even with the virus, my doping is still heavy in the headlines.

*"Sparks is Sparking up Something Else,"* one magazine headline reads alongside the picture of me out cold on a bed I don't remember being in. A big red circle magnifies a part of the room so you can see a couple joints sitting in an ashtray. Next to that, a mirror has two lines of cut coke and a rolled dollar bill lying on its side.

It really does look bad. The only thing I can hope is that the medical tests clear me. I don't give a shit what anyone says. I'm going to have Polly release the full report sans my social security number. Have the club doctor share the results in a live press conference.

Fuck yeah, that's a great idea.

For the millionth time today, I look at Sadie's empty balcony. I'm now soaking wet and it's later in the afternoon. She's not coming and the more I want her to, the less likely she will. Good things don't happen to assholes like me.

My phone messages ding and I glance down.

From: Jake

To: Evan

*No. Sadie's hot and sweet, but she's a recluse. Totally not your type. She's the kind of girl you take home to your mom. Don't ruin her. You'd break her heart.*

Pushing off the hood of my sweatshirt, I let the rain pelt my hair and face.

*Don't ruin her.*

*You'd break her heart.*

The words soak into my soul the same way the rain is on my body. The rain should be cleansing but it only makes me feel more like a loser. Standing out in the rain to catch a glimpse of a girl I have no business wanting.

She deserves better.

Shaking off the rain the best I can, I go back into the lonely apartment. Once I've showered and changed into dry clothes, I sit on the couch and flip on the TV. Gloria comes and sits on my lap, digs her claws into my thighs, and holds on for dear life.

Ignoring the pain, I pet the damn cat.

♡

## SADIE

A neat line of M&M's sits along the side of my work desk along with hand sanitizer, a bottle of water, and my collection of vitamin pills. Vitamin B, because I gave up bread—carbs are so yummy and evil—and I probably need the Thiamine. C, because duh. And D, because I sometimes go days without seeing the sun once the words start flowing. Candy-wise, the yellows come first because they are my least favorite color. Next comes brown, red, green, and then blue. Blue taste best. Not sure why, they just do. It's science. This is how I get my job done—by bribing myself with a sugar fix at the end of every page.

Here we go...

*He's doing it again, working out on the balcony half naked. Biceps flexing as he curls the dumbbell. A subtle sheen of sweat glistens on his skin, reflecting the late morning light. His smooth tan provides the golden hues missing on this cool autumn day. It's simply undeniable— the man is a living, breathing fire all his own. He's breathtaking.*

*How the hell can I even begin to concentrate on my "Outlander" binge watch with this show going on outside? Eamon is his name and he has a body made for sin. Long and lean and lethal. I don't even like basketball, but I can definitely respect the effort he puts into perfecting himself on behalf of the sport. Greek gods would be jealous. High cheekbones worthy of the catwalk and lips just made for kissing. He grits his jaw with each upward motion, the concentration on his face both deliberate and all-consuming. I cannot tear my gaze away from him. This obsession with my new neighbor will surely be my doom.*

*He certainly makes swearing off men for the duration of this pandemic an issue. And here I thought self-isolation would mean no temptation. No chance of being enticed. At long last I could concentrate on my dreams of learning a foreign language and writing a film script. Perfecting the art of making chocolate chip cookies and maybe knitting a sweater or two. I had plans. Goals. Now I just have a sad and lonely fixation on my neighbor that's slowly doing my head in.*

*Oh no. Not squats! Have a heart, Eamon. Your ass is a work of art.*

*But the man doesn't even have a clue what he's doing to me. Jogging in place in his sweatpants, his sizeable junk bounces around with joyous abandon. It's magic, really, the ways in which his body moves. I* don't think I've ever been this fascinated by anything in my life. I'd feel mildly dirty if I wasn't so damn turned on.

Question: Is it morally dubious to order binoculars to enhance my view?

Answer: Yes, girl. You're a pervert. Embrace the fact.

Though it's not entirely my fault. Let's be fair here. It should be illegal for a dude to be this hot. What chance do us mere mortals even have in the face of such sweaty perfection? We must drool and stare. There is no other option. For certain, his daily workout sessions have fast become my favorite offline porn. Yes, siree. The panty forecast is damp for the foreseeable future. And a girl can dream. After all, a guy like that wouldn't even notice an IT nerd like me in the real world. Not even in the most desperate of times such as these.

How did my ex describe me again? As being not only socially, but image-challenged too. And since that particular memory cuts like a knife, I haven't forgotten a single damn word. Is it any wonder I've turned only to my steadfast and true personal massager for love and comfort over the past few months? Plug it in to charge once a week and it's good to go whenever I am. No need for tedious conversations or awkward first dates. Not *even a single unsolicited dick pic. It's the truth. My vibrator loves and respects me for who I am while real men do little other than suck. And not even in the good way.*

*I'm much better off just admiring Eamon from afar. My hopes and dreams can't be crushed if I never actually attempt to get to know the guy. Both my ego and heart can stay safe. In my mind he can be a masterful lover, a best friend, a hero. But in real life he probably has mommy issues and an unfortunate rash downstairs. You know I'm telling the truth.*

*No. I will not go out onto the balcony and introduce myself. I won't even risk a conversation.*

My poor messy heroine, Katie, is so fucked. Literally and figuratively by the end of the book, God willing. Lucky thing. I toss a yellow M&M into my mouth. I'm like one of those trained seals. Years of practice throwing candy into the air and catching it with my mouth. If my writing career grinds to a halt, I can always join a travelling circus and take it on the road. The amazing mouth-catcher lady. Throw it high and watch her dodge and weave! Blue candy is her favorite. Watch what she can do when you offer a blue morsel of candy-coated chocolate!

Sounds great. *Not.*

Which is why this book is so important. I'm months behind on my business plan, what with the muse going AWOL and all of the anxiety that is life in the year 2020. The fact is, you need a certain number of releases per year to stay relevant in the indie publishing world. Competition is fierce and the market is flooded.

Staying on top of writing, publicity, and running a small business is no mean feat. Though the words are flowing now, and that's what matters. Thank God.

But back to the subject of Evan/Eamon. I've never actually gone for a jock. However, you've got to figure their stamina would feature heavily in any sex sessions—which can only be a positive. So long as they're not a selfish lay, of course. And our hero could never be that. Who the hell wants to read about a man who doesn't believe in the fundamental laws of foreplay or declines to go down on a lady? No. Way. There's enough of that kind of asshole-ishness in the real-world dating scene, thank you.

That's probably why I stayed with Sean so long. A whole eleven months out of my twenty-eight years due solely to the fact that the dude didn't leave me hanging in bed. You'd think I was led around by my clitoris. But the sad truth is, finding someone you're sexually compatible with can be hard. No pun intended. And despite my mistaken attempt, you can't base a relationship around your partner's ability to make you come. Occasionally, you have to converse with them. Discuss your day. Share your stories. Act like you're in a relationship outside of the bedroom. Jesus, was Sean dull. The boy was bland through and through. It's like he actively resisted having anything interesting to talk about. Only ever read the financial news. Never stepped beyond the borders of his nice, neat, sensible, organized life. Bleh.

Then there was the whole thing where he said he supported my career, but showed absolutely no interest in anything outside of sales figures and the like. Didn't want to hear me talk about possible plot ideas or share a little industry gossip. And it didn't just relate to my job, either. He wouldn't even listen to me whine the time someone keyed my car. And while I get no one wants to hear you talk about yourself twenty-four/seven, it seems only polite to not let your eyes glaze over the minute your woman mentions something about her life. Because why would we talk about my life when we could talk about tax breaks? The excitement! Ugh.

Now I'm actually sounding like a bitch. Sean wasn't all bad. He was polite to my parents and occasionally held the car door open for me. A couple of times, he even bought me flowers. Maybe I'm being too harsh on him. Maybe my mother is right.

Nuh.

My computer chimes and a message box pops open on Facebook Messenger. And no, I wasn't getting distracted by all of the fear and gloom on my timeline. I was watching important and educational kitten videos. For reasons. They're so funny the way they wiggle their little butts right before they pounce. It never gets old. Instant mood enhancer each and every time.

**Zahra:** You better be writing.

**Me:** You know, for an editor you're both bossy and unsupportive. I'm going to lodge a formal complaint.

**Zahra:** You pay me to kick your ass. You also ask me as your friend to kick your ass. And I'm my own boss so that complaint will be lodged straight into my wastepaper basket where it belongs.

**Me:** Haha.

**Me:** And yes, I'm writing. I've got words happening! Hooray!

**Zahra:** Woohoo! I'm so excited. You were really going through a dry spell there.

**Me:** I sure as fuck was. Can't tell you how relieved I am that it's over. So, this hot guy moved next door and I'm kind of writing about him, but not really because that would be wrong. Coincidence. Fiction. Etc.

**Zahra:** You wouldn't be the first of my authors to draw inspiration from their own lives.

**Me:** That's what we'll call it, inspiration. As Anne Lamott said, you own everything that happened to you. And boy did he happen to me on my own damn balcony.

**Zahra:** So, you're into him, huh?

**Me:** No no. I'm not. I mean, I am. I have eyes, ears, and a libido. But nothing's going to happen. We've only talked a couple of times. Had a beer together. He seems okay, but no.

**Zahra:** Want to protest some more or are you done for now?

**Me:** Shut up. I'm through with men. For now, at least.

**Zahra:** Tell me, Miss DEFINITELY NOT INTERESTED IN THE NEIGHBOR. What makes him so special?

**Me:** Body like you wouldn't freakin' believe, dude. His muscles have muscles which in turn have even smaller baby muscles that are harboring tiny soon-to-be muscles in the near future. But not steroid-y looking. Just a nice balanced level of ridiculously fit and healthy. And he has a nice face. Granite jaw. Very lush lips. Incredible ocean-blue eyes. Swoon-worthy.

**Zahra:** I need a picture.

**Me:** Creeper shots creep me out.

**Zahra:** Say it's for your mother and tell him to smile.

**Me:** Ha! Mom is still hung up on Sean and me riding off into the sunset with a healthy investment portfolio. Don't even get me started.

**Zahra:** Ugh. How are you doing on the quarantine front?

**Me:** The snack situation is kind of dire. I might have to venture out for groceries sometime soon. How about you?

**Zahra:** Kids are driving me insane and we're down to our last roll of toilet paper. At least we're all healthy.

**Me:** That's what's important. And if you're gentle, kitchen paper shouldn't chap your ass too bad. I'll order some toys online and send them to you for the kids.

**Zahra:** You don't have to do that.

**Me:** I know I don't have to. I want to. Poor, babies. It's not easy having to stay home. They must miss their friends something fierce. They're not natural shut-ins like you and me.

**Zahra:** They sure do miss them. And thank you. Let me know when you've got something for me to read.

**Me:** Will do. E-mail should be hitting your inbox in a day or two. I just want to get the first few chapters down while I'm on a roll. <3 Get it, roll. As in toilet paper roll. Something you don't have. lol

**Zahra:** Bitch! I see this book will be funny. Keep up the good work! I'll look forward to it! xx

I toss another M&M into my mouth feeling incredibly proud of myself. Mm. Yummy. And setting things up with my beloved editor basically qualifies as finishing a page of writing. Sort of. Don't question me. I'm the boss here.

"Gonna need more snacks," I mumble, turning back to the computer screen. "Time for you to accidentally burn your dinner and be forced out onto the balcony due to the buildup of smoke in your apartment so you can properly meet the hot neighbor, my voyeur heroine. And of course, all of this will happen when you're chilling at home wearing just a T-shirt and panties. Skimpy lace panties that let him catch a glimpse of your ass cheeks. Yeah…you saucy wench. Go get him, girl. Grr."

With my brain engaged, my butt in the chair, and my fingers on the keyboard, I get back to work. This story is shaping up great. Just great. Thank you, Evan Sparks.

# Chapter
## FOUR

### QUARANTINE: DAY 4

SADIE

I T'S ONE IN THE AFTERNOON WHEN I STUMBLE OUT ONTO THE balcony with a cup of coffee in hand. Ah daylight, my old frenemy. I squint and slide on my sunglasses. I pulled one hell of an all-nighter, writing until four in the morning. But when the muse is on a roll, you'd have to be stupid to get in her way. And when it comes to my career, I try very hard not to be stupid. Smutty? Yes. Smartass? Hell, yes. But stupid? No, thank you.

The yummy scents of food and the lure of fresh air beckon me outside. Along with a healthy dose of curiosity regarding the welfare of my neighbor. Oh, fine. So, I want to ogle him again. Hear him laugh and listen to him tease me. He's a fun guy to be around and it's not against the law to have a tiny crush on the new guy next door. Seeing him brings the added benefit of aiding my writing process. Hanging with him could even be considered research. Therefore, necessary to the development of my plot… along with being a good time. Win.

"Hey!" I grin, giving him a wave.

Evan stands at a grill, a plain black apron on and tongs in hand. He is not smiling. In fact, his granite jawline seems set in especially cranky and unimpressed lines this afternoon.

"Hi," he mumbles, without looking at me.

"How are you doing? Whatever you're cooking smells delicious."

A grunt from the big man is all the reply I get.

Maybe he didn't sleep well or something. These are stressful times all around. I lean on the railing, taking another sip of coffee. "I got so much work done yesterday. My word count is dazzling, I tell you. Didn't get to bed until almost dawn."

Evan flips one of the slabs of beef and turns a couple of cobs of corn. My mouth waters from both the view of him in a tee and jeans—I know it's his usual, but he wears them so damn well— and the scents of real food. Unfortunately, he doesn't even look at me. My new friend is distinctly unhappy.

"What did you get up to yesterday?" I ask.

He just shrugs.

Ruh-roh.

Gloria slinks out of the apartment and up to the railing on my side. Giving me a loud meow in welcome. At least someone seems happy to see me.

"She missed you." He waves the tongs in the cat's general direction.

"Precious floofy girl. I missed her too." I smile at the ginger cat, wishing I wasn't allergic.

"Then why didn't you come out all day? I was waiting for you," he says, then freezes and frowns. "We were waiting for you. I mean...I was just keeping an eye on her. Idiot cat, standing out in the rain, getting all cold and wet. It was pretty fucking pathetic."

Huh. "I'm sorry."

Another grunt. As if he could not care less about my apologies. Oh boy. His shoulders are up, his scowl fierce. I've really stepped in it. Everyone's toughing it out right now. Having to stay indoors, not being able to visit with friends and family. I'm the closest thing Evan has to real human contact with a pal and I let him down. I didn't mean to, but still.

"I, um… Sometimes when I get all caught up in a story I kind of lose track of the outside world," I explain. "But if I'd known you two were waiting for me, I'd have definitely taken a break and come and said hello."

He gives me a quick side glance. Not exactly happy, but no longer quite pissed either. Maybe I'm making some headway.

"I didn't mean to leave you hanging like that." My tone is filled with as much compassion as I can muster because I do feel really bad.

He sighs, his broad shoulders lowering a little. "Whatever. So, you got some work done?"

"Heaps. The book is going really well. I have a good feeling about this one. It's like the hero and the heroine have taken on a life of their own. I'm typing as fast as I can to keep up, you know?"

"Yeah? That sounds positive."

I smile. "Absolutely. There's real chemistry on the page with these two. I think readers are going to dig it."

"You writing a romance or something?" He raises a brow.

My chin juts up. It's instinctual. People love to shit on my genre which sets me off instantly. "What if I am?" My inner scrappy brat rises to the surface, ready to go to battle.

"Nothing. Just curious."

"Yes, Evan. I'm a romance writer. And proud of it." I'm now projecting my voice and using the official fuck-with-me-and-die-a-slow-death tone. Reserved solely for those times when people commit a serious social faux pas such as cutting in front of me at the grocery store. Or when morons make jokes about my job. Shit not on the books I love—or I will end you. I should probably get that tattooed on my forehead. Nah, maybe a wrist or something. More feminine.

Only Evan doesn't seem to be doing that. He just nods, expression serene. "Okay. Great. It's good that you have a job that you love and are passionate about. I've never read a romance, so I can't really comment. But it seems like you're seriously devoted…that's all you can hope for with a career, right?"

"Right." So maybe I went straight to DEFCON one somewhat unnecessarily on this particular occasion. For various reasons, his opinions of me and my work apparently matter. Interesting. I stare off into space, pondering this unwelcome development. My stomach takes this opportunity to grumble loudly.

"You're starving, aren't you?" he asks with a chuckle. "You're staring at my grill like it's your long-lost lover and I could have sworn I heard that stomach growl all the way over here." He clanks the tongs together astutely.

"I may or may not have been existing only on candy for the past twenty-four hours."

"Candy? Sadie, we can do better than that. All of that sugar is bad for you." His brow is pinched together, and his head is cocked to the side as he stares me up and down. "Explains the curves though." He grins wickedly.

"As you just experienced, I apparently need all the sweetness I can get. And these curves are fine, thank you very much!" I put my hands on my rounded hips. Are they getting bigger? No? I've been doing yoga and running in place to keep awake. I frown.

He laughs heartily. A girl could get addicted to that sound. All deep and low and inviting. Everything in my stomach flips at the noise. My center is once again aching and wet and it's all his fault. It's disconcerting how easily he gets me hot and bothered. One salacious word, a lustful look, a sexy laugh, and I'm a goner. Surprises me how much I want to please him. Because you could say it's just me recognizing that in these shitty times human interactions matter more than ever. Whether I was out here on the balcony yesterday or not, he was foremost on my mind all damn day.

The whole Evan/Eamon conundrum. When your muse and hero live so close to home it's a little scary, to be honest. Not only am I making up rude and intimate scenarios involving the man in my mind, but I'm committing them to the page. And boy, are they explicit and filled with emotions. Social distancing on this particular occasion may not save my poor heart. Only enhance the chance of future breakage. I don't want to be disappointed again. Please not so soon after Sean.

It's depressing as all heck when an affair blows up in your face like that. Especially when it's your own damn fault for ignoring the warning signs. Like almost falling asleep at the dinner table because he's tedious as fuck. Like allowing someone who is supposed to care about you to sideline and belittle your career. And that reminds me, I need to stop dwelling on my ex.

Life would be easier if Evan was just another gym junkie himbo. Except he isn't. He's not only hot, but he's funny and entertaining and sexy and many other things I'm still discovering.

Houston, we have a problem. I am officially experiencing *feelings* and I don't like it. Make. It. Stop.

Meanwhile, Evan is loading up a plate with a huge steak, a giant cob of corn topped with butter, and half of the large container of potato salad which was sitting on the small outdoor table. The plate is heaped, bowing beneath this mighty load of assorted food stuffs. They don't even serve meals this big in Texas.

"Wow. Do you really eat that much?" I ask, eyes wide with wonder. "Where does it all go?"

"No, this one's for you. I'll leave it outside your door." He picks up a set of cutlery neatly wrapped in a paper napkin. The man is going all out with this.

"Evan, that's very kind, but you've got like half a cow on that plate. There's no way I'm going to be able to eat all of that."

"So put the rest in the fridge for later."

"I do have food in the apartment, you know. You don't have to feed me."

"It's not a big deal. I cooked too much anyway," he says, halving part of the bowl full of green leaves on top of the monster meal. The man is like Martha Stewart on a mission.

"But…" I try to find anything I can say that will sway him, but really, it looks so good that my mouth is already salivating.

"Let me guess. You were going to eat some crappy microwave meal? Or maybe have a bowl of sugar-coated cereal." He grimaces.

"I'll have you know that eating cereal outside of breakfast time is one of the true joys of being an adult. Don't knock it until you've tried it. Repeatedly."

He shakes his head and if he had a hand free, I think he would have waved a pointy judgey finger at me too.

"Well, now you can sit outside in the sun with me and eat a decent meal. Doesn't that sound nice? You can't live on candy and cookies, Sadie. Shit food like that doesn't fuel you. Like Cookie Monster says, they're *sometimes* foods." He flashes me a grin and disappears through the slider, I assume heading back into the apartment to deliver the food.

Before long, I hear two loud knocks at my door.

Gloria blinks her gorgeous green eyes at me expectantly before settling herself in a sunbeam for a nap. Tail curled around her. Head resting on her sweet little paws.

"He's feeding me. I'm not sure a male has ever actually cooked for me before. Do you think this is part of some sort of mating process or just a friendship sort of thing? What's your opinion, fluffy baby?"

Only the cat is already fast asleep. I'm on my own with this one.

♡

## EVAN

After I knock twice, I set the food down in front of her door. It's definitely piled high, but that woman needs to get some real food in her belly.

I make my way back into my home away from home, grab a couple cans of beer, and bring them outside. The grill still smells amazing. I set the remaining New York strips on the higher half to ensure I don't overcook them. Plans for a steak and egg scramble for tomorrow have me doubling up on the beef today. And if I was being truthful, something I'd never admit to Succulent Sadie, I did hope the scent of grilling meat would bring her out of her hidey-hole.

Grinning like a loon, I make my way back onto the balcony where Sadie is already chowing down.

"Didn't your mama ever teach you any manners?" I tease.

She stops with her fork halfway to her mouth. Her plump, pink, soft-looking mouth. Mr. Happy once again takes notice. Sweet Jesus. Every time I look at this girl, I have to fight a stiffy.

"What?" She shovels the bite into her mouth and chews, then closes her eyes and moans. Loud.

Tonight's spank-bank material just came to life right in front of my eyes. My dick hardens painfully in my jeans as I memorize her gorgeous face and that heavenly sound.

I hiss, adjusting myself while gathering what I need to pull the remaining steaks off the grill. I set all but the one I plan to devour into the ceramic dish I brought out. Then using the tongs, I take my cut of cow off the fire and wedge it onto my already stuffed plate.

"You're supposed to wait for everyone to get their meal before eating," I admonish playfully.

She frowns and purses her lips. "Says who?"

"Everybody."

"Well I'm somebody, and I say 'to each his own.' And, I like my food hot! And, thank you, Sparky. This is incredible. Where did you learn to cook?" she asks before sinking her teeth into her corn.

I cut a piece of meat and stick it into my mouth. The savory flavors of the meat and rub I used mingle together on my tongue. "Damn, this is good." I mumble around my food, and then finish chewing and swallowing. "Dad taught me. And Curt, my little brother, from the time we could peek our heads over the Weber."

She laughs sweetly and it sounds like a song. Or maybe it's just that I'm into this girl. Really into her. I haven't so much as touched a hair on her head or held her hand and I can already feel my need to please her. To make her laugh. To feed her.

"Well I'll have to send a thank you card to the man because this," she points to her plate with her fork, "is amazing. Even the ruffage is tasty. Did you make the dressing?"

I grin. "Yeah, but it's just a touch of olive oil and balsamic. Healthier."

She pokes several leaves and a tomato. "Do you always eat healthy?"

I sip my beer and hold it up. "Not always."

"Besides beer. I think enjoying beer might be part of the male DNA." Her eyes sparkle as she smiles.

"When I'm training day in and day out, I can take more liberties, because I need a lot of calories. But if I don't want to spend extra time in the gym, I try and eat right."

She nods and continues eating.

"How about you. Any siblings?" I ask, eager to find out any little morsel about my mysterious neighbor.

"Only child. My dad is a dentist in Dallas. My mom works in his office as his receptionist and office manager. He has two hygienists and a couple office assistants. Unfortunately though, he's only supposed to go into the office if there is an emergency. He cancelled all his clients for the next three weeks—thank God!"

"Why you thanking the big guy upstairs?"

She blows a breath of air over her forehead which pushes a blonde lock of hair off to the side. "They haven't been taking this as seriously as they should. I'm worried about them. They're in their early sixties and, well, they just don't listen."

I nod. "Yeah. I read online that the virus is really dangerous for people with compromised immune systems. I've been telling my dad to stay home but he works in a cannery that makes food. They're considered essential employees."

"And your brother?" She sips from a glass of water.

"Manages a bar in the same town. The state hasn't required shelter-in-place yet, but Dad says it's coming. Curt is freaked. It's his only income and he only gets paid if he works."

"Oh no. That's really scary. I'm sure there are so many in his position right now. What about you?"

"Oh uh, I'm good. I've some in reserves and plan to send home a few thousand to my bro to cover him for a month or two."

"Wow. That's awfully nice of you." She sets her elbow on a tray table she brought out and rests her pretty face in her hand. "What did you say you do for work?"

I clench my teeth and look out over the view trying to figure out a way to avoid it. Though if I do, all she has to do is go online and search for my name. My ugly mug is still plastered across the celebrity sites—even with the virus making more headlines every day.

"I didn't say." I tip my beer back and glug down the rest.

She crosses her arms over her chest. "You don't have to tell me. Though I did tell you what I do."

"What do you think I do?" I grin and run my hand over my hair, loving watching her consider the question.

"Something physical."

"Oh?"

"Your body is ridiculously built. That takes a lot of work and constant upkeep. The obvious guess would be a fitness trainer."

I tip my head back and laugh. "Obvious, huh? I could train *you*. I saw you doing yoga the other day. Looked like you could use a spotter, all that wobbling around on one leg." I tease her and watch while her face turns bright pink.

"It's a new thing I'm trying! And I'll have you know, Mr. Muscles, not everyone can spend their life in the gym."

"True, true. And I don't spend my life in the gym, but I am required to spend a lot of time exercising. What's your next guess?"

She pouts and then narrows her gaze. "Basketball player."

"Basketball, huh? Ever played?"

"No. Have you?" she fires back instantly.

I snicker. "Yeah, babe, I have played. And I'm not a basketball player. Close, but no cigar."

"So, if not basketball, then what?"

"Football." I watch her face to see if there is any hint of recognition or a spark of any kind.

She wrinkles her nose. "I don't watch sports. And if I did, it would have to be a live game. Then it's an event. Something you're going to and experiencing with the players. On TV it just seems so…" She shrugs. "I don't know, boring."

"Boring? You think professional football is boring? Aw man, you got me!" I cover my heart and tip my chair back pretending to have been shot in the chest.

She laughs and continues to eat her food, though she seems to be slowing down. I glance at her plate. "Girl, you *were* hungry. Your body is probably starved for real vitamins and nutrients. What did you eat for dinner last night?"

Her eyes widen. "Dinner?"

"Breakfast?"

She winces and scrunches that nose again.

"Sadie, babe, this is not good. How are you able to work without fuel in you?"

Pressing her plate back away from her, she pulls one foot up into the chair and I can see her brightly painted pink toes. "It's always been like this. Ever since college. I'd study all night, go to school, then finally come home, eat, and crash. Then repeat. When I started writing novels, I just put my fingers to the keys and let my mind wander."

"And why does that prevent you from eating?"

"It's not intentional. But when the muse is active and going, we writers take advantage. Get as much down before it's gone, in a way. And before the quarantine, I was having a pretty serious case of writer's block. Now I'm not."

"Basically, you get lost in it."

She smiles wide. "Yes, exactly. The characters start talking and I get to typing."

"I can understand. When I'm on the field, everything but the players, the opposing team, and the ball disappears. We can have an entire stadium filled with fans screaming their hearts out and it all just fades away the second the ball is snapped."

"Totally."

"It's really neat what you do though. I couldn't imagine attempting to write an entire story from start to finish. Are you at a loss for ideas?"

She hums and it's almost as sexy sounding as the moan from earlier. "Sometimes. Ideas come and go rather quickly. It's the ones that really stick with you that you have to pay attention to. I can have an idea going to the mailbox to get my mail, but if it's not meaty enough, or speaking loudly to my muse, then it's nothing more than a passing thought. Does that make sense?"

"Not really." I laugh. "What's the new story about?"

Her face pinches and her eyes fill with something akin to fear. "A man and a woman."

"I figured that since it's romance. Not that it couldn't be two dudes or two chicks. Love is love, as they say." I hold my hands out in a placating gesture to ensure she understands I'm cool with people being people. Doing their own thing. Loving who they want to love. No skin off my nose one way or another.

She covers her mouth while laughing at my backpedaling.

"What's the plot?"

"It's still formulating," she says quickly. "What team do you play for?" She is changing the subject. Maybe she's one of those writers who works on masterpieces and won't share until it's just right? That's the way it looks in the movies.

Deciding to give her a get out of jail free card, I move on to her question. "Oakland Marauders."

"Cool," she says, as if it's all the same to her, poking at the small amount of scraps still left on her plate.

"So, what do you plan to have for dinner tonight?" I ask.

She leans back and covers her belly. "I can't even think about dinner with this much food in me. It will definitely be light if I eat anything at all."

I cover my ears and sing, "La, la, la, la la," until I can see her laughing but not hear her. "Don't say it. My heart can't take it. How about tomorrow we venture out together to get some groceries? I'm getting really low as I wasn't planning to stay quarantined here."

"We're not supposed to leave for much and we're definitely not supposed to go together."

I smile and tilt my head. "Do you always do what you're told?"

Her brow furrows. "Yeah, if it's going to save my life and the lives of others. You bet your ass I do."

I stand up and clear my plate. "Okay, Crazy, settle down. I was merely suggesting we go together. Doesn't mean we have to hold hands while doing it." Not that I wouldn't like holding her hand. I'll bet she's chilly-cold and needs a warm-blooded man like me to keep her from freezing. Probably has cold feet too. Boy, would I love to find out.

I lick my lips and think of all the other things I'd like to do with her. The visions flash across my sex-riddled mind in a series of delectable images.

Kissing her lips and finding out if they're as soft as they look.

Tunneling my hands into her long golden hair, holding her to me.

Gripping her hips, digging my fingers into her curves.

Plunging inside her wet heat until we both lose our god-damned minds and forget all about being quarantined.

"Hello, Earth to Evan?" her sing-song voice takes me out of my sex-starved stupor. "I said, tomorrow we can meet downstairs at ten a.m. on the sidewalk. As long as we walk six feet apart, we can go to the store together."

"Deal," I agree immediately. That's a couple feet closer to the woman I've been lusting after for four full days.

I can hardly wait.

# FIVE

## QUARANTINE: DAY 5

EVAN

S HE'S LATE. I CHECK MY CELL PHONE FOR THE UMPTEENTH time.

10:15.

I sigh and pace the sidewalk in front of the building wondering if she's going to stand me up like she did the other day. Then again, she didn't actually stand me up. I had hoped she'd come out and chat with me. It was my own damn fault that my expectations were so high.

10:20.

Christ, where is she? My heart hammers away in my chest and annoyance fills my veins. I turn around and watch the streetlights change rhythmically from red, to green, to yellow and back through its rotation. It's weird to look out on the streets of a normally bustling city to see it devoid of people. This area is usually packed with city slickers from all walks of life. Though it's good that people are taking this virus seriously.

10:25.

I grit my teeth and run a hand through my hair. Just as I think she's not coming, she flies out the door and stutters to a stop a few feet away from me.

"I'm here!" She pushes her shoulder-length golden hair out of her face. "I'm so sorry. I got carried away working and uh, yeah. I'm here."

Boy, is she ever.

I scan her body from her tight skinny jeans that mold to every curve spectacularly up to a long-sleeve cardigan with a lace-trimmed camisole under it that leaves all kinds of cleavage for me to stare at. Her creamy skin is luminescent in this light making me want to touch and taste. On her feet are a pair of brown suede boots that go up to her knee, no heel. Smart. Perfect for walking.

"It's okay. I understand, but give me your number, so next time I won't worry." I hold out my cell and wait.

She purses her lips as if she's weighing her options before blurting out her number. I enter it in and then send her a quick text. Her phone buzzes from inside a brown suede slouchy purse that matches her boots. I can't help but stare at her. She's wearing a bit of makeup for the first time and it enhances her already gorgeous face. Pink glossy lips and rosy cheeks. Her eyeliner is done in that pointed cat-like style. Basically, she's just topped off an already perfect masterpiece.

"You look beautiful."

Her cheeks turn a brighter pink as a flush covers the exposed skin of her neck.

She sucks in both her lips and takes in my appearance rather shyly. It's the closest we've been. What I wouldn't give to take her hand and walk proudly down the street with this angel at my side.

"Thank you." She blinks and looks away rather shyly which is surprising. This girl has been anything but demure, though I find it suits her. This shy nature. As if removing her from the safety of her home and balcony has brought out another side. A side I'm eager to learn more about.

"Shall we?" I motion toward the vacant street ahead.

She laughs and shakes her head. "The market is that way." She points behind us.

"Shit. And I was trying to be all gallant. I should have checked Google maps for directions."

Waving her hand, she spins around and starts walking. "I live here. I know where to go to shop. Follow me."

"You got it, gorgeous." I fall into step about four feet away, needing to be closer. A hint of lavender and fresh-cut mint swirls in the air around us. "You smell that?"

She frowns. "Smell what?"

"It's like flowers. Lavender and maybe mint?"

"You've got a good sniffer." She points to her nose. "My body wash and lotion."

"It smells fuckin' amazing." I lean closer and inhale her scent deep into my lungs. Fuck. I can't get enough.

Quickly she sidesteps off the curb and into the street. Shit, she shouldn't be on that side anyway.

"Six feet, buster!" She reminds me while pointing a finger. "I don't want your corona-cooties."

Letting her get back on the sidewalk ahead of me, I switch our positions making sure I'm on the side of the sidewalk that's nearest the street.

"Are we dancing now?" She eases closer to the buildings but once again, we're only four feet apart.

Being two feet closer is a true win but I keep that tidbit to myself, so I don't scare the woman away.

"Nah, I'm just making sure you're on the safe side. My late mother would kill me if I didn't treat a woman like you right."

"A woman like me?" Her blue eyes are dazzling with mirth and her cheeks are still pink, but I gather it's the nip in the air that's giving her the rosy hue.

"Yeah, a good girl. A woman you woo and bring home to the family."

"As opposed to a woman you just hit-it and quit-it with?" She cocks an eyebrow.

I suck in a sharp breath and hiss. "You caught me."

She shrugs. "I get it. There are a lot of women in the sisterhood who do not do themselves any favors. Though I'm not opposed to a woman getting herself some if she desires it. Each to their own. I think it's just there's a different societal expectation for women than men. If a woman has a healthy sexual appetite and takes advantage of a consensual night of fun with a man she's just met, she's a slut or a whore. It's bullshit."

"And if a man does the same?" I prod, interested in her take. Especially since up until this past year I'd been a serious man whore myself.

"It's just different. They're slapped on the back by their buddies. And if a woman doesn't put out within a certain number of dates, she's a prude or a cold fish."

"I can see that."

Her eyes blaze a white-hot fire as she looks at me. I'm actually a little afraid for my life.

"I swear I don't prescribe to that philosophy myself! Please don't incinerate me with your laser eyes, princess."

"Mmm hmm. Most people do. It's unfair when you think about it. Women have the same sexual desires and needs as a man does, but we're expected to hide that side of ourselves or push it out the door and try to find a happy medium between a slut and a prude. And then there's the man's take on sex. They want a lady to bring home to Mama, but they want a pornstar to fuck."

"Jesus, how did we get here?" I laugh while once again discreetly trying to adjust my cock. The damn thing is all too happy to discuss ladies and pornstars, but preferably naked while in bed with Sadie.

"You've gotta admit it's true." She looks both ways and then darts across the empty street even though the red light is showing on our side.

I think about it for a minute or two. "Maybe. I mean it's definitely got merit. Personally, I try not to worry about it too much and just go with what feels right when it comes to a woman I'm interested in."

"And what type of women do you normally go for? The good time gal or the type of you have to put the time in to woo?"

"Honestly, before this past year, I was all about no strings attached sex. I haven't taken a woman on a date in years. With my job, it's hard to find a person that isn't into me for the money or notoriety that comes with dating a pro football player."

"Huh, I guess I never thought about it. Probably a whole different world for you. I mean, if you're good at your job, you probably make a good living."

"I do."

"Which means there's likely women out there that want to hook their ball and chain to something like that. Interesting." She says the words as if she's cataloguing the information or taking notes.

"Not really. I'm not usually at a lack for company, but none of that company is worth spending time with. Other than a roll in the hay, you know?"

"Not really. I haven't been sexually active since my last long-term boyfriend."

I grind my teeth at the mention of an ex.

"Were you, uh, was it serious?" I follow her across another side street and keep pace with her shorter stature.

"Sean was killer in bed. Though I'm not sure we were actually compatible in any other way. My parents loved him though. Far more than I ever did."

"So, you did love him?" The hairs on the back of my neck tingle and I start breathing deep.

"I wanted to love him. How about you? Ever been in love?"

"The only love of my life has been the game. I've lived football since I was a toddler. Dad had me playing from the time I could hold a ball. Took to it like a duck to water. I played all through grade school. Was scouted right outta high school with a full sports scholarship."

"That's awesome! Where did you end up?"

"It was. Life-changing. Living in Indiana, I wanted to get the heck away from snow and cold weather. Accepted the deal UCLA offered me. Moved to California and went to college."

"Did you love it?"

"It was rough. Academics weren't my go-to. Though the team had tutors available at all times. Coasted through college with a C average but was once again scouted by the NFL. Chose the Marauders because I wanted to stay on the West Coast. Much to my father's dismay. He wanted me to play for Indiana, but I love the sun."

"You must miss your family?"

"I do. My brother is a few years younger and often needs a little guidance. He had Mom the least amount of time so I try to be there for him any way I can."

"That's right. You said you lost your mom. I'm sorry, Evan. I couldn't imagine what that would be like. My mother drives me bat shit crazy, but she means well and loves me to distraction. What happened to your mom?"

"Icy roads. She commuted to Indianapolis for work. Was a secretary for a law firm downtown. Got caught in bad weather. Ended up being part of a ten-car pileup. She was one of eight that died that day. I was fourteen and had just started high school. Curt was only nine. My dad has never been the same. Says he married his one and only love and he'd be her husband until the day he dies."

"That's heartbreaking for him and you and your brother." She reached her hand out to take mine but then closed her eyes and pulled it away.

I wished she had forgotten about the six feet rule. After sharing, I could use her comfort.

"Yeah, well it was a long time ago and life goes on," I say.

"That it does. Still, we should never forget. What was her name?"

"Why?"

"Because she lived and she still lives through you, your brother, and your dad. And I'd like to know a little more about the woman who made such a good man."

My eyes tear up a little as my chest tightens painfully. "Isabella. Everyone called her Bella."

"Isabella. A beautiful name."

I nod and shove my hands in my pockets to not only ward off the chill but in order to not reach for her hand the way she did mine.

"Eureka!" she exclaims. "We're here." She points to the big *Market* sign about twenty yards ahead.

Right at the door is a store attendant wearing a protective mask. He has a bucket of them and hands one to every customer. Not that there are many people in sight. It's like entering the Twilight Zone with everything so quiet and deserted.

"Keep for future use," he tells each person as they walk in.

When we come to the door, he holds up a hand. "Can't go in. We're keeping the numbers down to only thirty or so people at a time. You need to wait over there. See the blue tape on the sidewalk. Stand on one of those lines and we'll let you in after someone exits."

We both take a mask, put it on, and stand on a blue line.

"Does this mask make my ass look big?" she jokes, but the smile doesn't reach her eyes.

"Your ass is perfection."

"Thanks."

Someone walking on the opposite side of the street coughs and she flinches. We both do.

Shit just got real.

It is easy to pretend nothing much is happening when you are on the twentieth floor of a high rise, happily carrying on about your life. Safely away from interacting with the world at large. It is a far different story when you're boots-on-the-ground, being told you can't grocery shop without a mask, and that you must do so in small numbers.

"I'm scared." Sadie's eyes are on me, her hands trembling as she lifts them and crosses them over her chest. "This is all so...I dunno."

"I wish I could hold you."

"Me too. The thought that something as simple and everyday as grabbing a carton of milk and a loaf of bread could mean catching a super contagious virus that's killed thousands is insane." She turns around and faces the clerk.

More people stand in line on the blue strips behind us. It's six people deep when two customers exit the store and we're waved in.

Once inside, we each take a small cart and use antibacterial wipes that the store has provided on the handles and around the rim of the cart.

We pass by the grocery store clerks and I notice a five-feet-wide by three-feet-tall piece of plexiglass separating the clerk from the customer. That's new. Kind of like sneeze shields when you go to a deli. Still, the whole situation is like something out of a sci-fi film.

"Evan..." Sadie's voice is small, coated in concern.

"Just breathe through your mask and start with the cheese section. Everyone loves cheese."

For a minute I watch her stand there and just breathe, then she straightens her spine and puts one foot in front of the other. There is no stopping this girl.

I'm proud of her. And grateful as fuck that I have her in my life right now.

♡

## SADIE

Okay. I can do this. After all, if football is Evan's choice of sport, shopping is mine and shops are my natural habitat. Though online shopping and having things delivered to your door is my favorite, I love it all. The thrill of the hunt. The sheer joy of running down the perfect purchase. And sales! Nothing can compare to the rush of a bargain.

In this case, the purchase is cheese. First comes mozzarella because pizza is life, yo. Cheddar for when I get the nibbles, and also some Monterey Jack. Next come Kraft Singles because I'm apparently trying to relive my childhood.

"That's a lot of cheese," mumbles Evan, standing back the requisite six feet.

"Cheese is healthy."

"Sure. Sort of. In much smaller quantities." He grabs his own block of cheddar and a package of swiss cheese singles.

"We're meant to be stocking up for a week or so, right?" I ask with a shrug.

He tips his chin. "Are you part mouse? Because if some small cute percentage of you is rodent, I think I'd prefer to know sooner rather than later." He grins.

"Quitting football to go into stand-up comedy, I see. Can't say I'm a hundred percent behind that decision." I raise my chin trying to give my best haughty appearance.

"Got to have something to fall back on since you axed my singing career." He chuckles. I can see it in his dreamy blue eyes. They're a dark hue like the deepest, wildest uncharted parts of the ocean.

It's hard to be scared when he's making me laugh. Internally, of course. No need to actually encourage him. Being with Evan is like when you're on a rollercoaster and about to go over the edge. Your belly is a mess of excitement and you don't know whether to laugh or shout. Exciting and scary and unexpected.

But we should just be friends. That would be wise.

I move my cart along, inspecting the pre-packaged deli meats, trying to focus. All the bacon is wiped out—not even one straggler. Hmm, ham sounds good, along with some salami. Both make for quick, easy snacks when I'm working.

Evan's gaze flits over the cheese selection and he grabs two huge tubs of cottage cheese. Bleh. What's that for I wonder. I move onto the next cold case while he all but empties out the cold cuts. All of that meat. He's such a caveman. All brawny efficiency as he makes his way through the cold goods section. I can just imagine him hunting yaks or something in a fur mankini, striding across the plains with his spear in hand. And by spear I mean the actual weapon—that's not a euphemism or anything. Keep your mind out of the gutter, Sadie.

Yes siree, he'd have a club in one hand, dragging me off by my hair to have his wicked way with me with the other. My skin instantly turns to goose flesh at the thought. Rough, uncivilized sex with Evan. His big strong hands positioning me, holding me firm, ready to take his huge throbbing—

"Hello? Sadie?"

I blink. "Hmm?"

"You buying yogurt or what?"

"Right. Yes. Yes, I am. Love the stuff." And that is a total lie.

Yogurt is gross, right up there with cottage cheese, but I grab a tiny container to save face and push my cart into the fruit and vegetable section. I glance over my shoulder to see he's smiling while putting a couple huge containers of the plain stuff into his cart.

Damn, I can't believe he busted me having sex thoughts. How embarrassing. Hopefully he just thinks dairy goods get me overly excited. Even that would be less humiliating than him knowing I was dwelling on his manhood. What we can summarize from this is that when it comes to Evan, I am apparently a terrible friend.

I grab some strawberries and blueberries. A couple of red apples and a ready-made salad. A packet of carrots and celery sticks with some hummus. Yum.

"C'mon. You cannot be serious."

"What?" I look back over my shoulder at him.

His sigh is so long and heavy it might carry its own zip code. Like I'm slowly crushing the life out of the poor man with my bad food choices. "Step away from your cart, Sadie." His voice is authoritative and brooks no argument.

A little shiver ripples through me at the deep, sexy timbre.

"Ugh. Fine." I take several steps back and cross my arms. "It's not like I didn't get any fresh fruit or vegetables. Crudités count."

I glance at the clerks that are restocking each section with the fresh stuff while other patrons are grabbing what they can as soon as it's put out.

He doesn't even bother responding. Instead, he gets busy tossing a couple potatoes (so carby), a big bunch of kale (bleh), tomatoes, an onion, broccoli, cauliflower, and four huge cobs of corn into my cart.

"Evan, you've gone too far. I don't do cauliflower."

"We'll bake it covered in a cheese sauce. You'll love it."

"You're so bossy when it comes to food." I grumble, but deep down, this is fun. It's nice having him look after me like this.

Having him care about my health and the contents of my pantry as opposed to just my panties like so many other men. Though if he stuck to my thong, my heart would be safer.

I didn't really do domestic things with Sean. He had a housekeeper to deal with all sorts of necessities. Someone to handle the shopping and making meals. And then he had me to deal with his dick, and to be available as his plus one at business functions. The man sure had his life sorted into neat and tidy boxes. Pity it sucked so hard being a part of it.

"You'll at least try it, right? For me?" Evan flashes me a smile and my knees go weak. Oh, the things I wouldn't do for him when he looks at me that way. This is ridiculous.

"Fine," I say, letting my head and shoulders sag for good measure.

"That's my girl."

Next, he fills his cart with healthy food. Way more than I could ever eat in two weeks let alone one. I push my cart a little farther away and scan the paper products aisle. It's wiped out completely. Not a single roll of toilet paper. Thank God I buy a huge thirty-six count package every few months. Still, it takes me out of my happy little sphere thinking about all the people who don't have any.

Powering forward and skipping that aisle completely, I move on. Pasta, rice, canned goods, and so on. There are very few options in the pasta aisle. Which I guess in the grand scheme would make sense because it lasts a long time and is filling. A good way to feed large families.

Grabbing a single box of spaghetti and a jar of premade sauce, not my normal brand, but you get what you get and you don't throw a fit, I shift my mind back to what we talked about on the street. Namely him. My new favorite subject to dwell on. How would that affect you, losing your mom so young? Having to learn to cook and everything. Taking care of his little brother while his dad was at work. It's obvious he's a nurturer by nature. A giver. Despite what he says about having previously restricted sexual relations to hello/bang/goodbye.

Though if he pours all of his energy into football, then he wouldn't have necessarily have the time or the emotional energy for a real relationship. Perhaps when he left home for college and then the big leagues, he was focusing on his first love, the game, and didn't see any need for a second. Making up for the time he'd lost having to grow up fast after his mom died, maybe. Indulging in some of the partying he missed out on during high school.

Perhaps Eamon, the hero of my book, could be an orphan. Grew up fast in a series of foster homes, trying to protect the younger kids. Hardened to life from all of those tough times. That could work. A heart of gold hidden from the world. Buried deep behind sarcastic comments and his all-consuming commitment to the game. Hmm. It could work. An unwelcome thread of guilt moves through me. But it's not like I'm actually writing about Evan's life or anything. Selling his secrets. He's just my muse.

I add a box of cornbread mix and snag the last bag of flour tortillas. Because what even is life without Mexican food? Moving along, I head to the canned soup and toss in a can of stew just in case I get desperate. Preppers buy canned food and bottled water. They also buy truckloads of guns and ammo, but I'm not going there.

"I think that in an apocalypse situation I'd last approximately five to six minutes," I blather, knowing he's following my every move and judging each item I add.

Evan nods, scooping up a bunch of cans and some packets of quinoa. I can't even comprehend how that is cooked. I'm not even sure I've ever had it.

"That sounds about right." He snickers.

"Some friend you are. You're supposed to offer to protect me with your rockin' body. Shelter me by throwing footballs at our attackers and tackling them or something." I laugh quietly. The store, the whole situation, seems too somber for anything louder.

"My rockin' body, huh?"

"Oh, stop," I drawl. "You already know I admire your physique. Don't make a thing out of it."

He chuckles. "As long as you're not just after my mind. I hate it when chicks do that."

"Ha." I throw a few more things into my cart before heading into the next aisle. And here we are, nirvana. This is where I come into my own. This is where I truly belong.

Behind me, Evan groans. "Why don't we skip this aisle?"

"Hell to the no, boy." I park my cart to the side and wave a hand at him. "Step back. I'm in control now."

He mutters an assortment of swear words, but does as he's told.

When snack shopping, it's important to cover all of your basic food groups. Three or four bags of Doritos each, because I know they're a favorite for him. Then a selection of candy. M&M's (with and without nuts), Reese's Pieces, Hershey bars, and Skittles. Next come the cookies, a necessary part of any balanced crap diet.

He groans some more. Is it wrong that I like that sound? Because I really do like that sound coming from him. "Man, I can already feel my arteries clogging, my heart slowing down."

"Hush, Evan. I'm concentrating. This is important work."

"I can just see you in the oncoming apocalypse, going from store to store, desperately searching for your next sugar hit. Not even caring about the chaos on the streets or the cannibals hunting us down."

"Wait. There are cannibals in this apocalypse now?" I wrinkle my nose and scan all the beautiful packages of brightly colored cookies.

"Sure, why not? Ever seen *The Walking Dead?*" He winks at me, unrepentant.

"Tell me, in the ruins of this forgotten city, are you valiantly protecting me with all of those muscles while I search for a Snickers? Because you know I'm dead otherwise."

At this, he strikes an old-school Arnold Schwarzenegger strong man sort of pose and flexes. Even beneath his long sleeve Henley this is an impressive sight. I'm half tempted to fan my face. He just oozes this sexy confidence and masculinity. Help me, baby Jesus. Certain parts of my anatomy just caught on fire.

"Tell the truth. Is that your Tinder profile pose?" I ask.

"You like it?" He waggles his brows and continues to add different flexes for my benefit.

"Oh yeah, big boy. You work it."

And he really does, which has my mouth watering and taking in his stunning form. He really is a work of art.

He laughs, watching me for a long moment. And then we just stare at each other. Everything feels warm and lovely. Until he turns away. "C'mon. We better get a move on, other people will be waiting to do their shopping."

Shoot. He's right.

It's amazing how he can take me from scared to giggling in fewer than two grocery aisles. How lucky am I to have him willing to walk at my side (six feet back) and hang with me (on his own balcony) during these hard times? So many people are alone and afraid. Sick and waiting for treatment in a crowded hospital. Not even in my wildest nightmares did I ever imagine we'd be living through something like this. A pandemic. The knowledge of how messed up everything is right now does my head and my heart in. Just the thought wipes the smile from my face. But it's not like anyone can see what's happening behind the mask. Stay strong for another few aisles and we'll be back in the safety of our homes.

"You okay?" he asks, voice concerned.

"Yeah," I say, choked up for some reason. "We should hurry up."

"You can always flirt with me later," he offers sweetly.

I grab a couple of boxes of Oreos off the shelf and try for a smile. Even if he can't see it, he'll know somehow. I know he will.

"It's a date, Evan."

# Chapter
## SIX

## QUARANTINE: DAY 6

SADIE

MY CELL GOES OFF AT SOME UNGODLY HOUR OF THE morning. I gaze blearily at the time. Seven-thirty. How uncivilized. I didn't stop writing until well after midnight and was counting on sleeping in to recharge my body and brain.

"Hello?" I rasp, my voice thick from sleep.

"Sadie?" The sound of Sean's voice on the other end of the call is as unwelcome as fuck. "Is that you?"

"No, Sean. It's an alien pretending to be me, wearing me as a skin suit. How are you?"

He sniffs. "There's no need to be like that. I just wanted to check you were okay."

I slump back on the bed and stare up at the ceiling. Rain is coming down hard, rattling the window. My linens are happy shades of blue and I'm surrounded by about three billion pretty decorative pillows. It's the Disney princess in me. *Beauty and the Beast* was my favorite growing up. I always wanted the library and the huge dramatic bed. So now, books line a whole wall of my living room and my bed is an extravagant California King. It's a lovely sight. But not even my beloved bedroom can make this phone call a happy one.

"Sorry," I lie. And I don't even put much effort into the fib because he just doesn't deserve it. "You know I'm not a morning person."

Another sniff.

"Are you sick? What's with all of the sniffing?" Shit. Does he have the virus?

"I am not sick," he snaps. Good Lord, this conversation is off to a great start.

"It would be okay if you were, Sean. It's not actually a moral failing. Germs happen, you know?"

"I'm not sick." I can almost hear him grinding his teeth. "I'm in perfect health."

"Okay. Great. Well…I'm fine too."

"Good."

Silence.

"Was that all you wanted?" I ask, on the verge of death from lack of caffeine. If I'm awake, then the coffee should be flowing. It's the law.

"Work has been busy, though we've all relocated to our home offices along with the rest of the city. The initial upset was challenging, but we've all settled back into the flow of things now." Of course, he wants to talk about that. He always wants to talk about work in the most patronizing and supercilious tone possible.

"Yeah? My writing is going well too."

"A lot of clients are taking the opportunity to catch up on things while the market goes through this lull. Shore up their defenses and evaluate their finances to better weather the upcoming storm."

"The words have just been pouring out of me." Since he completely ignores my contribution to this conversation, I ignore his. Childish maybe, and yet, I don't care in the slightest.

"I seem to go from one online meeting to another lately. Some of it's just hand-holding, but almost all of our clients are seeing a sharp downturn due to current events. You can't blame them for being concerned. And if they're willing to pay my hourly rate then I'm happy to listen to them worry and whine."

"And my characters are coming along great. Thank you for asking." I yawn overly loudly in the hopes that he'll get the hint.

Nope. He continues undaunted.

"I trust you've made plans to ensure your finances will survive a possible recession?"

Here it is. The big reason he called. Probably wants me to invest with him. Been there. Done that. Threw away the frickin' T-shirt, thank you very much. "I'm not going to discuss money with you, Sean. You know that. That's a hard boundary."

"A sensible person would make use of help when it's offered by an expert."

We've only had this argument a thousand or so times. It's as old as Moses so I keep my trap shut.

He sniffs again. "Anyway, things have been quite shaken up by all of this. It set back our trials of a new accounting program which is disappointing."

"I'm thinking my hero and heroine will bang soon."

Insert dramatic pause here. "I'm well aware of what you write. There's no need to be crude, Sadie."

Every time we speak, I swear to God I should get down on my knees and give thanks that I dropped this loser. "You know, Sean, as I recall, we fucked a time or two. More even. Most people do. It's an important part of relationships and how couples communicate physically. For sure, it's the only thing that kept us together so long. But go ahead, dismiss me and my interests and life, talk *at me* some more about you and your work. You do you."

"There's no need to be like that. I merely wanted to check on you and see if you're okay."

"What would you do if I wasn't?"

He stutters for a moment. I actually used to find it endearing, the way certain things would throw him. Things usually having to do with emotions and humanity and other items outside his comfort zone of topics. Truth is, Sean lived his life behind some mighty high, anally retentive, self-involved walls long before the lockdown happened.

"What if I was sick?" I ask.

"I'm not going to play games with you, Sadie. I don't have time for that."

"You know, a new guy moved in next door. We're getting along so well. In the few days I've known him, he's been more of a friend to me than you ever were. More supportive and sweet and funny. Oh my God, he's so funny. We always wind up laughing when we're together, even with everything so dark and scary these days. He's just more everything, you know?"

"You're seeing someone new?" he asks, and I can just imagine the expression on his handsome face. Because Sean is hot in his own buttoned-down way. If only his personality wasn't the worst.

"Okay. Thanks for calling, Sean. This was actually really enlightening and reinforced all the reasons why I dumped you in the first place. Just on the off chance I was having second thoughts. Which I wasn't."

"Sadie, if memory serves, you said we could still be friends!"

"When you've worked out what it is to actually be someone's *friend*, Sean, feel free to give me a call. Stay healthy and safe, okay? Bye."

And that's that. Phew.

I tie back my messy hair in a ponytail and empty my bladder. Then I wash my hands while singing the first half of "Don't Start Now" by Dua Lipa because girl power and you can't be too careful. You got to spend quality time with the soap and water these days.

Next, I wander through the living/kitchen/dining area

straight to the glass doors leading out onto the balcony. It's wet as heck out there. Raining cats and dogs. No sign of Evan. Sad face emoji. Probably for the best given I'm only in my panties and a faded old tee. Bet I look stellar. Given the time, he's probably still sleeping. Or maybe he's on the running machine, what with the crap weather. It's not like he can do his workout on the balcony today.

In a just and humane world, if I have to be awake at this hour, I should at least get to witness the splendor that is Evan performing lunges. The man has the most amazing thighs. Yesterday he invited me to time my workout with his at nine o'clock. Which I thought was an excellent idea. I could do my yoga while he lifted the weight of all my expectations, emotional baggage, and sexual needs.

All right, so there's a little dark cloud hanging over my head today and it has nothing to do with hearing from the ex. Mostly. It's just that for some reason, I have the worst feeling Evan has friend-zoned me. It's nothing he's said or done exactly. Just this weird feeling I have. Our flirting is all playful and fun, but... I don't know. Is it actually going anywhere?

Maybe I'm overreacting. It is a hobby of mine. Not to be indelicate, but the boy is making me horny and it's not like you can invite someone over for intimate relations these days. Six feet of separation doesn't allow for anything. Evan and I have talked more than the ex and I ever did and I'd very much like to get closer to him. Problem is, it's not allowed.

How do you date during quarantine? I guess you don't.

With a sigh, I head over to my coffee maker. Time to pull my head out of my panties and start my day. First up is to check on Mom and Dad to make sure they're not planning on inviting anyone over to play cribbage or something. Then answering e-mails, checking messenger, and catching up on social media before I start getting the words down. I may also stress-buy a pair of new jeans or a couple of bottles of wine somehow. You never know. There're a lot of great sales on right now and it's important to support local businesses! I also love getting packages in the mail. It feels just like Christmas.

It doesn't even occur to me until later that I actually chose catching a glimpse of my neighbor over getting an immediate caffeine fix. Huh. How about that? Not many things come between me and my coffee.

*A cool wet cloth slides across my fevered brow. That's the first thing I feel upon waking. A sharp pain fills my head, wiping out all chance of coherent thought. When I open my heavy eyelids, it's to the sight of a handsome chiseled jawline and worried blue eyes.*

*It's my new neighbor!*

*I'm lying on a messy bed in a stranger's room. We're in his apartment, I guess. He must have carried me up the stairs in his thick, strong arms. Just the thought makes me weak all over again. How he must have held me against him. How close we must have been.*

*"W-what happened?" I ask in a breathy voice.*

*"You were mugged," he says in his deep rough voice. "It happened on the street. I saw it all. Someone pushed you over and stole your groceries and your purse."*

*"Damn. That was Dior."*

*"Bummer," he mutters.*

No. Okay. I'm having a little too much fun with my characters now. The last two lines can get deleted.

*"The last thing I remember is walking back from Trader Joe's. I got their last roll of toilet paper!"*

*"I'm so sorry the bastard got away." His expression is tortured—brow furrowed, and mouth a fine line. Is it angst or anger? The man is a complex mess of emotions that I cannot wait to untangle. Much like his beautiful mussed hair. "I'm sorry I didn't get there in time."*

*"You tried." I give him a smile. "That's all any of us can do in times such as these. My name's Katie."*

*"Eamon," he says.*

*"I know. I…I heard you on the phone one day."*

*His smile is wicked and knowing. More of a smirk, in truth. As if he's aware of exactly how I've been spying on him. All the hours I've spent holding a glass to the wall, straining to hear him speak. And that expression on his handsome face, the heated knowledge in his eyes… I feel it all the way to my quivering loins.*

With regards to the last couple of words, Zahra will make me change it to pussy or center or something more eloquent. Still, I thoroughly enjoy strategically placing both the words loins (especially when they're quivering) and moist throughout my work. It irritates the absolute crap out of my editor and never fails to amuse me. And when you work alone, occasionally amusing your-self is important. Bosom also warrants a small but passionate ti-rade from her. I'll have to remember to include it sometime soon.

Back to the words.

> *My nipples instantly harden to peaks sharp enough to cut diamonds. Eamon knows I've been a bad, bad girl. And what's more, he likes it.*

"Oh, you two crazy kids. Get a room already." I toss a Starburst into my mouth. Which is when my cell rings for the second time today. Give me strength. Since when did people feel the need to talk when they can text? Another sign that the world is spiraling out of control. Then I see the name flash up on screen. Since we just spoke a short while ago, this cannot be good.

"Mom? Are you okay?"

♡

## EVAN

"Polly, tell me something good." I huff through the pain. I'd set the treadmill at an incline and have already been going for half an hour. With this rain, knowing I'm not going to be seeing Sadie for a balcony rendezvous, I'm a bit edgier than normal.

"Well hello to you too, Mr. Sparks. I can hear you working your body to the maximum. That bodes well since I do in fact have great news."

I lower the speed to a fast-paced walk. My heart is pound-ing, but that could be adrenalin or the surge of fear as I anticipate whatever my publicist has to say.

"Lay it on me."

"Received the report direct from the team doctor."

"And?" Not that it's going to show much of anything—because I haven't done anything wrong. I may have smoked a little cannabis from time to time, but that shit's legal in the state of California. And only socially after the season ended. It's not like I'm a closet pothead. I'd never consider doing anything regularly that could affect me long term or prevent me from being in top shape come game time.

"Cleared of all steroids. No sign whatsoever that you'd been doping."

"Thank you, God!" I smile. "And the other drugs?"

"That's where things get a little tricky."

"How so?" I hit the stop button and jump to the side until the treadmill stops. I wipe my face with the towel I've got hanging over the unit and focus on every nuance of her voice.

She hums as though she's reading or doing something. "According to the report, it says here you had high levels of Rohypnol in your system."

"The date rape drug?" I blurt, shock prevalent in my tone. "I don't recall being given anything."

"Didn't you say the last thing you remember was going into a bedroom with a woman who handed you a glass of whiskey? In a dark liquid you may not have noticed any visible change. Especially if you were already drunk. All she had to do was slip the pill in and then offer it to you."

"No shit?"

"Yep." She's quiet for a minute. "Says here you tested negative for everything else."

"Release it. Along with a statement that I was drugged."

"Really? You want to go with the entire report?"

"Hell, yes! I want my name and reputation cleared, Polly."

"Doesn't change what the coach found in your locker. If you

weren't taking it, one could question whether or not you were selling it or helping your team's advantage by giving it to players that are less talented than you." Her words are compassionate and yet truthful all the same. Unwelcome as all hell, but I'd rather know exactly what I'm up against.

I run my fingers through my sodden hair. "For now, it will clear me of the doping allegations. The press doesn't know about the locker."

"So far. Your team knows. All one of them has to do is leak it and we're back to square one."

"Fuck!" I grip the roots of my hair. "It's like I can't catch a fucking break!"

"I know, I know. It's definitely a start. I'm sorry you're dealing with this, Evan."

"Someone is setting me up."

"Do you remember anything about the woman you were partying with?"

Closing my eyes, I think back to that night.

*Levi and I were shooting the shit in the backyard. We were at a friend of a friend's birthday bash in a swank old school style home in Berkeley. People were smoking a heavy amount of pot and others were dancing or playing pool. There was a game of poker happening in the dining room and Levi and I were enjoying stogies and far too much whiskey.*

*Out of nowhere, Coach appeared with some of the cheerleaders and a tall drink of water I'd not seen before.*

*"Hey fellas, brought you guys a little something sweet." He grinned wildly around his horde of women. None of whom were his wife. The guy was a total bastard. Great coach. Knows exactly how to win games and make the right plays. Though he is a total douche bag womanizer when it comes to the opposite sex.*

"Aw, Coach, you shouldn't have," I said, rather serious. I was enjoying my time with the guys.

Levi on the other hand lifted his arms out wide in a T and said, "You definitely should have. Come on over here, beautiful ladies!"

Two of them left the coach's harem and cuddled up to me and Levi.

"Hi, I'm Mindy," the sexy blonde murmured, her hands already sliding up my chest.

With the amount of alcohol in my system, I was thinking only with my dick, so I looped an arm around her and palmed her ass. She snuggled closer.

Things got a little wild after that. Coach's wife showed up and Levi and I headed her off before she could locate the coach who I was pretty sure was in the guest house banging a cheerleader or two.

We chatted his wife up, and then at some point, Mindy encouraged me to follow her. And I did. She grabbed a glass from one of her friends and we went to one of the empty bedrooms. There she pushed me onto the bed, ripped off her shirt, and straddled me. She sipped from the drink and then handed it to me. I drank heavily from it while she pushed down the lace of her bra cup and played with her tits.

"Keep drinking," she said in a sexy timber I couldn't do anything but follow.

So, I drank. And watched her play with herself until things got blurry and I got too tired to keep my eyes open.

That was all she wrote. I don't remember anything after that. "Shit. It was Mindy that drugged me. But she drank from the cup too! At least it looked like it did."

"Who's Mindy?"

I start to pace the workout room. "I don't fucking know. Coach brought her to the party with two other cheerleaders. I'd never seen her before."

"Sounds like you have a call to make to the coach and those cheerleaders. See if we can pin down who this girl is."

"Got it. In the meantime, are you going to release a statement along with the results?"

"Absolutely. Just keep in mind, it's not a cure-all. It definitely clears you of taking the drugs and establishes that you were drugged. Outside of that, we'll just have to see how this rolls out."

I grind my teeth. "Thanks, Polly. I know you're working hard to clear my name."

"It's my job. No thanks needed. How are you holding up?"

I glance out the window at the dark sky and rain clouds coating the city in a dreary melancholy. "Fine. I'm safe. Got groceries yesterday. It was bad."

"Yeah. New York is discussing shutting down. Confirmed cases are running rampant. I'm already working from home and have stocked up on what I can fit in my postage stamp-sized apartment."

I smile, thinking that she is right. I've been to her place. The entire apartment could fit into my living room in Oakland. Even this apartment is three times the size of hers.

"Be careful, Polly."

"You too. I'll be in touch soon and e-mail you the link when the press release goes out across the wire."

"Thank you, Polly. For having my back and believing in me."

"Again, it's my job and I love doing it. We'll talk soon. Be safe."

"Will do."

She hangs up and I immediately pull up Coach's number.

"Sparks, I've seen the report, son. It's good news."

I make my way into the living room and sit on the couch. "Yeah, I'm relieved."

"Unfortunately, there's still the matter of the contraband found in your locker. What was it doing there?"

"Coach, I have no idea! I swear on my love of the game, I did not buy those steroids."

The coach sighs heavily. "That doesn't solve the problem. It was in your locker. Now we have to test the entire team. The guys are pissed."

Fuck. If they didn't already hate me for believing I was juicing, now they're going to hate me for putting them through unnecessary testing.

"I am too! This is my whole fucking life, Coach. I've worked my ass off to be here and someone's trying to take it away."

"Just tell the truth. You're selling it," he states flatly.

"Are you kidding me! NO! I said I'm not dealing, and I have no idea who put that there. I'm being set up and I'm going to find out by who!"

Coach pauses and another sigh can be heard. "Not sure what to say. We have rules."

"I'm going to clear my name! Speaking of, do you remember the girls you brought to the party that night?"

"Son, they're cheerleaders on our team. Of course, I remember them. Tiffany and Jessica. That Tiffany is a good girl, but naughty as fuck. One of my favorites," he says smarmily which has me trying to hold off the bile rising in my throat. Dirty fucker.

"Not Tiff and Jess. Mindy, the other one."

"Hmm, Mindy. Can't recall. She just appeared at my side at some point and then left me to go hang with you."

"So, you don't know where she came from?"

"Nah. I entered the party with Jessica and Tiffany arm-in-arm. You know how I like a twofer when I play."

I have to swallow and breathe through my nose hearing the way he talks about women I consider my friends. Though I've also fucked Tiffany—hell, half the team probably has. She likes to party. To each his own, I say, but still the way the coach views women is just gross.

If I had bigger balls and wasn't afraid to be kicked off the team, I might say something. Except these women are of age. They make their own choices. No one is forcing them to do anything. I actually checked in with Jess and Tiff about it in the past. They enjoy having a pool of men to party with and have wine and dine them. They feel safe with the team. Something about living it up in their youth too. Far be it for me to rain on their parade if it's what they want to do. Honestly, it's no different than how most of the guys on the team are.

"Mindy is the one that doped me with the Rohypnol, Coach. I've got to find her and find out who put her up to it."

"Shit. Good luck, son."

"Yeah, sounds like I'm gonna need it. What happens now team-wise?"

"We test every player. If any one of them has juiced, they're off the team. Breach of their contract. Since we're still investigating, even your contract is uncertain."

Fuck me. Just as I suspected. Still, needing to hold onto my last hope, I make the suggestion. "Maybe whoever planted the dope is trying to frame me? It's hard to believe, though. These guys are like brothers to me."

"You never really know a person, son."

And that right there is the problem. People do crazy shit for all kinds of reasons.

"Well, I hope you're wrong. Polly is sending out a press release with the full medical report. That should take the heat off me in the press."

"It's a step in the right direction."

"Yeah, I guess."

"Keep your chin up. Only time will tell."

"Thanks, Coach. Stay safe and keep me posted on what you find."

"Will do."

My mood plummets as I ease back against the couch and cover my eyes. This time next year I could be unemployed and un-hireable. Though so far, I'm not feeling sick so I should be counting my blessings.

Entering the kitchen, I pull down the huge bottle of whiskey and drink straight from the bottle. I walk over to the stereo system and put on Red Hot Chili Peppers' "Suck My Kiss."

Fuckin' A.

It's going to be one of those days.

Booze. Music. Rain.

# Chapter
## SEVEN

### QUARANTINE: DAY 7

EVAN

I t's still raining. Means no Sadie. I grimace as I plop three ibuprofens in my mouth and suck them back with a full glass of water. Last night's pity party for one sure did a number on my head and heart today.

Hitting the fridge, I pull out strawberries, spinach, yogurt, and an apple. I've left my giant container of protein powder on the counter for easy access. I pull a banana off the caddy and toss the entire thing into the blender. One after another I add the ingredients to make my morning smoothie. Except today, I double the amount, adding two scoops of protein powder and more strawberries than I normally would.

I know she likes her sweets.

The thought of Sadie makes me smile. I'm starved for any form of interaction with her. Because of the rain I can't wait for her on the balcony. Did that once. Only thing I got out of it was wet.

It took everything in me not to reach out to her yesterday, but I don't want to seem pathetic. Today all bets are off. I'm going to call her. Right after I leave my sweet healthy treat at her doorstep.

Good thing I slept in today. She doesn't seem to be the type to get up early. And really, no one should call anyone before ten. That's just rude.

Once I've added the ice and mixed the entire thing together, I pour two huge glasses. Taking a sample, I note it's definitely sweeter than I normally enjoy, but it still has a green hue from all the spinach. Guess it will have to do.

I slip my sneakers on my bare feet, and head out my door and over to hers. After I set the drink down, I return to Jake's apartment and dial the number she gave me the other day.

Anticipation of hearing her voice sends a tingle to my stomach I haven't felt in a long time. Maybe ever.

"'Lo," she mumbles.

"Good morning, sunshine! Are you awake?"

"Begrudgingly, yes." Her tone is off and lacks the normal chipperness I've come to associate with talking to her.

"I left a present by your door."

"Is it donuts?" Her voice rises a little.

I chuckle and grab my drink from the counter. "Fried bread covered in sugar? Uh, no. There isn't anything nutritious about a donut."

"Then I'm not leaving my safe place to get whatever it is you left."

"Your safe place?"

"Mmm hmm. I've wrapped myself in my favorite blankets, surrounded myself in pillows, and have a bag of peanut M&M's to live off. I'm good right here. Here no one can harm me."

"Harm you. What's wrong?" Anxiety twists inside my gut.

"I don't want to talk about it. If I talk about it, it makes it real." Her voice catches and my stomach drops.

"First of all, Sadie, go get the damn drink I left at your door."

"Is it coffee? If it is, this may be true love." Her voice is teasing now but it doesn't carry her normal spirited vibe.

Fuck, why didn't I think to add a cup of coffee? I enter the kitchen and put one of the pods into the machine and get the thing started.

"You'll have coffee in about sixty seconds." I laugh but hear crickets on the other line. "Sadie, you're scaring me. What's wrong. Are you feeling sick?"

"No!" She sobs. "My dad is. H-h-he has flu-like symptoms and they're not testing him for COVID-19." She chokes on her words.

"Oh honey, I'm so sorry." I grab the now ready cup of coffee, take it outside, and set it next to the smoothie that's rapidly melting. "There's a cup of Joe at your door. Come out of your cocoon and get it, yeah? Then we'll talk."

She sniffs and makes a snotty sound. "O-o-okay. Only because I need the caffeine."

"That's good. Get your coffee."

I wait while I hear her shuffling around, and then I hear the unmistakable sound of the door opening and closing.

"You made me a green drink? I thought you cared?"

"It's a smoothie. I want you to drink it. It has tons of vitamins and protein. It's going to give you an awesome boost."

"I don't want a boost!" she snaps childishly. "I want my daddy to be okay!"

"Breathe, Sadie. Just breathe. Sit on your couch and tell me what happened." I follow my own advice and hold the phone to my ear, not wanting to miss a second of what she has to say as I get comfortable on the couch.

"Do I have to drink the icky-looking one?" she asks, the disgust clear in her tone.

"You have to taste it. And I'd be very pleased if you at least drank half of it."

I wait in silence for a full thirty seconds.

"It's actually not bad. Tastes like strawberries and bananas. Could use some whipped cream though, and a new color. No one willingly thinks, *oooh green drink. Yum.*"

"As you said, it tastes good. Ignore the color and no, absolutely no on the whipped cream. Drink your drink, sip your coffee, and tell me what happened."

She sighs heavily and then inhales. "After dealing with an insanely annoying call from my ex Sean yesterday, Mom called."

"Why did your ex call?" I pinpoint that bit of information immediately. My hackles rise. I wonder if she'd willingly give me his number.

"It doesn't even matter. He doesn't matter. The man is so self-centered. He was more worried about my retirement status during these trying times than he was about me. Eventually I told him to piss off."

I smile wide and cross my knee over the other. "Atta girl! Good. You don't need him bringing you down."

"No, I have enough of that without him." Her tone goes back to sounding hurt and worried.

"Tell me what's going on with your folks."

"Mom called yesterday. Told me Dad had been feeling under the weather for a couple days. It got worse. He was throwing up, couldn't keep food down, has the shakes, and was running a high fever."

"Oh, Sadie."

"Mom took him to the hospital, and she said it was insane. They waited hours and hours to eventually get a space in a room filled with ten or more other people. The staff are overrun, everyone is wearing masks, gloves, and smocks. Said it felt like she was inside that movie *Contagion.*"

"Jesus. I'll bet she was really scared."

"Yeah." Her voice is small, but she continues. "They tested him for influenza A and B, not COVID-19 though."

"Why the hell not!" I stand up and pace the room feeling like an animal stuck in a cage. He's in his early sixties. Seems like they should be testing anyone and everyone that's sick just to rule it out. I keep those thoughts to myself.

"Apparently he wasn't having chest pain or shortness of breath with the other symptoms."

"You're kidding me."

"I wish I were. He tested positive for influenza, but he still could have the virus. I'm so scared. They sent him home after pumping him full of fluids and acetaminophen. I'm worried he could end up dying because they wouldn't test him and treat him for the virus." She breaks out into bone-wracking sobs that have my knees weak.

"I'm coming over!" I head to the door.

"No! I won't open the door. We haven't been in quarantine for fourteen days. They say symptoms arise within a two-week timeframe."

"I don't care, Sadie. You need me right now."

She lets out a shaky breath. "No, no. We can't risk it. I'd feel horrible if I ended up being sick and then gave it to you. It would destroy me. We can't be selfish right now."

I press my head to the wall that connects with her apartment.

"You know he's going to be okay, right?"

She inhales long and slow before letting it out. "I want to believe that, Evan. From your mouth to God's ears."

"Just think positive thoughts, yeah? Would your Dad want you worrying like this?"

"N-no. He'd be pretty upset. He doesn't ever like to be seen as weak. And he's normally in such good health."

"Let's focus on that. Besides, people get the regular old flu all the time. Right?"

"Yes, they do."

"And usually lots of fluids and being on your ass while getting pampered does the job. I'm sure your mother is tending to him like a badass nurse."

"How did you know?" She chuckles.

"I love hearing you laugh. Brightens up my entire day."

"Even with it raining outside?" She sounds a little more upbeat.

"This is so fucked up. You know what I want more than anything?"

"What? Tell me?"

"I want to hold you, tell you everything will be okay. Kiss your forehead…and your lips. Christ, what I wouldn't give to taste your mouth. Make you feel what I'm feeling deep inside."

She gasps but then whispers, "I wish that too."

I press my palm flat to the wall trying to feel her energy, her presence, just beyond the barrier. "Sadie, this thing between us. It's growing every day. Do you feel it? Tell me you feel it too and I'm not alone?"

"I…I feel it too. I don't understand it, but I can't deny it's there. The attraction…"

"Is off the fucking charts." I shake my head and press harder into the wall.

"We've only known each other a week and we haven't so much as touched. How can this be real?"

"I don't know, sweetheart, but it's more real than anything I've felt before. I *crave* you. I lie awake at night and imagine what you taste like. How your skin would feel against mine. What your hair smells like. How you'd sound when I kiss your mouth, your neck, shoulders, and *lower*. I'm obsessed with thoughts of being with you intimately."

"My word, Evan. The pictures you paint." Her voice is lower, more seductive.

"Do you want that, Sadie? My mouth on yours. My fingers teasing your skin?" The vision of touching her flashes across my mind and my dick aches.

"Are you trying to turn me on?" Her question is breathy and filled with what I hope is desire.

"Is it working?" I run my hand down and cup my hardening shaft.

"Yeah," she admits. "But I'm not sure about this."

"Just let me try and take your mind off things for a minute or two, okay? Ease some of that stress. It's just you and me. And you know you're safe with me."

There's a pause, but then she says, "Okay."

"Are you sitting down on the couch?"

"Y-yes."

"Are you imagining me kissing you? Touching your skin. Running my fingers along your sides, up your ribcage."

"Oh my…" Her breath is coming a little faster.

"Are you touching your breasts?"

"I am now."

I bite down on my bottom lip at the vision of her splayed out on her couch, holding the phone to her ear, and touching herself to the sound of my voice. "Good. Play with your pretty nipples for me. Tell me what they look like. What color are they?" I shove down my workout shorts and let my hard dick fall free. I grip the base and stroke up once, imagining her touching her sizable tits. Even just hearing her excited breaths like this is a dream come true.

"I've never had phone sex before."

"No? But it feels good, doesn't it? It feels right. My voice leading you, encouraging you, telling you what to do."

"Y-yeah." She pants.

"Now focus, Sadie. Your breasts. Tell me all about them. I'm fucking dying here, needing to know."

"They're uh…pale pink, about the size of a quarter each. Though the tips are hard right now."

Hearing her talk like this… It's official, there isn't a drop of blood left in my head. Braindead from phone sex with Sadie. What a way to go. "I'd suck them into tight little berries. Make them red and burn with the heat of my mouth. Pinch them like I would."

She moans so loud I swear I can hear her through the wall. I press the phone closer to my ear. "I'm so hard for you."

"Tell me," she half sighs and groans at the same time.

"Long and thick. I've got my hand stroking up and down. My arousal is beading at the tip. God, if only your mouth was in front of me."

"I'd flick that drop with my tongue and take you deep into my mouth. Wanting you weak with desire at the control I'd have over you," she promises.

I hiss through my teeth. This is going to last like thirty seconds max. We're both too on edge. And it is perfect. "You like control in the bedroom, baby?"

She hums. "Sometimes. I enjoy socking cock. I'd enjoy sucking your cock."

"Jesus, you're gonna make me come. Dip your hand into your panties and tell me how wet you are right now?"

"Oh, Evan. I'm wet. Very wet."

"Are you dripping for me? Spin two fingers around your hard little clit. Over and over. Can you feel me touching you?"

"Yes, fuck. Yes, I can."

"Good. I'd plunge two fingers inside your heat and then use the moisture there to make your clit as slippery as my tongue. Then I'd repeat the move until you were begging me to fuck you."

"I'm close…" She sighs and her breath comes in short bursts through the phone.

"Me too." I grip my dick harder and thrust my hips, creating the perfect friction, ramping up the speed as I listen to her little mewls and sighs. "Fuck, I'm gonna blow, baby. You want to hear me come while you finger fuck yourself?"

"You're so dirty," she drawls languidly.

"I can hear how much it turns you on. Fuck yourself harder. It's my fingers inside you plunging deep, twirling around your hard clit. If I was there, I'd suck your little bundle into my mouth until you scream."

And that does it.

Sadie cries out. At the sound of her release, my cock shoots off. "Fuck yeah, Sadie. Baby…" Rope after rope of my essence jets onto my hand and the wall I'm facing. I don't even try and quiet myself. I want her to hear it all.

"Good Lord, that was good." Her breaths are still fast, but I can hear the joy in her tone. It makes me feel like a king. Like a god that I could give this to her. "Was it good for you, handsome?"

"I just shot my load all over the wall in Jake's apartment." I laugh dryly.

"Aw, you were pressed against the wall?"

"Wanted to be as close as possible to you," I admit. This woman makes me crazy for her. If I could go outside, I'd be carving our initials into a tree. It's insane.

"That's quite romantic for a man that just took me from crying over my parents to crying out in orgasm in the span of a phone call. Rather impressive."

"I'll take that as compliment and raise you one with an important question."

"Which is?"

"When are we going to do it again?"

♡

## SADIE

After the stellar phone sex, we simply move into regular conversation. I find Evan to be a great conversationalist. When he asks about my book, I can't help but fill him in on all the details—sans the part where the hero and heroine are loosely based off of us.

"They should do it doggie style."

I burst out laughing. "No, Evan. Sheesh. The sex has to further the story and say something about the hero and heroine and their relationship. You have to hook the reader, engage their minds and their emotions. Sex in a romance is a reflection of the hero and heroine's growing intimacy."

"Evolution through screwing, huh?"

"Basically, yeah. So you can't have them doing doggie the first time they hit the sheets. Where's the romance in that? It's a straight up horny porn position. Him behind her, out of her line of sight. That takes a certain amount of trust that probably hasn't yet been established between them. And her staring at the headboard or pillows or whatever. She's not getting to see how she's affecting him, if this moment is as important to him as it is to her. Maybe he's just getting off. Maybe he's thinking about his ex. She doesn't know."

"Hmm." The man does not sound convinced.

"Later on in their relationship when they're just going at it hard, sure, great. But for their first time? That doesn't work."

Since the horrible scary news about Dad, I've gotten no work done. My head is an even bigger mess than normal. I've done little but pace and cry my heart out since Mom told me. And it's not like I have tissues to spare for blowing my nose after crying jags either. An old tee has been sacrificed to the cause.

Luckily, Evan snapped me out of the panic spiral for the time being. With phone sex of all things. I did not see that one coming. I'm even smiling a little, though my parents are never far from my thoughts. Dad has got to be okay. He's *going* to be okay. I couldn't handle it otherwise. And poor Mom—stuck at home alone dealing with a seriously ill person and all of this. Unfortunately it's too late for me to fly home to Texas, so there's no point even worrying over it or feeling guilty. Doesn't stop the negative thoughts from filling my mind and affecting my mood. I couldn't be more thankful for Evan's support right now. He's slowly easing his way into my heart as well as my panties.

"I strongly disagree. I think there's plenty of romance in smacking and tapping a gorgeous round ass. Sliding your hand up a woman's spine and grabbing her hair, giving it a tug. It's a beautiful thing. How can you not see that, Sadie? Where's your imagination?" He chuckles.

I finish off the last of the coffee and take another cautious sip of the smoothie. So green. My body won't know what hit it with all of this healthy stuff. "Doggie style is pure smutty fun sex. I have nothing against the position. It definitely has its place in the bedroom."

"Or the living room, dining room, maybe even the kitchen." His words are laced with innuendo.

"Yeah, but then you're dealing with possible trauma to the girl's knees. Stop and think. How is she going to wear a flirty short skirt out to dinner with the hero in the next scene if she's got carpet burn or scratches from tiles, huh? Sheets and a mattress are just kinder all round."

He chuckles. "You've given this a lot of thought."

"It's my job. I dissect relationships and sex for a living. Ponder the secrets of life and love. Figure out new ways to come at one of the oldest stories there is—two people falling for one another. Or more than two. I don't write poly, but I sure read it."

KYLIE SCOTT & AUDREY CARLAN

"You're open to a threesome?" he asks, quick as a whip.

"I didn't say that."

"Hmm. On second thought, I don't think I'm interested in sharing you. Forget I asked."

"Will do. For what it's worth, I feel the same. When we finally get to be in the same room together, I don't think there needs to be anyone else, thank you very much. But back to the story…"

He clears his throat. "Right. So they meet during the lockdown and live near each other?"

"That's right." No need to go into too many details. Besides, I'm not exactly sure how I'd explain how semi-autobiographical certain aspects are. One major life disaster/concern at a time is best for now. "He rescues her from a mugging. Takes her up to his apartment. Offers comfort that evolves into sexual shenanigans."

"Meaningful sexual shenanigans," he corrects helpfully. Such a boy scout.

"That's right. You have been listening." I smile.

"Sadie, baby, I hang on your every damn word. How have you not noticed this yet?"

Oh God. My stomach drops through the floor. It kills me when he talks sweet to me. How his voice goes all husky, the volume dropping so that he's whispering to me in a way that makes it seem like we're the only two people in the whole wide world. The man goes to my head faster than champagne. I take another sip of the evil green drink to ground me. "I'm noticing, trust me."

"Good."

"You know, I was a little worried you'd friend-zoned me."

"Really?" he asks. And there's something in his tone. Something not quite right.

Wait. Did that sound bad? I think that sounded bad. What if he thinks I only want him for sex? Like only his ridiculously hot body matters to me. Shit. "Not that being just your friend wouldn't be wonderful and fulfilling. I just hoped maybe we'd become more than that, you know? But friendship with people is great too and we all need someone at our back. Especially during hard times like these. Attraction isn't everything. That we can spend time together just chatting and getting to know one another is great. And we laugh a lot together, right? We enjoy each other's company. Which is really important to me, I want you to know that."

Nothing from him.

"Evan?"

"Are you finished freaking out there or did you want to reassure me some more?"

"I just didn't want you to think that...you know. Don't tease me, you brute. I'm stressed out enough as it is."

He chuckles some more. "I live to tease you. And I don't think that. Relax, sweetheart. We both have a strong desire to be intimate with each other and that's a beautiful and natural thing. It's what adults do to express a deep and abiding affection—they get naked and bang each other's brains out."

"Aw. More romance. Have you ever considered writing poetry? I think you have a gift."

"You do? Let me see," he says, making a noise in his throat. A thinking noise. "How about this? Roses are red, Sadie likes blue, you're not going to walk straight for a week, once I get my hands on you."

I almost fall off the sofa from laughing so hard. "Oh my God, Evan."

"You like it?"

"That's hilarious. And you wish, big boy. I have seen nothing yet to make me think you're packing all that. I think someone's been fawned over by one too many cheerleaders."

And then there's another one of those silences. Awkward and

long. Either I'm the worst conversationalist in history or there's something going on.

"Shit," he finally mumbles. And he sounds so sad. Like all of the happiness and good times have been sucked straight out of his world. I've seen him happy and grumpy and several degrees between. But this is something entirely different. "Sadie, there's something I have to tell you."

"What?"

"You're probably going to see things on social media once the test results get released, anyway. Better that you hear it from me."

"Hear what from you?"

"I guess hearing about your dad getting sick and all, you haven't gotten around to Googling me, huh?"

"No, I haven't. I don't know that I would have. It seems kind of invasive. I've had the occasional overzealous fan try to track me down and things like that. Respecting people's privacy matters. Anything I need to know about, I'd rather hear it from you than read it online. Whatever it is. Evan, you're scaring me. What's going on?"

"Just…try and keep an open mind, okay?"

For the next hour Evan dumps a shit storm of epic proportions on me. It's so heartbreaking I feel chewed up, spit on, and tossed out like yesterday's garbage and it didn't even happen to me.

Poor Evan.

We end the conversation with the promise to call one another tomorrow but I can tell he's concerned with how I'm going to stew on the story he shared.

The reason he's in hiding. The reputation-destroying image splashed across the media. Being roofied. The steroids found in his locker. Him being set up. It's all so much. Far more than I ever anticipated he'd be managing alone, in complete silence, locked away in a home not of his own. Add the virus, the uncertainty hovering over everyone's heads right now like a dark cloud, and you've got dire straits.

Evan has hit rock bottom and right now it seems I'm the only good thing in his life.

A heavy place to be.

# Chapter
## EIGHT

### QUARANTINE: DAY 8

SADIE

**Zahra:** He says the girl drugged him and someone placed steroids in his locker?

**Me:** Exactly. And this is top secret, Zahra. You cannot repeat a word of this to anyone. He's trusting me not to sell him out to the press and loose lips sink ships. But I had to talk about it to someone and you're my best friend.

**Zahra:** My lips are sealed. Don't worry. The press is certainly skewering him. Some of these articles are damning as all hell. Goes to show how fast you can go from golden boy to the gutter.

**Me:** I know. I saw. I mean, how could I not after he told me everything? They're so cruel the way they're tearing his reputation apart.

**Zahra:** They're just doing their job and trying to sell ad space.

**Me:** Yeah, I guess. Do they have to be so overzealous about it though? Kind of makes me wonder how some of them sleep at night. The way they jump to all of these conclusions and how willing they are to write off his whole career. Even releasing the results from the drug test hasn't convinced all of them. God knows how it'll blow up if they find out about the stuff in his locker.

**Zahra:** It sure doesn't look good.

**Me:** I know.

**Zahra:** Question is, do you trust him or not?

**Me:** I've known him for exactly a week. But yeah, I do. He's a straight up guy so far as I can tell. And this is hurting him, bad. You should have heard him talk about it. The man sounded absolutely gutted. The way his teammates have turned on him and everything. They're like a family to him.

**Me:** On the other hand, I haven't always displayed the best judgement when it comes to men. The evidence is damning.

**Zahra:** Girl, we've all been there. Each and every one of us messes up sometime. And usually more than once. What does your head tell you? More importantly, what does your heart tell you?

**Me:** It tells me there's every chance I'm in over my head when it comes to this man.

**Zahra:** That's not necessarily a bad thing.

**Me:** How so?

**Zahra:** As I recall, your heart didn't have a damn thing to say about Sean. Nada. Nothing. Not a peep. At least it's paying attention this time.

**Me:** True. Even from the mandatory six feet away Evan Sparks has managed to get under my skin. He's a dangerous man. I've got to get off messenger. It's time to call Mom to see how Dad is going. She'll only let me call at designated times twice a day, so I don't drive her crazy checking up on them. Fingers crossed his temperature has come down.

**Zahra:** He'll be in my prayers. I'm here if you need me. Keep the pages coming. The story is fun and that's what people need right now. A little lightness and hope.

**Me:** xx

Once I've called my parents (Dad is doing better) and pre-pared Evan's treat, I pick up my cell and dial Evan's number. I'm standing behind my closed front door so I can hear everything that happens. I'm a little overexcited. So? Sue me.

"Sexy Sadie." He all but purrs.

My skin immediately turns to gooseflesh. How the hell does he do that? "Evan, you have a delivery. Go check your front door."

"Do I now?" The sound of his bare feet against the polished wooden flooring echoes through the quiet of his apartment. "How'd your work go today?"

"Excellent, thank you. But even better, my dad's fever broke."

"Honey. That's great news. You must be so relieved."

"Yes, I am. So, we're celebrating."

I can hear his door opening followed by a low chuckle. "Well, now. You've been busy. I wasn't entirely sure I'd be hearing from you again."

"What? Why not?"

He sighs. "Because of what I told you, about the whole fucking mess my career is in. You barely know me. Why the hell should you trust me to believe I'm not cheating the system and taking drugs when some of my oldest friends have turned their backs on me over it?"

"You're right, we haven't known each other long. And maybe

this is just a fling, a fun time between two consenting adults. Maybe when the world starts turning again, we're going to find we're not the least bit compatible and this was just a temporary isolation type thing. A Band-Aid to help get us through this situation." I pause and take a deep breath. Just the thought of this being a bust hurts more than I anticipated. Those pesky damn feelings again.

"But, Evan. I've seen you out on that balcony almost every day working your ass off to keep fit and strong. I can't even imagine how much time you spend on the treadmill and bike in Jake's spare room. I've seen how you eat clean and look after yourself. Most importantly, I heard in your voice how much this has hurt you. How wrong this all is. Not only do I believe you, I believe in you. Okay?"

"Okay. Thank you." His voice comes through both on the cell and more quietly down the hallway. We're so close, but not close enough. And the man needs a hug. I can tell. What he's going through is awful. That I can't be with him to comfort him sucks.

"Now pick up your food and take it inside while it's still hot."

The door to the neighboring apartment snicks closed. "Thank you for the beer. Without sounding like an ingrate, are you sure what's in this bowl is food? Because it doesn't look like food."

"This is as close as I get to cooking, buddy." I settle on the sofa, my own meal already set out in front of me. "I even did a side salad for you. You're welcome."

"Sprinkling parsley on top of orange macaroni isn't a side salad, baby."

"Close enough."

"This came out of a box, didn't it?" he asks, but I can hear the smile in his voice.

"Two boxes, actually. No expense spared. A toast," I announce, picking up my vodka, soda, and lime. "To our families' health and to us."

"I'll drink to that."

"Now put your TV on. *Lord of the Rings* is about to start and it's one of my favorites." I unmute my TV just as the wonderful opening music begins. God, I love this film.

"Never seen it," he comments.

"No? Well get comfortable because they're showing all three so we're here for the duration."

"Is this a date?" His voice is a low, sexy rumble. The kind I imagine might come with a saucy little grin.

"Of course, it's a date. Every time we come near each other it somehow winds up being a date," I say with a laugh, filling up a fork with gooey carby goodness.

"This is about wizards and shit, right?"

"Yes, it is, and you're going to love it. It's such an epic tale. The world-building is amazing. Not to mention that Aragorn is smokin' hot. For you, there's some eye candy in the form of warrior maidens and winsome elvish ladies fluttering their lashes. Plus, there's heaps of battle scenes. Helm's Deep is my favorite. It's so full on."

He chuckles around what I assume to be a bite of food. "Okay, okay. You've sold me. We're watching it," he says. "Except you know what this means? Next time I get to choose."

"Sounds fair."

"And you have to watch a ball game with me sometime."

"By ballgame do you mean porn?"

"Ha ha. Very funny. You're watching a sport with me, Sadie. I'll explain all of the rules and everything. It'll be fine. You'll like it. Trust me."

"Can't we just watch porn? I think it would be far more educational…for you." I tease while laughing, knowing he's going to jump on me like cheese on a hamburger.

"Are you suggesting I might need some sex education? Because

I thought I proved everything is all A's in that department just yesterday. I mean, I made you come without touching or kissing you. I'm thinking that's some phenomenal prowess."

"Fine, you win. Still when it comes to the sport, football for me has always been this odd event that happens before and after a cool mini-concert once a year. Lady Gaga was my favorite though Shakira and J. Lo were awesome too."

"You're killing me."

"And we all gather together with drinks and lots of different snacks to watch the mini-concert and cool ads. Then dudes run around a field doing something. I'm not sure what. Never really paid attention to that part of things."

Evan groans loudly. "You have so much to learn. I would have thought the guys running around in tight pants would have at least caught your interest."

"It's true. I do admire their thighs."

He chuckles. "You're going to learn about football, Sadie. And you're going to like it. You can't date a baller without going to the games. Assuming all of this shit gets sorted out with the pandemic and I get to play professionally again. Someday."

"It will be, Evan. Do not give up hope. I won't allow it. You're a great player."

"How do you know? By your own admission, you've never even watched a game."

"I don't care. I know things. Important things. And this is one of them. This whole doping scandal and whoever set you up is all going to get sorted out. Your career is not over, and you will be exonerated! Do you understand me?" My voice brooks no argument with how strongly I feel about this.

A pause. "Yes, ma'am. Hell, I wouldn't dare disagree. You're kind of scary when you get going. Sexy scary, but still a little teeth-rattling."

"I'm sorry I had to use my 'fuck with me and die' voice on you. But this is important."

"You have names for your different voices?" he asks.

"Indeed, I do, and you just heard one scarily close to DEFCON one, my friend. That's reserved for people who commit true acts of bastardry. Or if someone mildly inconveniences me when I'm hungry or something. It kind of depends on the day. Let's hope we never have to go there."

"You know we're going to."

"Hmm?"

"We keep this up, I'm going to hear you go ballistic one day. I guarantee it. At some hopefully long off time in the future, I will annoy the living shit out of you. In fact, I'm kind of looking forward to it. Which is a surprise, because I never hung around for that sort of thing before. But with you, it's different. It'll mean you trust me enough to go off because you know you're safe with me. And you'll know I'll still be there once you've calmed your ass down."

My heart doubles in size for some reason. It's pressing against the cage of my ribs, trying to hold in all of the emotions he evokes in me. Any day now it's going to burst and make an awful mess. There'll be clingy delicate feelings all over the place. I just know it. And after the year or so of nothing that was my relationship with the ex, the idea of feelings is more than a little scary. "That sounds dangerously like you're forecasting the possibility of a serious relationship between us, Evan."

"It does, doesn't it? I figure we're both old enough to know what we want." Once again that low rumble of his gets me every time.

"True." I wave a hand across my now heated face.

"Guess we'll just have to wait and see what happens between us. Which sucks because I hate waiting. I especially hate waiting when it comes to you."

I don't know what to say so I let him do the talking.

"Just don't go apeshit on me too often, okay?" His words hold a hint of vulnerability.

That vulnerability hits me right in the gut. "Okay," I whisper.

Soft chewing noises come over the line. "Thank you for making dinner for me, sweetheart. I really appreciate the effort, but this tastes terrible. I'm not sure it's really even food. Was this cheese originally in powdered form?" I can hear a gagging sound that has me giggling. "We can do so much better, baby," he says. "I'm thinking I should probably cook from now on—for both our sakes."

I snort. "The kitchen is nothing more than somewhere convenient to store my candy, cookies, and ice cream as far as I'm concerned. Have at it."

"Check out this dude in the gray hat. How many times a day do you think he knocks it on doorways, and it falls off?"

"He's a wizard. He has supernatural powers up to and including the protection of excessively pointy hats from any and all architectural structures."

Evan chuckles. Quite possibly my favorite sound in the whole universe. "Sure, Sadie. Whatever you say."

♡

# EVAN

"Hi, Dad. How's it going?" I ask while putting together my morning smoothie. Since I woke up so early, I didn't bother asking Sadie if she wanted one. Not that she would anyway. Eventually I plan on waking her up with some morning nookie which would then turn into having breakfast together and potentially even showering at the same time before we started our day.

Someday.

Hopefully.

"You're looking good, son. Fit as a fiddle." He coughs into his hand and I frown at the laptop screen I have sitting on the opposite kitchen counter running Skype. Thank goodness Dad has Curt still living with him. My brother set up the technology so I could connect with them face-to-face from anywhere.

"I am, thank you. Working out. Holed up in Jake's pad."

My dad coughs again and he hits his wide barrel chest with a closed fist.

I narrow my gaze and note his pallor is a little off. "Dad, why are you coughing?" My heart pounds right out of my chest. I stop everything I'm doing and hang on every breath my father takes to see if there is anything off or strange.

"Relax, son. I don't have the virus. I'm fine. Jesus. Everyone is going crazy about this flu."

"Dad, it's not a flu. It's a virus with no known cure, vaccine, or treatment plan other than to let it run its course or being hospitalized. Do you have a fever? Any other symptoms?"

"No, boy. I have this cough because I've been working myself to the bone. The cannery is working overtime and I signed up for as many shifts as possible."

"Why the hell would you do that! I have enough money to float both of us for the rest of our lives! You don't need to work, Dad. I've told you that a million times."

He scoffs. "What? And leave people in need? Reports are saying the stores are getting wiped clean out of canned goods all over the nation. We're a big supplier, son. I need to do my bit to help. This is me doing my bit to help. Understand?"

I grind my teeth and breathe through my nose. "Dad, I'd prefer you limit your access to other people. What kind of safety measures do they have going down at the cannery to protect the workers?"

He runs a hand through his white-blond hair and then his scruffy chin. The lines around his eyes seem deeper than usual and he just looks tired. Run down. "My company is taking it pretty seriously seein' as a couple people came down with the virus. They shut down work for an entire weekend and had a crew come in and do a detailed cleaning. We all wear coveralls over our clothes and have these face-shield type things. Which are a damn nuisance. Smelling your own breath all day. Breathing hot air." He scowls.

"Dad, those are in place to protect you."

"I know, and I'm doing my part, wearing 'em going in and coming out. We leave them in a heap by the exit on our way out and they do something to hose them down each night. We're lucky. Fellas in the break room are talking about some companies where they're just laying people off and not doing Sam hell to protect any of them."

Jesus. This thing is getting so much worse. I press a thumb and forefinger to my temples trying to ward off a tension headache. "Maybe this is a sign you're supposed to take early retirement? I'll make sure your account has plenty of money and you can spend your time golfing, playing cards, and hanging out with Curt at the bar. Hell, I'll buy the bar for you guys! You can run it together. After this pandemic situation gets better."

"Son…" He has that warning in his voice I have zero desire to hear.

"Just think about it, Dad. Okay? Talk to Curt, yeah?" I put a call to my baby brother on my radar for sometime today too. Get myself an ally. Curt would be happy to get Dad out of that back-breaking work in the cannery, but he may not take too kindly to his brother buying him a bar.

Hmm. What if I told them I needed the investment and they were going to own a third of it since they'd be the ones running it? Might make it sound more palatable. I'll talk to Sadie about it. Get her thoughts.

"I'll think about it," he says begrudgingly. "If you tell me what the hell is going on with all these media outlets claiming my boy is doing drugs."

I can't look my dad in the eyes. Even though I didn't do it, I still feel a ton of guilt my father even has to hear this crap.

"Polly's on it. We released my statement on the image along with the blood, urine, and hair test results that cleared me of doing anything wrong."

"Then why on God's green Earth are they saying you may lose your job on the Marauders? If you're cleared, you're cleared. End of. What does the coach have to say about all of this?"

"There's more than the jacked-up pictures, Dad. More you don't know about."

I glance at my father and note how his face changes from frustrated to concerned in a few beats. "Like what?"

"Coach had my locker searched after the party pics came out and found steroids." I toss in the ingredients to my smoothie and hit blend.

While I'm blending, I watch his entire face turn beet red. I hit stop and pull the pitcher off and pour my drink, afraid for the first time at how my father is going to respond.

"'Roids!" His voice is filled to the brim with rage. "Blasphemy! Who's got it out for you? No way in hell *my boy* would cheat the system and shoot poison up his veins to get a better record. That's not the son your mamma and I raised. Nut uh. No way. No how. You've got a bad seed on that team, son."

I close my eyes and set my arms against the countertop to hold myself up. The relief of hearing my dad refusing to even entertain the thought that I was juicing lifts a huge weight from my body and psyche. Tears hit the back of my eyes and a lump of emotion lodges in my throat.

"Thank you, Dad," I mutter.

"For what? Knowing my son isn't a cheater? Never would have crossed my mind. You're all about the game. It's the only woman you've ever claimed."

I grin wide, the worry and fear of moments before dissipating with my father's acceptance, belief, and mentioning a woman.

"Speaking of women, I'm actually seeing someone." I smile and suck back a nice portion of my drink. Shit, even the strawberry flavor of the smoothie now reminds me of my girl.

The realization hits me flat in the solar plexus. This is the first time I've ever thought of a woman as being *mine*. And I like it. A lot.

"Really? That's good news. Very good news. Means one day I might not die an old man with no grandbabies to call my own."

"Dad, you're fifty-two years old."

"And? I want little mini-Sparks running around when I'm young enough to chase 'em!" He smiles and winks.

"Man, I miss you. How's Curt?"

"Fine, fine. Tell me more about this woman you're seeing. And better yet, how in the world are you seeing her right now with the state being on lockdown?"

"You're never gonna believe this, but she lives in the apartment next door. We met on the balcony. Got to talking. Went to the grocery store together. Talk on the phone. Watch movies at the same time from our separate apartments. We even make one another meals and leave them by each other's doors."

"Shee-it. Sounds to me like you're courting her, son. That has to be a first for you."

I smile and rub at my chin. "You know what, you're right. We haven't so much as touched, but I swear I'm closer to her than any other woman in the whole world. It's like she gets me on a different level. And when she talks, she's so funny. The woman makes me laugh until my gut hurts. And Dad, she's fuckin' gorgeous."

"Oh? Make an old man happy and give me the details. Need something to talk about to the guys in the breakroom."

"Oh, man. Shoulder-length blonde hair. Looks thick and soft too. Big blue eyes I want to stare into for hours. A cupid's bow-shaped mouth that I can't wait to kiss." I smile thinking about her features, having memorized them. "My Sadie has these high rounded cheek bones that always seem to be a little pink and two small dimples just along the side of her mouth." I look off into the distance at the blank wall and let the vision of her fill my mind. "She's something else, Dad. And her body…" I whistle and grin. "Out of this world. Curves for days."

My dad smacks the desk in front of him. "Damn, son. The way you describe this girl, I feel like she might be Miss America."

"Better, because she's Sadie."

"I heard you say she was your Sadie. The way you talk about her leads me to believe you've got feelings for this girl that match the obsession with her looks, yeah?"

"Definitely. I'm not sure what's gonna happen or how long I can go before I lay my hands on her. It's killing me. She's content to wait for weeks. We're already on Day 8 and I'm jonesing for her."

My father nods and purses his lips. "Make a deal with her. Once you pass a certain timeframe, you come together."

I bite into my bottom lip and think about his suggestion. "That's a great idea. You're a genius!"

My father laughs and it fills my heart with joy. I've been feeling so heavy lately between telling Sadie the truth and worrying about telling my Dad, I didn't realize I'd been carrying so much emotional baggage. Now it's as though I'm a hundred pounds lighter.

"Well, son, I didn't win the prettiest girl in Indiana over being a dolt now, did I? And your Sadie sounds a little like your mama. Except the eyes. Your mamma's were as green as the grass in the height of Spring."

"I know. I remember. Thanks for the talk, Dad. With your suggestion, I've got a woman to call."

"Don't go right for it. Lead into it softly. No dropping any emotional bombs. Women get flustered when you do that. Take it easy, work it into the conversation. You'll figure it out. My boy is smart and savvy when he wants to be."

"Learned it from my dad."

"That you did. Love you, boy."

"Love you too, Dad. So much. Be safe and keep me posted. If I don't hear from you in a couple days, I'll be calling."

"And I'll look forward to that call. Bye now."

"Bye." I hit the button that shuts off Skype and think about all that Dad said.

If I want to get my girl to agree to let me into her world physically, I'm going to have to appeal to her logical side. She's incredibly astute and combative by nature. She'll put up a fight for sure. Though it's the war I intend to win.

And Sadie, she's the prize.

# Chapter
## NINE

### QUARANTINE: DAY 9

EVAN

"**G**OOD MORNING, SUNSHINE." I SMILE AS I STEP out onto the balcony while holding my phone to my ear. The sun is shining, and the breeze isn't too chilly. Perfect weather to be outside talking to my girl.

"It is a good morning. Spoke to Dad myself. He's already turning the corner and feeling heaps better."

"Baby, that's great! Good to hear. I talked to my father too."

"Really? How'd that go?"

"Come out onto the balcony wearing your yoga gear. Bring your mat and I'll tell you."

Sadie groans loud. "I'm already in yoga pants and a tank but I was planning on loafing today. The muse is being a pest and not playing well with others. Others meaning me. She's avoiding *me*, the cranky wench."

"Aw, sorry, babe. She'll come back. Maybe you just need a little sunshine. It's beautiful out. The sun is shining down on my face as we speak."

"Hmm. Are you shirtless?"

I grin. My girl likes my body. Huge plus. "I could be."

"If you are, I might be persuaded to come and get my eye candy fix for the day."

After putting the phone on speaker, I set it down on the small table and rip my T-shirt over my head. "Shirt off. Come hang out with me. Teach me some yoga. My back's a little tight from the lifts I did this morning."

"Would much rather massage all those muscles and work out another way," she grumbles, sounding very put out.

I chuckle. "Hey, anytime you're ready to break your rules, I'm here."

"They're not my rules," she snaps. "They come straight down from the highest level of government."

"Just come outside. I found a thick towel I can use and am ready to be trained."

She huffs. "Oh fine. Give me a few minutes. I need to brush my teeth."

"To do yoga you need to brush your teeth?" I laugh out loud.

"Shut up! Good oral hygiene is important, and I just had my third cup of coffee. I can't exercise with coffee breath."

"Third? Sadie," I start to chastise her, but she thwarts my efforts when she hangs up on me.

Shaking my head, I set up my towel longways on the concrete space and go inside to get a bottle of water and my shades.

When I make it back out, bottle in hand, I'm greeted by the sight of Sadie's rounded ass up in the air as she's bent over flattening her mat just so.

"Nice view." I bite into my bottom lip and tip my head wanting to imprint every curve into my brain.

Sadie pops up, spins around, and puts her hand to her hip. Her gaze is malicious, but her cheeks are already tinged pink and her mouth is twitching.

"Pervert!" She blasts and then smiles.

"Guilty. And I'm not even sorry."

She harrumphs and carries on organizing her stuff. "Let's start with some standing poses I learned recently. The teacher calls this one, Warrior One. Put your left leg out front and the right leg backwards in a scissor-like shape."

"Oooh, scissoring. Kinky." I follow along while facing her.

She grins and lifts her arms in the air. I watch fascinated as her full breasts rise up while she puts her hands over her head as if reaching for the sky.

I imagine putting my hands and mouth on those delectable-looking mounds. "Maybe this wasn't such a good idea."

"Get your mind out of the gutter and focus on the position," she reprimands. But the curtness in her tone and her sexy-as-fuck body have Mr. Happy paying far more attention than he should.

I adjust my cock to a more comfortable position and then raise my hands up but something else starts rising right along with them.

"Jesus, you're obscene. And sexy as hell. Stop it!" she demands, but I can see the fire and heat in her eyes.

Needing to rile her up, I turn sideways and allow my cock to tent my gym shorts in a graphic display of my desperate need for her. "It's your fault. Look at him. So ready and willing."

She scowls. "You're not playing fair."

"Who the fuck said anything about being fair? I want to put my hands on the woman I've been obsessing over for the last nine days. More so, you want it too."

"Evan," she groans and crosses her arms over her chest protectively. Instantly I feel like a shit.

"I'm sorry. I can't help wanting you. I think it might help if we had a timeframe or end date to this enforced celibacy neither of us want."

She sighs and rubs at her bare biceps. "The virus is dangerous, and it takes up to fourteen days sometimes for symptoms to show. And I think…"

"We've already survived nine days with nothing. Isn't that close enough to put us out of our misery?"

She frowns and shakes her head. "It wouldn't feel right."

"Then when would it?" I stretch my arms over my head and lace my fingers behind my neck, putting my entire body on display.

I watch while her gaze tracks all over my skin as if it were a physical touch. She puts her hands on her hips, and I can see her nipples bead up in tight little points against her tank. I'd give my left nut to put my mouth on those erect tips.

"Maybe another week? If we both don't have any symptoms whatsoever, I think it would be safe for us to see *only* each other."

My heart sinks as my mind starts counting back. "Baby, that's seventeen days not fourteen. How about ten?"

She laughs. "Tomorrow?"

"Deal!" I chuckle.

"No deal! That's only ten days. How about Day 15? Then we'll know for sure."

I shake my head and palm my hard cock. Her blue eyes sparkle and heat as I rub my dick through my shorts and groan. "Fourteen. Not a day more. I can't take it. Waiting five more days to touch you… Fuck, Sadie. It's gonna kill me."

She licks her lips and frowns. "I know. For me too. But we can do this. For the safety of one another, we can manage. Now scissor your legs, ignore your hard-on, and raise those massive arms over your head." Sadie does the same as she instructs. "Then lunge forward until you feel a nice stretch through your hips and back leg."

I follow along and breathe deeply, trying to calm not only my rapidly beating heart, but to chill out my dick. Blue balls are the real deal and Mr. Happy is now Mr. Grumpy due to not getting any action. I'll be taking care of that later tonight. Maybe I could talk Sadie into another phone sesh. Oooh better yet, a video sexca-pade. Now that has some merit.

"Next you want to pinwheel one of your arms out into a T. Stretch the back leg out in a wide stance and focus intently forward." She scrunches up her face with the effort. No half-assing it for my girl.

I do as she says and enjoy looking at her while getting a good stretch in. "So, tell me. What's your favorite food."

"Candy," she says instantly, and then moves into another pose.

I follow her movements fluidly without being instructed. "Candy is not a food, babe."

"It is to me. Let's see, there's Reese's Peanut butter cups. Good for breakfast, kind of like peanut butter toast. Then there's Snickers…all those nuts and nougat. So healthy." She grins. "Even the commercials confirm that it's designed as a meal replacement." Without so much as a stumble she moves into the next pose. Something that has one of her arms pointed up toward the sky and half her body bent over to the side as she rests one elbow on her bent knee.

"Baby, no." I lean over and do as she does. "This is so much worse than I thought."

"And of course, one of my personal favorite staples—peanut M&M's. All that good protein. And there's dairy in the chocolate. So, you've got protein and dairy all in one. It's a time saver, really." She smiles wide and I can tell she loves getting my goat.

"Your level of nutrition horrifies me. After yoga, I'm making you lunch. And dinner!"

She pushes up to a stand, puts her hands above her head in a triangle with palms touching, and lifts up one leg and sets it on the inside of her thigh. It's the same pose she was doing when I watched her the first time. Though this time she's not wobbling all over the place.

"Awesome job! You're not even moving. What's this pose called?"

"Tree Pose, I think. Yeah, I'm pretty sure."

I attempt to put my foot all the way up against the inside of my thigh, but it is not happening. She giggles as I keep trying and fail miserably.

"Start lower. Rest your bare foot against your inner leg or ankle. You're still getting a stretch and working on your balance but it's not as difficult. The more you do it, the more flexible you'll become. Before, I wasn't able to touch the ground when I bent over, now I can."

"Show me." I smirk.

She narrows her eyes. "Fat chance, buddy! You just want to see my ass or my cleavage."

"Yep."

"No lies, I like a man that's truthful and you've been very forthcoming with me. So much so, I think you deserve a little eye candy." And without further comment she rips her tank over her head and is left standing in a simple, almost sheer, workout bra. I can see the perfect quarter-sized shaped of her areolas and succulent tips.

"Jesus! You trying to kill me!" I groan but can't take my eyes away from all that flesh goodness. "You're fucking beautiful. Everywhere."

"Back to it. Everything we did you need to do on the other side."

I lick my lips. "As long as you face me the entire time, I'll do whatever you want, princess."

"You are such a boob man. I knew it! The way your eyes would slide down to them. I'm going to remember this boon."

I shake my head. "Call it what you want, but my woman has the most magnificent rack I've ever seen."

"Your woman, huh?"

"Yep. I decided that the day you made me come all over the apartment wall. If a woman can make me lose myself without ever having touched her, I know she is the one for me."

The she in question hums. "We'll see."

"I could see better if you remove the bra."

"It's practically sheer! Don't be greedy. Plus, there are other neighbors I'm not on such intimate terms with." She purses her lips and moves into another pose.

"Greedy? When it comes to you, Sadie, I'll never get enough. But fair point. I don't need the rest of the city seeing you."

Her chest moves up and down and my cock throbs with every inhalation she takes.

"I think we should video chat tonight," I say.

"Do you?"

"Absolutely."

"And you just want to chat?" She raises a brow.

I nod. "Yeah, but I think we should do it naked. As you can see," I gesture to my obvious desire. "I'm a man in need and you're the woman I need."

She presses her lips together and looks off toward the view. "I kind of like being the woman a big brawny man like you needs. Though I've never done anything like that before."

"Me either. We'll figure it out together. Make it a date."

"A date for sex?" She tips her head as though truly considering the merits.

I grin. "A booty video call." I laugh and her lips twitch. "Remember the phone sex was a first for us both, right?"

She nods. "And that was um…" A blush rises over her chest, neck and up through her cheeks. "Very hot. And fun."

"I think a video chat would be insane. And educational. You know, for your story. Maybe the hero and heroine could have some Skype sex."

Her eyes widen. "That's an excellent idea. We should do it for research purposes."

"Definitely. What time shall I call? Ten?"

"I don't go to bed until late."

"Baby, you're not going to bed to sleep. You're going to bed to fuck yourself on camera while I stroke myself and we both get off to the beauty that is building between us."

"Beauty?" Her head jerks back as though she's surprised.

"I believe all sex acts are beautiful in their own way. It's all about trust and passion. Caring about one another in a way that makes you want to express it physically."

She smiles wide, positively glowing under the sun's golden rays. "And what of love?"

"When two people are in that place in their relationship, it only adds to the fire they've built. Keeps it burning so it never goes out. At least that's the way I see it. Or I do now."

Everything I said bum-rushed my form the same as if I was on the field, running for the end zone and being taken down at the last second by the opposing team's linebackers. The wind left my body as though I'd had the breath knocked right out of me. My gaze on her became crystal clear and I could see the two of us in the future. A lifetime of laughing and teasing one another. Happiness in a forever kind of way.

In that moment, I realize I'm falling for this woman, and I've never laid my hands on her.

Mind.

Blown.

"I'm going to let you finish your routine. I've uh," I point to my situation, "got something to take care of. See you at ten." I blow her a kiss.

"I can hardly wait, Evan. I'll see you at ten."

With a flick of my fingers I head back inside and straight to the bathroom.

## SADIE

Ten minutes to ten o'clock and I'm a tingle of nerves and anticipation. Nervous because what if I do something he doesn't like, or it doesn't look attractive through the screen? What if my stomach makes that roll shape when I sit down? Everyone has a sit-down roll, I think? I crunch my stomach up and back in the attempt to see what Evan might see.

Groaning, I flop back on my bed, my laptop next to me. Why am I worried at all? He's a man. Men like naked women, and he's made it very clear he likes my shape and seemed rather fond of my breasts earlier today. Perhaps I can focus on those. Distract his vision with the boobage, a guaranteed crowd pleaser.

What if he wants me to put the camera between my legs?

Oh my God! No way am I doing that.

Probably not. Hmm. I'll want to see between his thighs most definitely. It's only fair that if he shares, I share.

Okay, maybe if things get super-heated, I'll give the ole crotch shot a whirl.

I clench my jaw and check the time. Eight minutes have passed and I'm lying on my bed in a teal satin camisole and panty set. There are lace triangles covering my breasts, but you can still see ample cleavage. Under the breasts the cami glides along my ribcage and over my abdomen. The panties are a stretchy lace thong that has a saucy satin bow at the top of my ass crack—as though I were offering my ass up as a gift.

Technically it's true. In a manner of speaking.

The notification that I'm receiving a video call flashes and I curve to my side on the bed and rest my head in my hand. I attempt to portray an attractive pose and an air of calmness I absolutely *do not* feel as I press the button to accept the call.

Evan's smiling gorgeous face and upper body appear on the screen. He's bare-chested and grinning like a loon. He must have the computer resting on his lap because I can see he's in bed, leaning up against a wooden headboard with a stack of pillows behind him.

I can't help but tip my head back and laugh instantly. "We're such dorks. You realize that, right?" I tease.

He grins and sits up straighter, eyes widening as he looks his fill. "Desperate times call for desperate measures, right?"

"Are we really desperate, though? I mean we're safe. We've got an excellent view to enjoy every day. The Internet, TV, phone, Candy Crush, you know, the important things. We're not destitute."

"No, we're not, but you forgot to mention the most important thing."

I tap my bottom lip and think about it. "You're right. Snacks. We have lots of snacks. We're set."

He groans but follows it up with a laugh. "Nah, sweetheart, we have each other. I look forward to seeing your face each day, hearing your voice. This may sound incredibly cheesy but you're the calm in my storm right now. Without you, I'd be losing my mind."

"Well, that's one way to get a woman to hop in bed with you. Too bad—I already have. As previously mentioned, neither of us is taping anything or doing screenshots etcetera and we both respect each other's privacy. Now show me your dick."

He laughs hard and I watch while every boxy abdominal muscle moves with the effort. His pecs and biceps flex delectably and my mouth waters.

"You go right for the good stuff, eh?" He purses those succulent, plump lips.

I shrug. "Isn't that how this is supposed to work?"

"It's pretty safe to say we make our own rules and I'm only

going to show you mine if you show me yours first." He shrugs nonchalantly.

"What! Good sir, I protest. How rude and ungentlemanly. I'm supposed to be the delicate flower you're wooing into having dirty video sex with." I pout for good measure.

"Is that how it is? Well how about this for starters. You stand up and show me that entire sexy number you put on for me tonight. Give me the full view and maybe I'll think about showing you more."

I lick my lips and sit up. "Fair enough." I back up so I can see his face as I stand in the center of the room with my hands on my hips.

"Show me," his voice drops to a lower timber that instantly has me shifting my legs together to create a bit of friction where I need it most.

I pick up the flaps of the satin covering my stomach and gift him an even better view of the panties and my belly.

"Come closer to the camera. I want to see those panties."

Inhaling full and deep, I sashay closer, so the entire screen reflects my lace-covered sex.

"Christ, are you shaved?"

"Guess you'll have to find out." And on that note, I slowly spin around. When I do, I know the exact second he can see my bare ass.

Feeling emboldened, I shimmy my hips.

"Fuck me, you have an incredible ass. I want to take a bite out of it like a juicy peach. Jesus, Sadie, you undo me."

I glance over my shoulder at the camera and see he already has a hand down his briefs. His hand is moving back and forth under the fabric in a vulgar display that makes me hot and bothered instantly. Heat and excitement ribbons through my body and settles hotly between my thighs.

"Remove the shorts, buddy, and I'll take off my top," I barter.

Instantly he shoves down his underwear and the prettiest, thickest cock greets me. Above average in size and length with a wide knobbed crown that I want so badly to put my lips on. I'll bet it's the softest skin I'll ever touch.

"Wow, you are packing something nice there." My voice shakes as I watch him encircle the head with his thumb and spread moisture all over the tip.

I moan and bite into my bottom lip.

"Your top. Take it off. Right fucking now." His voice isn't a request. It's a demand, and so fucking hot gooseflesh rises on the surface of my skin.

Wanting to make this good for him, I slide my hands up to my breasts and palm them. Then I pull the lace down to expose them for his viewing pleasure.

"I knew they were beautiful, but damn baby—those are some stellar tits. I'd suck on them for so long you'd come without me even touching your pussy. Pluck and pinch the tips for me."

I do so and cry out at the beauty spearing through my body. Arousal is coating my thighs and I rub them together while playing with my breasts.

"Top, baby."

I lift the cami over my head and toss it behind me.

"Get on the bed on your side like you were before but push the laptop back so I can see most of you."

Blindly I follow whatever he says to do. I'm so turned on I can hardly think about anything other than getting off and watching him do the same. "God, Evan, your body is insane. I want to run my hands and mouth all over you."

"I want that more than anything too. Take off your panties."

I close my eyes and just do it. I want this too much. Quick as possible, I push the lace down my hips and legs then kick them to the end of the bed. I don't allow any preconceived notions or pesky insecurities to take me out of the moment. I want to enjoy every second of this experience.

"Sadie, baby, look at me." His voice is ravaged and so deep I swear I can feel it weave through me like a physical caress. Tantalizing and exotic.

I open my eyes to gaze into his. They are dilated and far darker than they usually are.

"Sadie, you are stunning. I've never seen a woman more beautiful or perfect for me than you. From the top of your golden hair to the tips of your painted toes. You are gorgeous and I can't wait to worship you in person in a few more days."

His words fill me with such desire I can't help but run my hand down over my breasts and to my wet flesh.

He groans at the move. "Keep going. You're so fucking hot. Open your top leg to the side so I can see what you're doing between those thighs." He bites into his bottom lip the second I open my leg and give him a nice side view of my sex. "Fuck, yeah. Touch yourself."

I watch him drag his large hand up his thick length. He seems to be gripping far harder than I would and straining into each thrust. So sinfully wicked.

With him as my visual guide, I ease my fingers over my clit, twirling around the sensitive bud until I'm crying out in pleasure.

"Beautiful," he grates through his teeth. "More. Put two fingers inside. I want to watch you fuck yourself like I would."

His voice, his expression, his everything get to me. This is so much hotter than I ever imagined. Being shy or worrying over the dimples in my thighs never even occurs to me. Evan just is that inspiring and like a duck to water I go for it, plunging two fingers deep. I thrust my hips wanting it deeper, pretending it's him fingering me, in and out, just the way I like it.

I watch enraptured as Evan runs another hand down between his massive thighs where he grips the two round globes hanging heavily just under his upright cock.

"If I was there, I'd lick and kiss each ball then drag my tongue all over that steely length, ending with sucking on the tip, running the flat of my tongue along the underside until you go crazy and shoot off in my mouth. Then I'd lock my mouth around your tip and swallow it all down until you aren't able to move."

"Jesus!" His hands pick up the pace. "If I was there, I'd plunge my fingers so deep and hook them up and find that magical spot inside you. When I found it, I'd be relentless, tugging and tickling it while wrapping my lips around your clit and sucking until you couldn't stop humping my face. You'd come over and over, baby, so much I'd be able to sink my tongue inside you and drink deep. I can almost taste the sweetness already. Fuck, I'm gonna come," he warns.

I pick up my pace, turning to my back, but keeping my head to the side so I can watch him go off. The second the first jolt of his essence appears, my body convulses, the orgasm racing through my system, sending shocks of pleasure coasting along every nerve ending. One orgasm barrels right into another one as he coats his abdomen and hand, his neck and body arched powerfully in the most graphic display of virility I've ever seen. And it was the sight of me that did that to him. What a heady thought.

Eventually we both come out of the extreme wave of beauty that befell us and just lie there breathing, our chests rising and falling as though we'd run a marathon.

Evan blinks open his eyes and gifts me the goofiest, loveliest smile.

I give him one of my own, grinning happily.

He reaches for a washcloth on his nightstand that he must have prepared in advance and wipes down his chest, hand, and cock. I pull back the covers and slip underneath, my eyes never leaving him.

When he's done, he slides under the covers and moves the laptop to the side of the bed the same way I have so we're facing one another, face-to-face close up.

I smile.

"Most beautiful thing I've ever seen," he whispers softly.

"Video sex?"

"No, the smile you just gave me after sharing one of the most intimate moments of my life. Thank you for experiencing that with me."

I snuggle against my pillows and cuddle the blanket to me as if I were holding onto him.

Yawning, I close my eyes. "You're gonna make fall in love with you if you keep this up," I warn half-heartedly, my body languid and happily sated.

"I know the feeling. Goodnight, my Sadie."

"Goodnight, Sparky." I don't bother shutting off the video feed, preferring to fall asleep to the sound of his breathing. If he were here, it would be the sound of his heart.

For now, I'll settle for his life-sustaining breath.

## TEN

### QUARANTINE: DAY 10

SADIE

"Sadie? Hey, angel, you gonna wake up sometime?" A throaty, rumbling voice enters my subconscious mind as my dreams start to fade into ether.

"Hmm?" I open my sleepy eyes and blink at the video screen still open in front of me. Evan is right there, a soft smile spread across his handsome face. What a pleasant sight to wake up to. I don't even care what time it is. "Hey."

"You make little baby snuffly snore noises," he says.

"I do not." I scrunch up my nose.

"It's cute. Honestly." He grins. "Good morning, beautiful."

"Morning."

"I sure hope I have a lot of this to look forward to in future." His hair is a tousled mess and his bare chest is still as tan and mouthwatering as it was last night.

"Waking up to a laptop?" I joke.

"Waking up to you." His gaze heats as he looks over my shoulder. Bet my hair's a mess. I'm like the bed head queen twenty-eight years running now. And I barely even had any hair for the first year. Never mind. If I can't be real with the man, then we have no business even being in a social distancing relationship.

"My mom's going to want to show you embarrassing baby photos of me. Just to warn you."

He raises his brows. "Is she? I'll look forward to that. I'd like to meet your parents." His tone is honest and forthcoming. I think he genuinely does want to meet my family one day.

"They're seriously bad photos. Me with a gigantic bald head and stupid little pink bows sitting on top. They're the actual worst." I frown.

"I bet you were adorable." He puts his head on his hand, like he's getting more comfortable.

"Freakish big-headed alien baby with a bow on top." I paint a picture that is absolutely accurate. Though if he and I were to have children, his hot guy genes would have to take over. That's a plus.

He laughs. "You sure are random first thing in the morning. Not really an a.m. person, are you? Tell me more about these bizarre baby pictures."

"No. Not if you're laughing at me."

"I'm not laughing at you. I'm laughing *with* you. Big difference, sweetheart."

I pout. "That's just it. I'm not laughing, Evan."

"Aw, poor Sadie. Well I have something that will turn that frown upside down."

"Oh?" I perk up thinking maybe it's more sexy time.

"Your coffee and a smoothie are at your door."

"You've been up already?" I gasp truly horrified by how early this man wakes. Is the sun even out yet?

"I knew you'd want your caffeine fix pronto," he says with a smile. "Got to look after my girl."

"Thank you." I sit up and stretch. And Evan's eyes widen appreciably at the sight of my naked breasts.

The man licks his lips. "Well, hello there."

"Such a tit man." I grab my discarded cami and slip it on over my head, and then pull it down. The fact Evan turns his head and follows the material's progress with a slightly panicked expression is just damn funny in all the ways.

"Now you're laughing at me," he says in an amused if accusing tone.

"I am. It's true." I sit on the mattress, slowly bringing my sleep-befuddled brain online. Waking up is hard, yo. "Do you want babies?"

He freezes.

"It's okay. You can not be ready to discuss this topic. I kind of sprung that one on you out of nowhere and it is the honeymoon phase with us, technically speaking."

"No, I uh…I do want kids. And I think we'd make some seriously beautiful babies. Even if they do have abnormally large heads to start out with like their mama."

"Ha-ha. Yeah. Me too. I mean, I don't want them right now. But eventually. In a few years or whatever." I sigh. "Sean didn't want children."

"The ex?" He scowls. The man is even pretty when he does that. Damn, I'm lucky.

I nod. "Children cost approximately a quarter of a million dollars to raise and that doesn't even include college!" I bark out, doing an approximation of Sean's highly aggravating, preachy tone of voice. "They're just not a sound investment, Sadie."

"Huh. What a douche."

"Imagine being the kind of asshat who thinks of children as an investment. Sheesh."

"He sounds like a fucking cock-splash if I ever heard of one. You definitely shouldn't go back to him. And I say that as both your friend and your current boyfriend." He gives me a wink.

"Now go get your coffee, sweetheart, before it's stone cold. We can plan our baller baby dynasty later."

Instead of ending the session, I grab a pair of sleep shorts from the floor and slip them on, only allowing him a speck of an ass shot. Then I pull out the power plug and carry the laptop into the open living area of my apartment.

"Lots of books and blue. Exactly what I'd expect from my Sadie. Nice place. Homey."

His compliment makes me feel proud. I have worked hard and given myself the life I want. "I'll have to see your actual house sometime. And baller baby dynasty?" I ask with a cringe, setting the monitor down on a coffee table.

"Sure. I'm thinking six, minimum. Three on each team for the daily football practices in the backyard."

"So much no," I mumble, walking out of view to grab the coffee and smoothie from my doorstep. Oh, God. It's green again. I'm sipping hesitantly when I walk back in. To show appreciation, I try to act enthused, but obviously that doesn't work because Evan snickers. "Dude, I'm trying."

"You're doing great. And your body's going to love you for all those vitamins and minerals." He's also moved and is now sitting on Jake's bro-home black leather sofa. Hetero men. Like a splash of color and a few throw cushions would kill them. Honestly.

After downing about half of the lukewarm coffee, I smile. "Thank you, Evan."

"Looking after you is my pleasure." There's so much warmth in his voice it makes me tingly. I never stood a chance against this man. He's so sweet. And I do like my sweet things. "Meet you out on the balcony?"

"I'm not going out on the balcony with my butt on display."

A heavy sigh. "Come on…you put on those little shorts."

"That show a lot of cheek!"

He grins. "I know." He waggles his brows. "I had to try. You know I had to try."

"Mmm hmm." I slump down on the sofa, alternating sips of coffee and smoothie. "And I appreciate your enthusiasm for seeing my cellulite in the cold light of day."

"I love your curves, baby. You're perfect from head to toe and I refuse to hear any different."

"You're awfully good for my ego, Mr. Sparks."

His voice drops by about an octave as he says, "I intend to be good for you in a lot of ways."

"I'll hold you to that."

Gah. My mind has officially melted. "That's the smile I need for my cell wallpaper. That exact one."

"Later on I'll send you a picture," he promises.

"Why thank you."

"Finish up your breakfast and I'll see you on the balcony for yoga, okay?"

"It's a date."


*My cell chimes and a picture of Eamon appears on screen. He's grinning and flexing an arm. Oh, my. So many muscles. And he knows what the sight of his body does to me. Since we're both still isolating for fourteen days for safety, I'm back in my own apartment. I'm not sure if this is the right decision or not. The man muddles up my mind and stirs my hormones to peak crazy conditions. But at the end of the day, we barely know each other.*

*He says he wants to get to know me. So, I'm going to let him. From a distance.*

*We may have gotten much closer than six feet as a result of the mugging and him recusing me. However, a little caution now won't hurt. I don't want to be a momentary distraction for him. Nothing against one-night stands, but this time I want more. As scary as things are right now, he makes me feel things. Good things. Things I don't want to take for granted. Or get prematurely attached to in case he changes his mind.*

*"Come out on the balcony," he texts.*

*After first fluffing up my hair and applying a little lip gloss, I do just that. And he's waiting, looking so good it ought to be a sin. He has this dimple in his chin that drives me wild. And then there's the knowing look in his eyes. Like he has a hand down my panties and knows exactly the state they're in. My face heats at the thought.*

*"Katie, you're blushing." He grins and my knees go weak.*

*"I was just…doing things."*

*He tips his chin. "What sort of things?"*

*"You know, cleaning, scrubbing the tub," I lie. Because staring into space and daydreaming about him was the only thing I've successfully accomplished so far today. Also, I am obviously a conversation mastermind. Next, I'll give him a step by step about cleaning the toilet. "How about you?"*

*"You can definitely give me a good scrub in the shower anytime you like." There's a smile in his gaze. A particularly heated one. "Ain't No Sunshine" by Bill Withers plays softly on his stereo and the song only adds to the atmosphere building between us.*

*My mouth hangs open. He did not just say that. "Eamon. I…the things you say. This is all happening so fast."*

*"Beautiful, you've been spying on me for the last week."*

*"That's so embarrassing. You knew all along? I can't believe you didn't say something."*

*"I not only knew, but I liked it. A lot," he says, a hint of a growl in his voice. As if men like him even considered getting in deep with girls like me. "Don't stare at the ground, Katie. Look at me. See me."*

*Emotion all but chokes me. "I do, Eamon."*

*"And I see you too."*

*All I can do is sigh. This is a dream. It must be. My prince charming stands across from me on his balcony in basketball shorts and nothing more. His proud manhood tents the front of them so large and erect it's vaguely threatening. Could a girl even hope of witnessing a more glorious sight? The passion he has for me. The fervor.*

*Immediately, his expression turns to one of pure conviction. "Come to me, Katie. Come for me."*

*"I can't. You know I can't." I swallow hard, my throat so dry it's painful. "We have to be apart."*

I re-read the page I just sent Zahra via e-mail and click back over to Facebook Messenger and watch the little bubbles as she types on her side of the world.

**Zahra:** Good God, this couple is hilarious. And hot.

**Me:** Thank you, ma'am. Figure we could all do with laughter right about now. Sending more pages soon. How are you?

**Zahra:** Children are running amuck and I'm on the verge of day drinking. The prize at homeschool today will be awarded to whichever student manages to not annoy the living shit out of their principal and teacher—moi.

**Me:** Yeah? What's the prize?

**Zahra:** Some candy left over from last Halloween that I found at the back of the cupboard. Lol

**Me:** AWESOME PRIZE

**Zahra:** Thank you for the puzzles and toys. It kept them occupied for a full five minutes before they started running around the house yelling like lunatics. How's your father?

**Me:** Better. I got to talk to him yesterday. Still a bit weak, but definitely hopefully on the mend. Mom is spooning bone broth into him at a scary rate while he bitches and demands a steak.

**Zahra:** I'm so glad he didn't have it. A college age kid down the road came back from spring break with it and is now on a ventilator. It doesn't look good.

**Me:** Oh no.

**Zahra:** At least his parents made him self-isolate when he got back.

**Me:** Fuck, this is scary. How the hell did we wind up living in times like these?

**Zahra:** I have no idea. Tell me about your hottie next door. Get my mind off things.

**Me:** We had a Skype date last night. We did things. Dirty things. Disgusting things.

**Zahra:** You ho. Good work. Glad to hear it.

**Me:** Thank you.

**Zahra:** So, what's the black moment in your book going to be?

**Me:** Eamon has been accused of sleeping with the coach's wife. But he was set up.

**Zahra:** Excellent chance for tension and emotional trauma.

**Me:** You betcha.

**Zahra:** Tho this fiction is awful close to your reality.

**Me:** Sports romance is hot. Scandals happen in sports all the time. As if Evan would actually read the book anyway. It's not really about him. It's fiction. He's just my muse when it comes to certain aspects.

**Zahra:** Ok.

**Me:** Who even knows if we even have a future?

**Zahra:** You need to stop the negative bullshit caused by your idiot ex from spilling over into now. You made a mistake staying with Sean for a year. You learned from it. Now move on.

**Me:** I know, I know. I just don't want to get my hopes up too high. Evan is so wonderful. But then Sean seemed okay at first too.

**Zahra:** Big difference between wonderful and okay.

**Me:** True.

**Zahra:** Just don't settle this time. Be smart. You're not afraid of being alone, so there's no need to put up with trash. Take that shit out and be done with it. Expunge him from your mind and move on.

**Me:** You're right.

**Zahra:** Of course, I am. And now my pupils have started a hair-pulling fight. I'll catch up with you later.

**Me:** Later. Good luck. Xx

♡

## EVAN

After the sexy yoga sesh with Sadie, I showered and then sat down in front of the computer. I pull up my e-mail and see one from Polly. Not good news. Apparently half the media believes the truth behind the drug report released and the other half think it's bogus, bought and paid for by the team.

I sigh and rub at the back of my neck. Tension filters back into my temples as I review the coach's report. Reading the details, I perk up. Fuck yes. None of the guys tested positive for doping.

I stand up and fist punch the air several times like I'm Rocky Balboa. Yes! Maybe now the guys won't think so poorly of me. Having that weight on my shoulders has not helped. Even though it sure has put a lot into perspective about the brotherhood. Instead of talking shit behind my back, they should have come to me. Asked what happened. I read through more of the e-mail and the coach says my contract is still under review with the legal team. What the hell? Shouldn't my innocence and that of the rest of the team clear me?

Picking up the phone, I dial Trina, the team secretary. She's always been like a favorite auntie to me. We've shared a bond since the very beginning when she found out I was motherless and all alone in California. In fact, I used to go to Friday night dinner at her house with her family at least once a month before this lockdown business.

"Hello, young man. I was wondering when you were going to get around to calling me." Her voice is hoarse when she answers.

"Hey Trina, how are you feeling?"

"Oh fine, just fine. A little tickle in my throat I haven't been able to shake the last couple days. Nothing to worry about. It's probably allergies."

Trina is in her later fifties and has three sons, all working in sports in one way or another. One is a sports doctor, the other a lawyer, and the last a pro baseball player. Each is fiercely protective of their mother, but none of them live in the area.

"How's Tom? Keeping an eye on you?" I ask, referring to her husband of thirty years. High school sweethearts and still devoted to one another. A love like theirs makes me believe true love does exist, you just have to find the right person. Maybe I have.

"Definitely. He's making me some herbal tea now. How are you?"

I groan. "You seen the reports?"

"Clean as a whistle as expected. I knew you didn't do those things. I know you like to party, but you've never been a drug user."

Well, I've smoked in my time but no need to go there. Besides it's legal so it's not a drug anymore. That's my story and I'm sticking to it.

"Yeah, and I wouldn't screw over my team by doping or pawning that shit off on my teammates. We win games with hard work, skill, and talent. Maybe even a dose of luck but never by shooting up poison."

"I know, I told that very thing to the coach. He said he wasn't so sure."

"Really? He said that?"

"Mmm hmm. Got me mighty pissed off, and you don't want to get me angry as you well know."

"That I do. So, what's the word you've heard around there?"

"Legal team is reviewing your contract and the parameters. The issue is image. The damage the scandal has done is being evaluated against the moral and ethical conduct clause in your contract. I assume you'd figured that out."

"Yes, but I was set up! By some chick named Mindy. She doped me at a party, brought me to that room, and must have taken pics then sold them to the media. Which is why I called. Wanted to know if you'd heard the name before. Any of the guys seeing a woman by that name?"

"Mindy? Got a last name?"

I sigh heavily. "No, unfortunately not. Maybe you can ask around some of the guys and cheerleaders when you have your calls?" Trina would be checking in on all fifty players and the entire cheerleading team. The woman was like the team Mom and we were all her baby chicks.

"Well, it's an uncommon name. I'll definitely bring it up and keep my ear to the ground."

"Thanks, Trina. I appreciate it."

She coughs and attempts to clear her throat. It sounds super dry. Hair on the back of my neck rises and a slither of fear worms its way into my thoughts. "You sure you don't have a fever?"

Trina groans. "Stop fretting. I'm fine. We're closing in on

April for goodness sake. They're shaking those damn almond trees all over the state. It's hell on my allergies. Farms don't stop working just because the rest of us are holed up. They need to feed the people."

"True. Just have Tom check you daily, yeah? For me? Just to be safe."

She hums, but it sounds more like a disgruntled animal groan than anything else. "Fine. Fine. I'll keep you posted if I hear anything through the rumor mill or any whispers down the line from legal. Keep a stiff upper lip, my dear. This will all work out in the wash."

"I sure hope so. Playing ball is all I've ever wanted to do."

"Perhaps you should consider this time to reflect and consider what you'd want to do after you retire from the game. Maybe put some time into other hobbies or interests."

"Couldn't hurt." The idea about buying that bar my brother works for comes to mind.

What else would I want to do if I wasn't in the game anymore? It's hard to even fathom not being a part of football in some manner. I've got years before I'm obsolete as a running back, but if I leave the game, I want to do so on my terms. Not because some asshole set me up.

"Thanks for everything, Trina. I'll think about it. Keep me posted on anything you hear."

"Will do, sweetie. Take care."

"You too."

I end the call and pull up my brother's contact information.

"Ev, how's it hanging, brother!" Curt's voice is a welcome sound that has me smiling where I sit.

"Staying inside. Avoiding the paps and this crazy virus. You?"

"Pretty much the same. Hey, got the wire of the five grand you sent. I normally wouldn't accept, but…"

"You're there helping take care of Dad." I remind him of the very real fact that I haven't been there to help support our old man physically in a long time.

"Me? Taking care of him? He'd lose his mind if he heard you say that." He chuckles.

"You mowing the lawns? Picking up groceries. Helping make dinner?"

"Fuck, yeah. You know I am. Just yesterday I had to crawl under the house to fix a pipe that was acting up."

"Exactly. If I were there, I'd be halving that load. Sending a little extra money is me halving that load. True?"

He makes a sound as though he were sucking breath through his teeth. "True."

"Then not another word about it, yeah?"

"Cool. Dad says you've got a woman. Sadie, I think he said?"

I smile wide. "I do. Met her on the balcony."

"How's that work? Dating a woman you can't touch?"

I laugh out loud and pound my knuckles on the desk. "It's tricky for sure. We do a lot of chatting on the balcony, phone calls, video dates. Shit like that."

"And the sex? How's that working for ya?"

"You'd be surprised, bro. Visuals and voice calls go a long way towards wettin' the whistle, if you know what I mean."

"Okay, okay, I get ya. Happy for you, dude. Cool as hell you finding something good to hold onto during all this shit with the world and your career."

"Which brings me back to my call. I want to get Dad out of that cannery and you out of working for someone else."

"Whatcha thinking?"

"Buying the bar you work for. Or creating a new one from scratch. Having you and Dad own it and work it together."

"And what would your role be?"

"Silent partner. I need an investment and you and Dad need something of your own. Win-win for the Sparks family."

"No shit, Ev? You want to buy us a bar?" I can hear my brother's volume ramp up which means he's getting excited.

"Yeah, man. You and Dad need to work for yourselves and I don't trust anyone else with my investments but family. What do you think?"

"I think you're handing me a fucking bar!"

I snicker. "Yeah, I guess I am. Though you have to do all the work. I'm just the investor. First thing—do some research. See if the bar owner is willing to sell. If not, look for another building. Find out rates and so on. Then when you've got something going, let me know."

"And Dad? How we gonna get him to quit a lifelong career in the factory?"

"Let's think on that too. The both of us. My hope is if you get it all set up, I put in the cash, then we tell him we need him to help run it. He'd love nothing more than serving drinks and shooting the shit with his buddies who would no doubt come in to drink where he serves. And it gets him working less hours. Doing something he enjoys for once. Let's just think on it. You do your research and we'll circle back around. Sound good?"

"Fuck, yeah. Sounds amazing. I'm all over this, bro. Appreciate your belief in me."

"Always. Now get to work. I want you to report back in a week and tell me what you find out."

"On it. And thanks, Ev. You're the best brother a guy could have. You will make it through this with the truth as your defense."

"That's the plan. Love you, bro."

"Right back attcha. Bye."

Pride fills my chest as I sit back and balance on two legs of the chair. My brother will go full speed on this, that's a given. Dad will be a bit harder sell, but eventually he'll see reason. He always does. I can't wait to tell Sadie my plan. Hell, I can't wait to hear her voice again, even though I promised her I'd wait until tomorrow so she could get some work done.

Turning back around, I face the computer and click on the cheerleaders' Facebook page to start my search for a blonde named Mindy.

# Chapter
## ELEVEN

### QUARANTINE: DAY 11

EVAN

I FLOP BACK AGAINST THE COUCH AND SIGH. SADIE'S gorgeous face is a mirror image of mine on the laptop screen. She has a content, whimsical smile that I wish more than anything I could kiss right now. Especially after sharing yet another round of stellar video sex.

Aside from the spunk on my abdomen, I could easily just sit back and snooze. Something I never do. Naps are a luxury I've never been afforded. Though this quarantine is teaching me to appreciate so many things I took for granted before. Like being able to go for a run. Lifting weights with my brethren. Seeing a movie. Going to the grocery store. And the most important, being able to hold and comfort the woman I'm obsessed with.

Sadie smiles, sits up from her spot on her couch, and puts her ribbed tank back on. After she taught me more yoga on the balcony, we agreed on a movie. The second we got settled, I told her to take her top off. She didn't so much as hesitate. We went at it fast and furious. She didn't even take her pants off, just slipped her hand beneath the waistband. One hand on her lush tit, the other between her thighs. It was beautiful.

"Ready to binge watch the *Twilight* saga?" She lifts a bottle of water to her mouth and takes a long drink.

I glance down at the mess I've made. "Babe, I'm gonna need a quick shower."

She grins. "That concept has possibilities. You could take the laptop with you; I could watch the Evan Skin-a-Max channel for my viewing pleasure."

I shake my head. "I've created a sex monster."

She shrugs. "Nah, I've always had a huge libido. I write erotic romance for a living. I like sex. Sex is good. Sex with you is awesome. Why not have it regularly?"

"Good to know…in exactly three and a half days."

"Oh, are you keeping track?" she teases.

"You know I am. Better yet, I know you are too. You want a piece of this bod as much as I want all over yours."

She purses her pretty pink lips. "Hmm. True."

I grin. "Let me hose down and grab a beer and some snacks. I'm feeling like loafing with my woman today."

"You're the perfect man. And I've got lots of snacks. What were you thinking? No!" She holds her hands up. "Let me surprise you! I'll make you a smorgasbord!"

I chuckle and stand up, not bothering to cover my junk or the mess I made in her honor. "All right. Try and put something healthy in there, yeah?"

She frowns and her entire face squishes up as though she's smelling something putrid. "Um…healthy? Huh."

Laughing I shake my head and leave the laptop where it is. "I'll let you think on that, princess. Be back in ten."

I rush through the process of showering off a great afternoon delight and tug on a pair of sweatpants and a red T-shirt. Once I've donned a pair of socks, I pad back into the living room and head for the kitchen. I snag two cans of beer and the fresh cucumbers I already peeled and cut along with the homemade hummus I made. Tagging my loot, I bring it back to the table and set it down.

"Check your door!" I hear her holler but don't see her face on the video screen.

This girl. I smile and go to my door to see the offering she left me.

Oh no, she didn't.

Grabbing the plate, I bring the lot back to the couch and sit my ass down. When I get there, she's got a clear bubbly drink in hand with a lime wedge shoved inside it.

"Soda, lime, and vodka. My favorite."

"Baby, what the fuck is this?" I lift up the plate.

She sits cross-legged on the couch and puts her own plate on her lap. "Okay, the square shapes are Triscuits with Cheez Whiz on top. You know, cheese...healthy." She beams while explaining. "Those brown things are dark chocolate-covered almonds. I know, I know. So good for you!" There is honest to God pride in her tone and I can't help sucking my lips between my teeth and letting her carry on with her joy. "Then of course, the *pièce de résistance*...the hunks of salami."

"What's in the center of them?"

She positively exudes excitement. Her cheeks pink up and her eyes are a stunning blue and shimmering beautifully. "Cream cheese and pepperoncini! It's a veggie! Look at me. Feeding my man the good stuff. Keepin' that body fit and toned! Mmm hmm." She wiggles around happy as a clam.

I do not have the heart to tell her that none of this is exactly healthy, but it's not all candy and that's a plus. "Thank you, baby. This is wonderful. Though I draw the line at eating canned cheese."

She frowns. "Really? That's the best part!"

I laugh and point at the TV. "What channel is this vampire story on?"

"Twelve."

We both turn on the TV and get to the right channel.

"Ohh we are right on time! It's just the opening sequence. Awesome! I can't wait to find out if you're Team Edward or Team Jacob. I'm firmly in the Team Edward camp but I can see the appeal of Jacob. I mean a wolf-shifter is all super alpha and hot. I bet you'd make a great shifter."

"Are you for real? A wolf shifter? I thought we were watching vampires?"

"We are. There are all kinds of paranormal things happening in the movies. The books are even better, but I think you'll find Bella to be sexy and sweet. You seem like you enjoy the girl-next-door types."

That has me cracking up. "I like curvy, gorgeous blondes who eat garbage, speak their minds, and make me laugh so hard my stomach hurts." I lift up the rolled bit of salami.

"Hmm, and I thought you liked me for my awesome phone and video sex skills. I slay at that!" She lifts her chin.

"Baby, you are unlike any woman I've ever known. Everything I learn just makes me like you more. Now eat your fake cheese and tell me why we're watching children in high school. I thought you said this was a romance with a lot of action?"

"Oh, it is! Just, you know, pretend they're in college. That's what I do."

I laugh. "They're clearly in high school, babe."

"The actors are older though. Anyway, they get out of school soonish. Just pay attention."

For the next two hours I get sucked right into her vampire-shifter world. By the time movie one ends I'm fired up to watch the second but hungry as a horse.

"Let's pause the TV and I'll make us some dinner, cool?"

"I could eat."

I lift up the laptop and bring it to the kitchen. "Babe, you can always eat because you survive off sugar and snacks that go in the system and have no staying power. Let the master show you how it's done."

"Ooh that sounds fun. I'll just watch you cook while I drink."

I chuckle while pulling out some ground turkey.

"What's that?"

"Ground turkey. For tacos."

She makes a face. "I thought you use ground beef for tacos."

"Not as good for you as ground turkey, but I promise it tastes the same."

"I'll give anything a whirl as long as I didn't have to make it. What else?"

I show her the seasonings I use and get the meat simmering while I cut up the tomatoes, green leaf lettuce, and avocado. "I've got a light sour cream and a low-fat cheese to go with it."

"Low-fat cheese. Does not compute, Sparky."

"It's good. You'll not be able to taste the difference."

"Uh huh." She doesn't sound convinced. "And what about that green stuff you got there." She points to the counter.

"Avocado and lettuce."

"Lettuce is practically see-through. That is dark green. Bleh." She makes a gag face.

"Baby, you're eating lettuce. Jesus. How have you survived before me?"

"What can I say? My body knows what it likes, and it isn't green in color." She blinks her lashes prettily as if that's going to get me off her case.

"You're eating it or I won't have video sex with you again."

Her mouth drops open. "That's torturing yourself as much as it's torturing me. And totally unfair. You can't use sex as a tool to get me to eat healthier!"

I grab a red pepper and start cutting it up. "I can and I will. I want you alive for a long, long time. Besides, what will happen when you're carrying my baller babies? A fetus can't survive on candy alone."

"Pshaw! If you take away all my candy you won't be getting any sweet time from me in order to get me pregnant in the first place. Ha! So there!" She huffs and crosses her arms over her chest.

"Are we honestly bickering about future babies and fetuses we haven't even created yet?"

"You bet your fine ass we are. If this body is going to carry your giant children—because let's be truthful, you're massive. Hot, good looking, and panty-dropping sexy, but you are huge! That's a con when considering future progeny. So you should be thanking me for even considering opening my womb up for business. Which means treats are life, and you will let me have as many of them as I want!"

"Fine, woman! Eat all the candy you want!" I fire back caving in.

A full minute goes by of us looking at one another with mock glares. Then I burst out into raucous laughter. I can't stop. The entire scenario is fucking hilarious and I'm so damn thankful I have a woman in my life who's willing to go head to head with me on any little thing that matters to her.

Before long she's laughing right along with me. "Man, being hangry makes me a whacko!" She admits with a shy note to her voice.

"You don't have to tell me, lady. I just watched you plead your argument and win your case all in one breath! Lesson learned. You do not have to tell me twice. I'll stay five feet from your candy shelf at all times. Swear." I cross my heart in a peace offering.

"That's right, buster! And don't you forget it. I'll defend my candy intake to the death! Now when are those tacos gonna be done? Your woman is starving!"

"All right, all right. Coming right up." I finish plating two fully loaded tacos. I load up four tacos for myself and set those on the coffee table before taking her plate to her door.

She's gone when I come back. Probably watched me from her peephole.

When she re-enters the screen, she's got a taco already half in the air going toward her mouth.

"Baby, you didn't wait for me again," I say like a wounded child.

She shrugs. "Snooze you lose." She mumbles around a mouth full of food.

"What am I gonna do with you?"

"Feed me. Water me. Sex me?" she offers, quite helpfully.

"Deal."

"And treat me with care." She finishes on a whisper that sounds a lot like a plea.

I look into her soulful blue eyes. "I will, Sadie. With everything inside me. I will treat you with care."

She smiles and it lights up my life.

I lift up the taco and salute her. "To Team Edward."

That has her fist pumping the air wildly. "Yaaaaaasssss! To Team Edward. Okay, ready…" We both hold up our TV remotes. "Go!" We hit the un-pause button at the same time, so the movie doesn't echo through both our speakers.

It works.

A good meal, a sort-of-interesting movie, and an amazing woman at my side.

I couldn't ask for more.

♡

## SADIE

I've been putting off sitting in front of my computer today for a good reason beyond just needing a break. The alerts on my cell were bad enough. First up is some hate mail from a reader telling me I write pornography. She goes on to complain about my characters swearing so often. English is apparently a beautiful, expressive language and I'm lazy and foul-mouthed and hell-bent on cheapening the written word. Paper shouldn't be wasted on my disgusting stories and my family is probably hideously embarrassed by my lurid attempts at literature.

Good to know.

Fuck me. People.

Just because you have an opinion doesn't mean you should share it. And if you want to put your thoughts about a book out there, that's why reviews were invented. But no. Someone has to dump it on your doorstep, throw it in your face. I'm not chocolate. I was never going to make everyone happy. Readers might like one book and hate another. Art is subjective. There are so many aspects about writing a book and having another person read it beyond my control. What my muse is willing to supply me with. What mood the reader was in the day they happened upon my story. The list is endless. Sending me hate-filled missives, however, is just trash behavior. I'll defend the romance community 'til the day I die. So many readers have been more than kind and supportive of me. But the Internet has made it too easy to be an asshole.

I delete the e-mail and fetch myself a glass and a bottle of wine. It just feels like one of those nights. Maybe I'm about to get my period. It would figure.

Next up, confirmation that every book signing for the summer has been canceled. It's like a hit to the gut. And I get it. Of course I do. It had to happen. But I earn a decent chunk of my income through signed book sales. People will still buy e-books, but people are also really distracted right now. And who can blame them? Life as we know it just went out the window.

At any rate, time to start reviewing my spending to see where the business can pick up the slack and keep me afloat. I need food, a place to live, electricity, water, and so on. My books need to be edited, proofread, and formatted. Covers need to be made and new releases need to be promoted. Everything else is pretty much on hold for now. Essentials only. No new pretties. And the new couch I was saving up for…that money can go toward the bills.

Also, I need to write more. I need to get my ass into gear and boost my productivity. Only staying inspired during the stress and panic of a pandemic is hard as all hell. Even my new friend/boyfriend can only inspire me so much. Keeping your chin up in times of duress is a bitch. The positives—I believe in romance and hope and love. I believe we're going to get through this. For sure, though, there are dark days ahead. Publishing seems to have been in a state of flux for the last decade or so, and things aren't settling down anytime soon.

I down a mouthful of wine and take a deep breath. At least I'm not going through this totally alone. So many people must be looking at months of lockdown with no comfort in sight. Layoffs, unemployment, and seriously hard times. I'm lucky. Evan's right next door. Dad is feeling better and Mom is just fine. Things could definitely be worse. As someone much wiser than me once said, I know everything happens for a reason. But what the fuck?

I try not to get hung up staring at the news, spending endless hours getting updates on the headlines and latest figures, but things are damn scary in Los Angeles and New York City. Hell, they're scary all over the country. The lack of ventilators and personal protective equipment rip my heart in two. Pictures from Italy of hospitals struggling to help the sick. The burial pits in Iran, so large they're visible from space. It's all so terrifying and heartbreaking. Hard to make sense of it all.

It wasn't that long ago that everything was normal and boring. How the hell did we get here? Then there are the people ignoring the warnings and still having get-togethers. I'd dearly love to rage-scream at them. From six feet away, of course. How the hell can people be so careless?

Times like these are a trial, all right. Maybe this was what it felt like to be alive during World War II. Or to send your son off to Vietnam, not knowing if you'd ever see him again. Living with this weight on your soul constantly threatening to drag you down. Humanity seems both stronger and more fragile than I ever imagined. And I mean, I think I'm healthy. Evan might have something to say about my diet, but that could be worse. This virus, however, seems to be taking people from all age groups. No one is completely safe. We can all only do our best.

Amidst all of this, however, there are glimpses of hope. Lights are still shining out there, showing us the way. People helping their elderly neighbors. Musicians putting on impromptu performances on balconies. Whole cities cheering and clapping for healthcare workers. Then there are the signs that even love will find a way. A boy sending messages to a girl in a neighboring building by drone. A husband standing outside his wife's nursing center holding a sign and balloons to celebrate their sixty-seventh anniversary.

Love and life will persevere. It has to.

In the meantime, I have wine.

Feeling morose and missing my parents, I pull out my cell phone and give them a call. Her voice is an instant balm to my battered soul right now.

"Mom, hey."

"Sadie? Are you okay? It's quarter to ten."

"But you were still awake, right?" I ask, because she doesn't sound sleepy. Slightly put out perhaps, but not sleepy. "I didn't realize it was after nine there already. Sorry."

"Your father and I were just reading in bed. How are you, sweetheart?"

Glass of wine in hand, I sit back in my seat, sock-covered feet up on my desk. Because comfort and liquid refreshments are important. "Fine. Good. Yeah. I was just watching a video about how to properly clean your groceries and wanted to make sure you were aware that you needed to be doing that."

A pause. "And this couldn't wait until the morning?"

"It's important."

Mom sighs. "I wasn't aware of it, Sadie. But rest assured, I'll look up the information tomorrow and see what they're advising."

"I'll e-mail it to you," I offer. Anything to distract me from the world and the book I should be writing.

"All right, dear."

"It's really important that we start doing this now, okay? How's Dad?"

"Much better. The book of crosswords you sent is giving him a headache, but the flu seems to be just about gone. He's still resting and taking it easy, though."

"Good. That's good." I smile even though she can't see me. "I have something to tell you. Something important."

"Besides the need to bleach the groceries?"

"You don't bleach them, Mom. You wipe everything down with a disinfectant wipe. Like Clorox or whatever you've got. Even the cardboard because the virus can live on all sorts of surfaces for longer than you'd think."

"Understood," she says. "So what's so important that you have to call us at this hour?"

"It's not that late," I grumble. Then I grin because this is happy news and I am determined to drag my mood out of the gutter. "Anyhoo, so I've met someone."

"You met someone? How on earth did you meet someone with all of this going on?"

"He lives next door. He's a professional athlete and a wonderful person and I think you're going to love him." I happy-sigh at just the thought of Evan. His smile. His body. His laugh. His everything. God, I'm so gaga about him. "We got to talking out on our balconies and really just sort of hit it off."

"What's Sean going to say about this?" asks Mom.

"Who gives a fuck?"

She clicks her tongue. "Sadie. Language. Have you been drinking, dear? You sound strange."

"No. Of course not." I take another sip of wine. "Well, maybe a glass or two. The point is, you need to forget about Sean. God knows I've been trying to, black hole of a man that he is. You know he rang me the other day to talk at me about his work. Not to me. At me. There's a difference. He's the most self-involved jerk I've ever met."

"Sean rang you?" She sounds so hopeful I cringe.

"You're missing the point here. Focus, Mom. Sean sucks, Evan rocks. That's the state of affairs here. Now you're up to date on my romantic adventures."

A deep sigh from Mom this time. The sigh of so much disappointment. It worked on me up until about age eight or so. Still, it's never stopped her from pulling it out of her arsenal. "All right, Sadie. Tell me about this new man. A professional athlete called Evan, I take it."

In the background, deep mumbling commences.

"Your father wants to know what sport?" she asks.

"Football. He plays for the Oakland Marauders."

Mom relays the information and Dad's mumbling increases

dramatically in both volume and duration. Oh, no. I have a sudden bad feeling about this. Dad follows sports, even those that aren't golf. Why didn't I think about this first? How best to break this information and present Evan and his recent troubles in the best light. Because I believe in his innocence and I am not going to tolerate any unnecessary, uninformed negative backlash.

If only I'd kept my mouth shut. Damn wine.

"Not...what was the name? Evan Sparks?" asks Mom, voice filled with concern. "Sadie, he's a drug addict. What on earth are you thinking? Your father says he's being kicked off the team for selling and using steroids. I know you took the breakup from Sean hard, dear. But is that really the kind of person you want to get involved with? Have you lost your mind?"

"He was set up, Mom," I say through gritted teeth.

"Well of course he would say that, wouldn't he?"

"I'm serious. Both of you, listen. Evan is a wonderful, kind, non-drug-taking person and I like him a lot. Like, a lot a lot."

"I'm not even sure I know what that means. A lot a lot."

"Guess, Mom. Just guess. Perhaps you can even tell from my tone of voice that this man is meaningful to me, hmm?"

"It sounds to me like you're feeling scared and alone, so you fell for the nearest man available. Paying absolutely no attention to what kind of person he is behind the smile he gives you. I knew you should have come home to Texas. You've always lived with your head in the clouds, Sadie. But you've never been quite this foolish before."

"Mom..." My jaw hangs open. Seriously. I'm gobsmacked by my parents' opinion of me.

"A drug addict. Good Lord." Mom's voice is terse and filled with reprimand.

"Firstly, stop. Secondly, you really need to stop."

"Sadie—"

"Jesus, Mom. Do you really think I'm that much of a naive idiot? So you're just going to automatically believe bullshit tabloids selling sensationalist stories over your own daughter's judgement, huh? Really?" I sit up, wine sloshing about in my glass. "I'm twenty-eight, Mom. I run my own business and have done so for years now. I'm a fully functioning adult with no small amount of dating experience and I'm telling you the papers are wrong about him. He's a good person. You're wrong about him."

"Surely the journalists would have done their research and know what they're talking about," Mom says in a huff.

"I honestly don't know how I'd have gotten through the last week and a half without him and you won't even give him a chance. Your mind is made up. No room for the truth."

The Empress of Pained Sighs lays another long and loud one on me. That should be Mom's new official title. "Sadie…"

"I need you to trust me about him. Can you do that?"

There's more mumbling in the background, but I can't make out what Dad is saying.

"I need you to open up your mind and consider just for a moment that maybe I'm not thirteen any more, giggling and making eyes at cute boys. In fact, that was a hell of a long time ago. I know what's best for me. I know *who* is best for me."

"Let's talk about this tomorrow when you're sober," she says. "We love you. Good night. Get some sleep, sweetheart." And then she hangs up on me. Holy cow.

Mostly I want to bang my head against the desk. It feels like the appropriate response right now. However in lieu of giving myself a concussion, I'm going to have another drink.

Because I'm an adult and I can. So there.

# Chapter
## TWELVE

## QUARANTINE: DAY 12

### SADIE

"BABY, WHAT'S WRONG, IT'S AFTER MIDNIGHT? ALSO, holy shit, look at you." Evan's eyes are wide as the moon highlighting the Bay.

I raise my wine glass to him. A cool night breeze ruffles my silk kimono. A friend gave it to me a few birthdays back, but I'm not a robe kind of person. I have, however, thought of the best use for it tonight because I am a genius. "Nothing's wrong, silly. We're drinking alfresco and enjoying the city lights, that's all."

"Really?" he asks, setting his cell down on the small table on Jake's balcony. "Your text sounded upset."

"How can a text sound upset? It's just words with no context."

"Okay. It sounded blunt. A little off, somehow. Not the normal you." His tone is laced with concern.

"Strongly disagree with you there, Sparky. I think 'I need your ass out on the balcony' is in fact a coy, charming, and warm invitation from a woman who admires you greatly. But she's also a woman who doesn't wish to overstate her growing emotions for fear of…stuff. It's complicated. Let's not get into it right now."

He just blinks. "How drunk are you?"

"Eh. A little. Let's label it tipsy. That sounds about right." Lie. I'm on my second bottle but it's the first glass and I've been drinking since my call with the parents.

After a nod, he pulls a chair up to the balcony closest to me and sits. Only he does it with his chest against the back of the chair and his legs spread wide in that way dudes do. "Okay. What's on your mind?"

"You're not going to have a drink with me?" I work hard to cover the slight slur.

"Sorry, baby. Cutting back. I need to watch my intake. But I'm more than happy to sit over here and keep you company."

I slump down on my own chair. "Fine. Spoil my plans."

"What plans would those be?"

"I was going to greatly improve this lousy ass night by trading you a flash of my boobs for a glance at your dick," I tell him very seriously. Because it's a very serious topic of conversation. I mean, I even put on makeup for this occasion. Smoky eyes and shiny red lips to go with my navy kimono. Black patent heels finish the whole look off just so.

"That's why you're all dressed up in that sexy getup?" he asks.

I nod. And pout. It's been that kind of night.

"While I fucking love how into my dick you are, darling, you previously said doing anything revealing out here on the balcony was a bad idea. And you were right. We do not want anyone accidentally getting a look at your gorgeous body. Let alone possible taking a picture of it, hmm? Besides, I have enough bad press."

"Oh, man. You make sense. I hate it when you make more sense than I do."

"That's okay," he says with an amused grin. "I'm sure you'll be back to making all the sense in the morning. And I'm definitely saving your idea of a peep show for another time. That is a most excellent idea. Now how about you tell me what got you in this bad mood?"

"My mom. We may have butted heads over certain matters." I shrug. "It's honestly not that unusual when it comes to us. Margaret hasn't been wrong a day in her life."

"So that's where you get your strong will from, huh?"

"You should see us fight over games of Scrabble. Dad calls it Word War whenever Mom and I sit down to play."

Evan laughs.

I take a sip of wine. "Ah, aged grape juice. So much Vitamin C. I'm almost as healthy as you are!"

"A little Cheez Whiz on a cracker and you're all set." He smiles and it's beautiful. And exactly what I need.

"You're mocking me. But I like you and I'm happy to see your gorgeous face, so I don't care."

"Nuh uh. I'm not mocking you. I'm admiring you and all of your idiosyncrasies. Keeps me on my toes, having a woman like you in my life." He looks out over San Francisco, I assume taking in the night sky and the tall buildings. "Figure I'm about the luckiest son of a bitch in this city right now, getting to sit here with you."

"Don't be sweet. I can't handle sweet right now. You'll make me cry." I sniffle not so delicately.

"Whatever she said, your mom sure upset you," he says in a low growl.

"It's not just her. I was looking at the headlines and some asshole sent me hate mail and all of the signings got cancelled and my muse was being a bitch and honestly everything just kind of hit the wall necessitating copious consumption of alcohol." I sigh. Woe is me. "Wine, meaning booze. And whine, meaning to moan and carry on. Wine, whine. Whine, wine. Hey, do you think there's a link?"

"Undoubtedly." He chuckles. "You're kind of hilarious when you're hammered. And I'm sorry your night took a turn for the worse. We should have just stayed sitting in front of the TV talking to each other on the phone. Much safer."

"True," I say glumly.

"What does signings getting cancelled mean to you?"

"Means my bank account will take a hit." I punch the air but instantly realize my mistake when the wine sloshes onto the concrete. Good thing it's white.

He raises his chin. "You need money?"

"Huh? No. Thank you. I'm fine."

"Sadie, are you sure? Because there's enough in life to be worrying about right now without you counting your pennies when I can afford to help you out."

"Absolutely not. My earnings will be down a little this year, but I'll work it out. I'll find a way, I always do. And I do not want your money." That's the last thing I want from him. I can only imagine how many women before me wanted him for that very thing.

"Yeah. But do you need it? That's the question."

"No, Evan. Just no. This conversation is over now. I mean this topic. It's done. Gone. Kaput. Goodbye."

He's doing the jaw tensing thing. I can almost see the little muscle jumping on one side. "We'll talk about this later when you're in a better and more sober mood."

"No, we won't." I take another sip of wine. "I appreciate you, but I am not going to mooch off you. Get that idea out of your head right now. Besides, there's no cause for alarm. I am writing—some of the time—which means things are moving forward. There's no reason to freak out just yet."

Nothing from the grim-faced man with the determined expression sitting across from me.

"My indomitable hero. You're awful cute when you're all put out like that." And he is. I wish I could climb into his lap, press my face to his neck and just breathe. I'll bet he smells amazing. He'd wrap his arms around me and just make it all better.

"Am I now?" Something glitters in his eyes.

I grin. "I could just sit and watch you for hours. You're fast becoming my happy place, Evan Sparks."

His shoulders sink a little as he relaxes. "You're mine too."

"Aw. Aren't we a pair?"

"And that's why this is so important. Because one day soon, you're going to be sitting on my lap wearing nothing underneath that pretty robe."

Oooh he took my little wistful vision to a saucy place. "Am I now?" I all but purr. That's one hell of a mental image I'll be replaying later.

"Oh, yeah. And when you refuse to be sensible and let me help you when you're in trouble, I'll turn you over my knee and turn your gorgeous ass pink." His corresponding grin is panty-dropping wicked.

My mouth falls wide open in surprise. "You did not just say that. The fuck you will, Evan." There goes the wine again spilling all over the place.

"The fuck I won't, Sadie." His hands sit on the high back of the chair, his chin resting on top. "I may not have a huge amount of experience at relationships, but one thing I know for sure. We're either in this together or not at all. We look out for each other. We have each other's backs."

"Backs, yes. Backsides, not so much, mister!"

He lifts his thick shoulders in a shrug. "If you're my woman then I'm going to want to look out for you. Get used to the idea."

"Looking out for someone does not include running roughshod over them. Partners love and support each other. They do not dictate to them."

"Partners also share what they have with each other. How about that?"

163

"No. Just no. I am not taking your money. I will not be one of those women chasing after you hoping you'll pay my bills. That is bullshit. You're supposed to be my boyfriend, not a damn sugar daddy. I can stand on my own two damn feet. And also, Sparky, you sure as hell are not spanking me." At least not without my consent. Hmmph.

I drain the last of my wine and get to said feet. Oh boy! These heels really are high and I'm just a tad wobbly. Bare feet might have been safer. But still, I stand tall, staring the beast next door down. "Evan, I'm going to bed now. I'll expect an apology from you in the morning."

And the man is not in the least bit fazed by my evil empress glare. Dammit.

"Good night, sweetheart. Make sure you lock the door and put a glass of water and some aspirin by your bedside."

Grrr. And he's so fucking calm it's rage-inducing.

I may or may not have flipped him the bird on my way back inside.

These things happen.

♡

EVAN

The second I wake in the morning I realize my day is already off to a shit start. It's raining. Again. That means no face-to-face with Sadie. Not that she'd be willing to see me after last night.

Maybe it was the booze? For her at least. For me, seeing her upset and worried does my head in.

I sit up and run my hand through the messy layers. I need a haircut, but that won't be happening any time soon. All non-essential businesses, salons and barbers included, are closed. Hell, I read last night they closed down all the schools in the state and are starting to do the same across the country.

This shit is becoming insane.

I read an e-mail last night from the team that they'd be suspending Spring training until further notice. At least that's something positive. None of the guys are practicing so I don't feel so put out by this scandal. The press is fifty-fifty as Polly expected. Half believe I'm innocent while the other half believe I'm lying through my teeth and paid off a specialist to doctor my results for the media's benefit.

Inhaling full and deep, I place my elbows on my knees and rest my head in my hands.

My career is on thin ice.

A virus is taking over the world.

The woman I'm falling in love with is pissed at me. And I can't touch her. Not for two more days.

Fuck me.

My phone buzzes on the end table. I pull it off the charger, hoping it's Sadie and she's ready to talk. A FaceTime request from Jake pops up.

I smile and instantly hit accept.

"Whoa. Hey, brother. You just wake up from a bender? You look like shit." His concerned brown eyes are a welcome sight.

I rub at my bed head. "Can't get a haircut and I just woke up."

"Ah, I see. How are you?"

"Been checking the papers lately?" I ask, fearful of his answer.

He offers me a sad smile. "I'm sorry, Evan. This shit with the picture and the planted dope stinks."

I shrug. "Yeah, but there's nothing I can do but try and figure out how to clear my name. The medical reports only got me out of half of the trouble with the team and my contract. There's still a moral and ethical conduct issue because I was seen like that."

"Ridiculous. How's my pretty princess?"

I turn my head and see her fluffy ginger ass lying on the pillow next to the one I slept on. Feeling generous, I move the camera so he can see her sleeping.

"Aw, my girl. I miss her." He frowns. "Are you being nice to her?"

"Dude, she's sleeping in the bed on the pillow next to my head. And that's only when she's not stealing the covers."

He laughs and wipes at his tanned, sweaty brow. His dark hair is a riot of espresso-colored curls all over his head. By the time we hit college together, he was the dark to my light. The ladies loved it. Like a physical yin and yang. Which is also how our lifestyles have always been. I entertain people, he heals them. Though we share a love of sports, beer, outdoor activity, good food, and family. We appreciate one another's differences and at the heart of us both, we have the same moral compass.

"Yeah, she's greedy. And she looks a little fatter. Have you been giving her too many treats?" He frowns and squints. I turn the camera off his beloved pet and back to me so he can't figure out the cat has definitely gained a pound or two.

I pretend to act innocent. "How many is too many? Five?" I lower the number I normally give her. I've won the little shit over with a treat every couple hours. She doesn't claw me, she gets a treat. No pain, she gains. It's working brilliantly and I'm glad that cat treats were the one thing they had at the store that wasn't running out.

"Five! You're giving her five a day! Jesus. She's going to be diabetic when I make it home."

"Speaking of making it home, when do you think that will be?"

He sighs heavily. "We're actually being sent to Europe tomorrow. Italy and Spain are being ravaged by this virus and they need all hands on deck."

"Are you fucking kidding me! No. Hell no. Do not go there, brother. You need to get your ass home where it's safer."

Jake's expression morphs to one of extreme sadness. "I can't. It's not in my nature. They need doctors. Medical professionals to help stay the spread. I took an oath, man…"

"Fuck that. Fuck that in the face! You are my family. My best friend. Do not put yourself in the way of further harm. Shit." I jump up and start pacing his bedroom. "I was already freaked out by you doing the humanitarian mission and that was supposed to be for two months. It's been six. Now you're going to further risk your health by going to the countries that are torn to shreds by a virus that is killing people left and right."

"Evan…"

"No. Don't Evan me. Jake, this is dangerous."

"Brother, it was already dangerous for me to come to Africa, but you know I needed to. I was aimless. Lost. Not sure what to do with myself. I hated the politics at the surgery center where I worked."

"So, get a different fucking job! You don't get on a plane and disappear for six months to Africa. Christ!" I grind my teeth and look at my best friend's face. I know it almost as well as my own, or my brother's, my dad's.

Jake shakes his head. "I have to do what I have to do. This is important. For the first time in my life I feel like I'm needed. Truly needed."

I point to my chest. "I need you. Your family needs you. Jake, come on, buddy. Come home. Don't go to Europe."

He shakes his head and a sorrowful expression mars his normally handsome face. "Sorry brother, I'm not going to do that. I was calling to tell you I need you to take care of Gloria. While I'm gone and if you know, anything happens."

"Fuck! I hate you so much right now. If you were in front of me, I'd punch you so goddamn hard in the face your teeth would rattle."

Jake laughs for the first time and the sound lifts my soul. "We haven't fought since we both accidentally dated the same chick at the same time without knowing it."

I grin. "Chelsea. She was a pistol. Seeing us both on the sly."

"Yeah and we both fucked her." He winces.

I suck a breath through my teeth. "Yeah, then she messed up and planned the same date with us both and we brawled on the sidewalk." I laugh.

"Yeah and when she came running out all hot and bothered by the show of our manly affections, she suggested the three of us hook up." He reminds me of what I already know.

"And we dropped her ass like a hot rock, went to a sports bar, drank our weight in whiskey, and crashed fully clothed in the same bed." I waggle my brows at him for shits and giggles.

He covers his mouth with a fist. "That's right. When we woke up, we turned to one another and started laughing our asses off at one another's black eyes and busted lips and then went out to breakfast."

"Good times," I say.

"The best." He tips his head. "I'm going to be okay, Ev. I promise."

"You come home in a box and I'll never forgive you." I issue the threat serious as a heart attack. This man is important to me. I cannot lose him. Especially when I'm about to lose everything else.

"That's a promise I'll endeavor to achieve."

"You better!" I growl. "Now I've gotta tell you something and I need some advice."

"Shoot," he offers instantly.

"I've been seeing Sadie."

"What the hell! You can't risk your safety like that." He instantly goes into doctor mode.

I jolt my head back and stare him down.

He groans knowingly seeing as he's presently risking his own health and safety every damn day.

"We haven't touched one another physically. Not for two more long days." I sigh.

"Two more days?"

I roll my eyes. "Yeah, she's making us wait until it's been the full two-week quarantine timeframe."

He nods. "I see. I mean, I'm not surprised you hit on her. She's gorgeous, as I mentioned. Though she's kind of bookish. I think she's a writer or editor."

"Novelist," I say with pride in my tone. What he doesn't know is that I've downloaded one of her books to my phone. The one about a soldier who has PTSD and falls for the counselor in his group meetings. "She's talented too." I'm already sucked in and it's not the shit I normally go for. Books being things I don't normally do. But she's got a way with words and I'm looking forward to when the hero and heroine finally hook up. It's painstaking how long it's taking. Something I should ask her about.

"Oh, sounds like you've gotten to know Miss Sadie rather well."

I grin. "I have. Very well. We not only talk on the phone but meet for chats and yoga on the balcony. I make her food and leave it at her door. She makes me these god-awful snacks she believes are healthy. The girl really needs a total overhaul of her diet. Though her curves are not something I want to lose."

"Her curves, eh? Should I take that to mean intimacy has been had in other ways?"

I bite down on my lip and can feel my cheeks heat. Fuck, I'm blushing talking about my girl. "Uh yeah, a few times already. Phone and video."

His eyes widen and light up. "Video? Whole hog?"

"Whole hog. And every inch of her is absolute perfection." I smile so wide my cheeks hurt.

"Lucky bastard! And here I am, sexless in Africa, about to get more sexless in Europe." He sighs.

"Sounds like your work is your woman right now."

He nods. "Too true. So, what's the advice?"

I enter the kitchen and go about pulling out the ingredients for my smoothie. "Well since the virus hit and everything is shut down, she claims all her signing events have been cancelled and people aren't spending as much on fun stuff like books. She sounded worried about her future income last night so I offered to help her out."

"Jesus, Ev. You can't do shit like that. You barely know this woman."

I frown. "Right now, I know her better than any woman I've ever known in my life, save my mother. We talk about everything. And last night she drunkenly shared some of her fears and it gutted me. I have plenty of money and can totally cover her. Better yet, I want to. It's the least I can do for the person that is making my life bearable through all this crap."

"I get that. Really, I do. Though as long as I've known Sadie, and that hasn't been well, but well enough to know she seems like she's the type to take care of herself. She may have just been venting and wanting you to listen. Not fix her problems—just listen to them."

His comment has me flinching. "Why wouldn't I fix it if I can?"

He sighs. "Man, you have a lot to learn about women."

"Says sexless in Africa."

He chuckles. "True, but I've been in a few relationships, and you have not. The most important thing to remember about a woman is to listen. Don't react. Listen to what she's sharing. Ask her how she feels about it. Ask her if there's anything you can do to help. If she seems like she wants the help, she'll make that message clear."

"This is stupid. She might need money. I have it. It's easy for me to fix her problem and make her happy. Why is that wrong?"

"Would you let her pay your bills if all of a sudden your money was frozen?"

"Fuck, no!"

"Exactly. It's no different for her."

I toss the rest of the ingredients in the blender and lean against the counter. "All the women that hang around the team seem to want a player to take care of them. They live for that."

"And are you interested in them?"

"No," I fire off.

"No. Because those girls want something from you other than your time. They want fame. To walk around in expensive designer garb with a baller on their arm. Sadie's not that type of woman. And I'd have to say, that's probably part of her appeal whether you realize it or not."

I slump against the counter and think about it. Sadie hasn't asked me for anything. She hasn't wanted to take a selfie or pictures of me to post online. I'm not even sure if she's told anyone about us. That information getting out right now could cause a whole host of other issues for me during this scandal. But it's been crickets. She's been there for me. Just me. Seems to want to spend time simply talking, watching movies, sexing, yoga, eating meals, and laughing.

"For the first time in my life, I find a woman I want to take care of, and she doesn't want it. How am I supposed to take that?" Sadness seeps into my pores and a heaviness grips my heart.

"Let her ask for help when she needs it, brother. Don't swoop in and try to save the day. You met this girl less than two weeks ago. Give it time. She takes care of herself. Has been doing so without a man for as long as I've known her. Though there used to be some asshole that came around. I didn't like the look of the guy. Seemed like a stuffy prick."

"Sean. Her ex. Real tool, but she's way over him. Though if the fucker comes sniffing around, I'll be handling that."

Jake chuckles. "You've got it bad, eh?"

"I'm falling for this girl. Shit, I may have already fallen. I don't really know what it feels like since I've never had it before."

"Falling in love is like that moment when you catch the ball in midair at the fifty-yard line. You look back and see a horde of badasses coming your way, but you turn the heat on and run. Fast. Faster. Until you eventually make it to the end zone. Except you're still tackled down to the ground, with three two hundred-pound weights each, on top of you, making it so you can't breathe, and you're in pain. And yet it's the best feeling of your life, knowing you made the score."

"Damn. You should write for Hallmark."

"Maybe in another life. Did I help?"

"Always, brother. Just seeing your face and hearing your voice alive and well makes me feel better. And yeah, your lesson to listen more and react less is how I'll move forward with Sadie. Thanks, man."

"Take care of my girl and stop overfeeding her."

"Um, yeah the line's getting a little static…" I warble my voice to make the sound.

"Dude, you're on video chat. There is no static!"

"Going through a tunnel, gotta go." I laugh.

"You're not driving! Jesus, fine. Good luck!"

"Be safe. Love you like a brother." I tell him because right now, with the uncertainty of his role, I want him to know how much he means to me.

"Same, man. We'll talk when I get settled in Europe."

I swallow down the sudden lump in my throat of worry for my best friend. "You do that. I'll be here. Taking care of big fat devil-kitty."

"Stop feeding my cat too much!" he yells.

Gloria takes this opportunity to scale her much bigger body up and onto the counter. "Fat cats are cuter."

"They are not! Come on!."

"Byyyyeeeee." I wink and hit the off button.

Gloria meows, stretches into a rainbow shape, sits, then stares me down. While doing so she lifts her paw, stretches out her sharp-ass nails, and licks them one at a time.

A warning.

Feed me or die.

"How's about a treat...or five?"

# Chapter
## THIRTEEN

### QUARANTINE: DAY 13

EVAN

S HE DIDN'T ANSWER HER PHONE ALL DAY YESTERDAY. Water poured from the sky like a waterfall so I couldn't catch her on the balcony either.

My girl is avoiding me.

And tomorrow is the day.

THE DAY.

I'm so damn excited I can hardly be in the same room with myself. And yet, the woman I'm obsessing over is ignoring me. So, I didn't apologize in my texts because I'd planned on doing so to her beautiful face. Jake was right. I went about things all wrong and after a full day of thinking it through, I eventually came to the conclusion that I was a bit of an arrogant dick. Trying to swoop in and save the day using my hefty bank account.

Sadie doesn't give one iota about money. Hell, the woman thinks football is a pastime before and after the Superbowl half-time show.

I pull up her number and hit call.

"Hello, person I'm not speaking to," she says in that haughty tone that makes my dick perk up.

"Baby, come on. I need to talk to you. Come out on the balcony. The sun is shining."

"Perhaps I can be persuaded. On the condition that you're planning to grovel? I'm talking down on your knees, completely repentant, begging me to forgive you. Do we understand each other?"

There's my girl. All sass and quick wit.

"You'll have to come outside to find out. Besides, I have a present for you."

"If it's a stack of money, I will kick you straight in the junk the second I can see you tomorrow. There will be no sweet nothings. No tongue touching. No hands, no penises anywhere near this body. You hear me?"

I laugh hard. "I missed you, sweetheart. Your voice. Seeing you. Yesterday was the pits, but I figured out a way to make it up to you. Now come outside. Pretty please with whipped cream and a cherry on top?"

"Hmm, only because I'm hoping there is actual whipped cream and a cherry magically sitting on top of a sundae on my balcony. And I swear if you're not shirtless, there will be consequences. Lots and lots of bad consequences."

"Got it." I put the phone down and on speaker outside and rip my shirt over my head. The wind is a bit nippy as proven by my now-erect man nips, but the sun is warm enough for me to tolerate. And for Sadie, I'd do just about anything.

She meanders through her sliding door. Her hair is in a ponytail on top of her head. If I was there right now, I'd grab that tail, wrap it around my fist, tilt her head back, and ravish her mouth.

I firm my jaw and stand with my hands on my hips, taking in her splendor.

"You're a sight for sore eyes." I scan her form until it's all I can see. Nothing else exists.

KYLIE SCOTT & AUDREY CARLAN

"Oh, please. It was only a day."

"In quarantine. A single day is like a full month and you know it."

She purses her lips and crosses her arms over her chest. "I missed you too," she huffs, and looks over at the view. Her side profile is elegant, with her pointed chin and long slender neck.

"First, I want to apologize for the other night. I didn't mean to be so overbearing. Your finances and your career are your business. I should have listened to what you were saying. I know you can take care of yourself, baby. You're the most intelligent and independent woman I've met."

"Thank you." She keeps her chin lifted as if she's not yet ready to back down, but I can see the cracks in her resolve to be mad at me tumbling down.

"Honestly, I don't know how this relationship stuff works. You're my first girlfriend since high school."

"You're kidding!" She loses all pretense and frowns.

"Went to college and focused on nothing but the game and doing my best to pass my classes. Sure, I played around on and off the field, but nothing concrete. Nothing anywhere near the seriousness of our relationship. Which means I'm gonna screw up with you occasionally."

Her blue eyes flash with a fire I missed so dammed much my balls ache seeing it.

"I'll probably screw up a lot. Not by cheating or anything like that so don't get all in a snit."

She giggles and it's the cutest sound in the world. "I wouldn't think you'd do that."

"Because I wouldn't. You mean something to me. And when you were talking about your money concerns my instinct was to fix it. Right away. I have more money than I know what to do with and you'd be surprised. My teammates are big spenders. I laid a

176

whack down on my house and car, but I have to. I live in Oakland. I'm considered a celebrity and safety matters. It's also expensive. Besides that, I'm all about hanging with the guys, working out, training, and playing the game."

"But you can see how high-handed it was to simply offer to pay off my debts like I'm incapable of doing the same for myself."

"I do and I apologize. I'm sorry." I give her my best puppy dog look until she gives in and smiles.

"Oh, all right. I forgive you."

"Thank you. All I ask now is that you work with me. You never back down in an argument and I love that about you. I want you to do that if something I say or do hurts you or your feelings. And I promise to do the same. This is unchartered territory for me, sweetheart. I'm swimming in an ocean full of sharks. Any wrong move and I'm shark bait."

That has her cackling in laughter. "Like *Sharknado!*"

"*Sharknado* is ridiculous. And awesome. We should totally watch it together."

"I'd like that."

"You forgive me?"

She smiles wide. "I'll forgive, but there's one more thing."

I sigh and take a deep breath. "Hit me."

"Where's my present?"

I grin and lift up a paper towel ball wrapped in cellophane. "Here, catch!" I toss the few-inches-wide ball I crafted the eight feet to her balcony.

She catches it easily. "I can't believe you just threw something over the balcony! You're such a rebel."

"Just open it."

She eases the plastic wrap open and unfolds the towel. "Oh my God. Is this what I think it is?"

"Chocolate chip cookies. Made by yours truly with all the

butter, sugar, and extra chocolate chips to boot! I was busy yesterday."

Without saying a word, she takes a ginormous bite, eating half in one go. Her eyes light up and she moans. "So good!" She finishes her bite and I watch as she stares at the small stack lovingly. "These are amazing. You never mentioned you could bake." She plops the other half of the first cookie in her mouth.

"I didn't know I could. It's actually something Jake is good at, but I found the chocolate chips stash along with a cookbook. Since I had time yesterday, I made three dozen."

Her mouth opens and her eyes go wide. "And where are the other cookies?"

That has me laughing. "Greedy girl. I put them in front of your door."

Without responding she dashes inside. I roll my eyes. That girl loves her sweets. Major win. I'll have to remember this moment when I'm in the doghouse again. Because it's inevitable that I'll be there again one day.

She comes out with the Tupperware and her stash in the paper towels. "This is the best present I've gotten in a really long time. So personal and appropriate for me."

"Glad you like them, baby. I wanted you to know I was thinking about you yesterday even when you were ignoring me."

She frowns. "Sorry about that. I was embarrassed for being so mouthy and drunk. It's just my mother and father found out we're dating and they're really unhappy about it and I just lost my mind a little."

"You told your parents about me and they're unhappy?"

"Um, it doesn't really matter. They're still stuck on Sean and…"

"Sean! Douchebag who doesn't give a shit about you, your work, or the things that matter in your life outside of your financial portfolio? I probably make a hundred times the amount of money that guy makes! More even!" Anger, white and hot, fires through my system and makes my blood boil. "And isn't he a pip-squeak? I could totally take him!" I growl through my teeth, putting my hands to the railing and squeezing as hard as I can to let off some steam.

"Baby, no. I'm sorry. I didn't mean to say anything. It's dumb. They don't understand. Sean was what they wanted for me: white picket fence and two point five kids. Perfect marriage material."

"And I'm not! What the hell is wrong with me? They don't even know me! I want kids and my house rocks. You'll love it. We could even turn the room over the garage into a private office for you to write in." I grind down on my teeth and breathe fire through my nose.

"Evan, it's stupid, but Dad follows sports and they know about the scandal and they think I'm making a bad decision dating a baller who's been pictured with a lot of different women. And then the picture of you passed out with drugs in the room. It doesn't look good and they don't know you like I do."

I hang my head.

"I'm not good enough for you," I say to the side of the balcony. "They're right. You don't deserve any of this. What I'm dealing with right now. Scandals. Drugs. A player. You're better than that. Sean is an asshole and I'm a fuck up. A woman like you, Sadie. Beautiful. Smart. Writes amazing books. Yeah, I've read one already and am on my second. You're so talented. You do not need the bad press or the shit that my life will bring to your doorstep. Dating a celebrity is not fun."

"I don't care about any of that. I only care about you. The man I've chosen. The man I want to be with. You. Just as you are."

I firm my jaw and shake my head. "No, you don't know what it's like. Being in the spotlight all the time. Bullshit is said about me and who I have on my arm the second I show up anywhere. I wouldn't want that for you. It's good that they don't approve. Now that I think about it, I don't approve either. You're better than all of this." I run my hands through my hair and turn around.

"Evan, no! That's not true. Please, don't leave me like this. Talk to me!"

My shoulders fall and I look at her face. There are tears in her pretty blue eyes and something about seeing those tears clocks me upside the head.

"I don't want to ever hurt you."

"Then don't do anything rash. Don't you dare believe all the hype."

"They're your parents. They care about you and if they don't like me…it will never work."

"I don't give a shit what my parents think. Besides, deep down they are good people. I promise. When they meet you, they will know what I know. That Evan Sparks is a hardworking, record-setting athlete who has devoted his life to his career. They'll know that their daughter is head over heels for a man that is strong, noble, kind, compassionate, and supportive."

"Baby…"

"Just don't push me away. What we have is more real than anything I've ever had in my life."

"For me too." My voice is hoarse and raw.

"Then don't do anything to fuck it up. You just told me not to let you screw us up. This is me telling you not to screw us up. If you care about me, you'll fight for me. You'll fight for us. It's me and you, Evan. Since Day 1 of this crazy new normal, it's been me and you. And when this passes, I want it to still be me and you."

I close my eyes and let her words sink in. "I want that too."

"Okay. I'm glad we got that settled. No pushing one another away. Besides, tomorrow is Day 14 and I'm looking forward to it. So much so, I think Day 14 of every month should be a day we celebrate. It will represent hope and anticipating good things."

God, this woman. She's everything.

"I'm sorry again for screwing us up."

She tips her head to the side. "It's okay. I'll be here to put us back together. Do you want a cookie? It will make you feel better." She smiles as she holds one out, though there's no way I could reach it even if I tried. The balconies are a full eight feet apart.

"No. Your smile. Your voice. Your wisdom. That's what makes me feel better."

She smiles softly. "Are we okay?"

I nod. "Yeah, Sadie, we're okay. As long as I keep a clear head, we'll be okay."

"I'll make sure you do. Now tell me more about the book of mine that you read! I want to hear everything." Her voice is filled with awe and joy. She sits down, crosses her legs, and bites into another cookie.

My girl. Life tosses her a doozy, but she gets past it and keeps on smiling.

♡

## SADIE

To celebrate the day before the big day, we go for a walk to get some essential items. Six feet apart, of course.

"This time tomorrow, I'll be holding your hand," Evan says with a grin.

I snort. "Yeah right, buddy. You'll be holding a tit, more likely. Don't try your faux-romance moves on me, you fraudster. You're a breast man from way back and tomorrow is day fourteen. Sex day. And we both know it."

Footsteps approach and a police officer stands against the building, ensuring we can safely pass him. With the city so silent, you know everything I just said carried straight to the man's ears. Speaking of ears, the tips of the young officer's are bright pink. Huh.

Evan holds back a chuckle not so successfully.

That's me. A freak in the sheets and a lady in the…never. I am never a lady. I am always just me. Such is life. "Stop laughing," I hiss at my way-too-amused new boyfriend. "You're making it worse."

Evan wipes a hand over his face, smiling up a storm. The ass.

"Evan Sparks!" The officer's eyes light up with recognition.

Evan's smile fades as he nods. He starts walking faster. "Morning."

"Hey. Psst. Slow down." I just about have to jog to keep up with his long-legged strides. He has his head down and his hands shoved into the pockets of his jeans. He is not a happy camper. Guess I just got my first look at the fame monster. Even in my comfy black leather booties, I'm struggling to keep up with the pace he's setting. Though I am happy with how my outfit came together. Skinny blue jeans, a sexy/baggy sweater that hangs off one shoulder revealing the strap of my white tank, and a red hairband. I was a little overexcited to actually get dressed and leave the apartment. Oh well. "Evan!"

He stops and turns. "Yeah?"

I skid to a halt, careful not to get too close. "I can't keep up with you. Please slow down."

"Sorry, baby."

"Are you okay?"

He sighs. "Yeah, I ah… Guess I got used to being left alone, you know? Not that I mind being recognized or having a fan say hi."

"It's just with all of the crap they're saying in the papers you don't know what to expect. I understand."

"I don't know, it's as if they get this look in their eye like they're trying to decide if I'm a scum-sucking cheating asshole or what."

I shake my head. "We're going to get through this. You're going to show them exactly who you are and there will be no doubt that you got set up."

He nods, and looks down the street where the police officer is climbing into his cruiser. "C'mon, gorgeous. Let's get moving and get this done."

Within minutes we reach the small store wedged between two skyscrapers.

Like most of my gender, I enjoy a trip to a pharmacy. And right now, any chance to get the hell outside is a beautiful thing. But this is actually fun. I peruse the boxes of hair dye. "Think I'd look good as a redhead?"

"You'd look good as anything," he murmurs.

"You're going to regret saying that when I shave my head due to a combination of sheer boredom and frustration over the state of my roots."

Evan stares at the top of my skull. "Bald would be an interesting choice. But whatever works for you, baby."

"Look at you being all supportive and wonderful." I grin.

"I'm not getting put in time out again. Not this close to game day."

"No. Stop. Do not compare our sex life to a sport. I forbid it." I point a finger at him, my packets of allergy medication safely in the other hand. One way or another, I'm probably going to get exposed to the wonderful fluffiness that is Gloria sometime soon. Best to be prepared. But back to the boy. "No, Evan. Just no."

He smiles.

I move down the aisle, checking out the selection of hair brushes and other things. "I was wondering about giving myself bangs, though. Just for something different."

"Don't do it, sister," yells a woman an aisle over. "You know you'll regret it."

"Yeah. You're probably right. Thanks."

The woman moves on and Evan gives me a look. "Do you know her?"

"No. But at times such as these, all us girls have to look out for one another. The sisterhood must live on."

His brows go up. "Okay."

"It's like when we go to the bathroom to pee *en masse*. We all need to be talked out of cutting our own hair at one time or another. After a break up, during a pandemic…you get what I mean."

"I figured you were always just talking smack about men when you went to the bathroom."

"Oh yeah. I'm not going to lie, there's a lot of that. But women are natural born multitaskers. We can reapply lip gloss, decimate a dickhead, and still make time for some hairstyle advice all while washing our hands."

"Right."

Next comes the vitamins because I'm low on C. Meanwhile Evan inspects a selection of multivitamins for women. "If you insist on eating processed crap instead of fresh fruit and vegetables, we should probably get you some of these. Just to be safe."

"I eat vegetables."

"Tater tots don't really count, sweetheart."

"Well that's harsh." I pout.

He reads the back of a bottle. "This one looks okay. You want to check it out?"

"No, I trust you. Chuck it in the basket."

"Did you want to talk some more about your parents?" he asks. "If so, I'm happy to listen. Without losing my shit this time."

"Thanks. But not really. I mean, they're wrong. It's pretty straightforward. They're working on limited and biased information instead of listening to me, their only child. The person who actually knows you and has spent time with you." My foot starts tapping. "You'd think my happiness would count for something with them, you know?"

"I'm sorry they upset you."

I scowl. "Ugh. It happens. Families…"

"Still, I hate seeing you down. We're going to do some definite hugging and comforting tomorrow."

"Oh yeah? Naked or clothed?"

"Naked, of course."

I laugh. Men. They're such sweet, simple creatures, really. Evan amply displays this in the next aisle. "Yes! Here we go, baby. Time to get serious." First he throws a couple tubes of lube into his basket, followed by carefully perusing the prophylactics. "Ribbed?"

"Sure. Knock yourself out."

"Flavored?"

"Ew. Pass."

"Glow in the dark?" He waggles his brows.

"Are you that likely to get lost?"

"Hell no." He moves along. "Any feelings about warming ones?"

I shrug. "Haven't tried them."

"Let's give those a whirl."

"Do we really need that many?" I ask.

He just looks at me, gaze serious. Wounded almost. Like he's questioning my priorities and general life choices.

I shake my head in wonder. "Okay. Fine. Keep going. But at this rate, you're going to have to carry me everywhere."

"I think that would be best. Keep you nice and handy for whenever we feel the need. And you can bet after the past few weeks, I definitely feel the need."

"That sex starved, huh?"

"Nope," he corrects. "I'm Sadie starved. There's a difference. No other girl will do."

"Aw."

"Studded?"

I wrinkle my nose. "I dunno."

"Another time. Edible?"

"I have cookies. Why would I even?" I cross my arms. "I think you've got enough. We should probably leave some for the rest of the city."

He inspects the heaped contents of his basket with a frown. "It'll do for the first week."

"Good God. Do you anticipate us ever sleeping or indeed doing anything other than having sex in the near future?"

He lifts a shoulder. "Meh. If you really want to. We could watch a little TV, I guess. And I'll cook meals for you. Got to keep your energy up, baby."

"I'm getting that. I can see me icing my vagina at this rate."

"Is that a problem?" And he's serious. The man is actually serious.

We finish up our purchases with the cashier giving Evan the bro-code version of a thumbs-up when he says, "Niiiiccceeee," at the sheer amount of sexual paraphernalia he's purchasing. I look around and notice one of the other cashiers giving me the side-eye.

She just wishes she had a hunk-a-licious like Evan stocking up to fuck her stupid. Too bad he's all mine.

"Don't worry, baby, we'll get more next week," I say loud enough for side-eye jealous girl to hear. Petty, but fun.

Evan follows me out the door and back to our place. Staying six feet behind me until I stop cold after exiting the elevator at our floor.

"Sean, what are you doing here?" I glare at the most

unwelcome of visitors standing outside my front door. Also, I desperately need to change the code for my personal entrance to the building. Pronto.

Behind me, I can just feel Evan bristling. Unfortunate after our lovely outing. We've been smiling and laughing, the day a success. Now this.

Wearing a gray pinstripe suit, a mask, and gloves, Sean just blinks at me, his black hair neatly slicked back. Then his gaze goes to the much bigger man standing behind me. It's wrong the way I objectify Evan and his large hot body. I know this. I'm a shallow and wanton creature. But right now, I can't bring myself to care. I've moved onto bigger and better things. Literally. And I'm more than happy for my ex to see that for himself—the asshat.

"I bought you a care basket," he says, gesturing to the flashy gift box of wine, fruit, and flowers sitting at his feet.

"You did? Why?"

"Well…because I care." He even sounds haughty wearing a facemask and gloves.

Instantly the idea of a gentleman serial killer coming after Eamon and Katie in my novel prods at my sleeping muse before I shake it off to pay attention to the situation.

"No you don't." I frown remembering all the times he didn't care. Book releases. When I hit the *New York Times*, when I sold my first book to another country. He's never actually given two shits about me and my life. Just how I fit into his.

"He pretending he cares because he's trying to get back in," growls Evan. "Dude, no matter what you say, it's not going to work. That ship has sailed."

Sean sniffs. "You're the drug dealing baller, I take it."

And then it all clicks into place with horrible, blood-boiling clarity. "Oh my fucking God! My mother called you. I don't believe this. Evan, baby, I'm so sorry."

"Not your fault," my man says through clenched teeth, staring Sean down as though if he so much as flinches he's jumping him like a hungry Rottweiler protecting its food. Only in this scenario, I'm the food.

"You can't be serious, Sadie. What the hell are you thinking? He's an over-hyped, panty-chasing, drug-taking baller with a tiny dick and an even smaller IQ. Grow up and choose better."

Evan's jaw is set, his gaze ablaze with fury. I can see him clenching and unclenching his strong hands into fists. "Do not insult her or I will end you."

"And don't insult him either," I add, stepping further into the open hallway. "Evan, I really am sorry about this."

He doesn't so much as look my way, blazing gaze set on the douchenozzle. "Not your fault. I already told you that."

"I know this is going to be very hard for you, and likely goes against everything you believe in, but would you mind going into your apartment and letting me deal with this? Pretty please? It'll only take a minute and it's something I feel I have to do on my own."

His brows draw down into one fierce and pissed line. "I'd rather hit him."

"Yes, but then you'd break social distancing rules and need to do another fourteen days of isolation to make sure you haven't caught anything. What do you want more, a piece of me or a piece of him?"

Sean scoffs. The idiot. As if he'd stand a chance against an enraged Evan. And my new boyfriend is beyond furious.

"He's not worth that. And you come first. Always." Frown still in place, Evan fishes out the keys to Jake's apartment from his jeans pocket and unlocks the door. "I'll be right on the other side organizing our condoms if you need anything. Quarantine or no quarantine."

Sean rolls his eyes and makes a gagging sound. "Classy."

"So helpful, honey. Thank you."

Then he turns to Sean. "You say one thing to upset her in any way and I will destroy you. There will be no discussion. Do we understand one another?"

Sean just blinks again.

"I think he understands," I say.

Evan disappears inside the apartment and I sigh. "You were brought here under false pretenses by my mother for which I apologize. But hear me now and make no mistake, Sean. I don't want to see you. I don't want to hear from you. And I definitely do not need rescuing."

"Sadie—"

"I was lonely and I thought having you in my life would fix things. That I'd feel more competent and accomplished or some such shit. Like my career and interests and friends weren't enough. It's hard to believe in love when it keeps passing you by. I think it was approaching thirty that made me panic. An image I had in my head of where I'd be by now in life. But I'm over that. And the truth is, being with you made me feel more alone than ever. The constant need to restrain myself, to censor myself, so I wouldn't be too much or too weird or too something for you. So I wouldn't be me and embarrass you. That's the truth of it. It was a messed up and shitty cycle to be caught up in and I'm done with it. Now, as for the other matter." I slip my cell phone out of my purse and dial up my mother.

"Sadie." She's smiling. I can hear it in her voice. And meanwhile my blood is basically boiling. Far the fuck out.

"Listen to me carefully and do not interrupt, Mom. I'm happy with him. Evan makes me happy. Do you get how big that is for me?"

"But, honey—"

KYLIE SCOTT & AUDREY CARLAN

"No. Listen. Just listen for once, will you, please? It's not because I'm having to isolate and am stressed and scared of the virus. Even though I am all of those things. It's because he's a good person and he's good for me. He accepts me as I am. All of my insecurities and quirks and everything." I take a breath and let it out slow. "So you're going to delete Sean's number from your cell and you will never pull this sort of thing again. I'm serious. You have hurt and embarrassed me along with humiliating Sean here. Someone that you apparently have more respect for than me. Then you're going to go and sit down and have a long think about the kind of relationship you want to have with me. I'll call you in a couple of days when I've cooled down. Please don't call me in the meantime unless it's an emergency." Then I hang up. Go me for getting the last word for once. Victory.

Sean's brows seem to have inched up into his hairline.

"I've made my choice and I regret nothing. I do not want you in my life in any way, shape, or form. We're over."

"But?"

"Over!" I practically screech.

He stares at me for a long time before closing his eyes. I think he finally might actually believe me. "I take it we understand each other now?"

He nods.

"Excellent. Take the fucking basket and go," I demand.

Finally, for once in the time we've known one another, he listens too. He grabs the basket and walks around to the elevator.

Once he's gone, a wave of exhaustion encompasses me. A moment later, Evan cracks his front door open and peeks out. "Safe to come out yet?"

"For you? Yes."

His expression is filled with compassion and I think a little pride. "You kicked ass, baby. Remind me never to get on your bad side."

I smile, but my shoulders slump. "I know you said you were cutting back, but can we just go sit out on our balconies and chill with a drink? Talk about the mysteries of the universe?"

His corresponding smile...so dreamy. "Whatever you want. I'm here for you."

# Chapter
# FOURTEEN

## QUARANTINE: DAY 14

### SADIE

I<small>T'S QUARTER TO EIGHT WHEN</small> I <small>KNOCK ON HIS DOOR IN A PAIR</small> of yoga pants and a tight white tee. Evan opens it approximately two seconds later.

Oh, the fire in his eyes. And baby, am I ready to burn. First he takes in me, from the fluffy socks on my feet to the messy bun in my hair. Then he notices all of the assorted shit surrounding me. A couple of boxes. My luggage. You know…stuff.

"What's going on?" he asks. "Thought I heard noises out here."

"Okay, so if we're doing this right, here's how things are going to be. Ready?"

He nods.

"So the rules say that if you're physically involved with someone…and I trust we're about to get physically involved?"

Another nod.

"Then we need to be self-isolating together, basically. I think that would be safest and make the most sense. If you agree, of course. Now Gloria is used to this apartment and I didn't want to upset her because she's a sweet floofy baby. Then there's your treadmill and all of your training gear to be considered. Hence my choice of this apartment. You also discussed at length that we're apparently giving up anything besides eating and sleeping in the pursuit of fucking from now on."

"It's a noble pursuit and we need to be focused."

"True. And being in the same space will make that easier. Though I do need to get some work done now and then. I packed my laptop and a couple of knickknacks off my desk so I can set up a little space at the dining table or wherever suits." I gesture toward one of the boxes and a bag.

His smile is slow and freaking divine. "You're moving in with me."

"I'm moving in with you. If you want." My stomach flip flops from nerves. I am never this brave. Though Evan makes me feel like I can scale mountains. I certainly want to scale him. But first things first.

"Oh, baby, it's safe to say I can't even remember ever wanting something as bad as this," he says. "I've been waiting out on the balcony for you since dawn. Got just about no sleep last night, I was so damn excited. Can I touch you now?"

I hold up a hand. "Just a minute. I'm not quite finished with the speech I prepared earlier. Also, we need to get my stuff inside."

"Step back and let me get that sorted," he says, reaching for the luggage and dragging it into Jake's hall. Next he picks up like all of the boxes, including the heavy ones full of books (as if I'd go anywhere without my books). Damn is he strong. "What else did you want to say?"

"Right. I've never lived with anyone before and I'm assuming you haven't either—"

"That would be right."

"So we're both going to make mistakes and step on each other's toes now and then. The important thing is to be open minded, patient, and keep the communication happening, right?"

"Right."

"Because neither of us know how long this lockdown could go on for. When you need some time to yourself or if you want me to go back to my apartment so we can take a step back from this for however long, you need to tell me. And I'll do the same if I need some space. Complete honesty, okay?"

"Agreed."

"Which brings us to back to the here and now. I had this idea of wearing a slinky dress and heels and looking all fancy for you. But the fact is, moving necessitated these comfortable, boring items of clothing."

His gaze runs over my body like an actual caress as he grabs the rest of my belongings. I've never been moved so fast in my life. The man is on a mission. "Understandable. Though nothing you put on that body could be boring, baby."

"I appreciate your vote of confidence, but I wanted to make this a special occasion. The truth is, however, I haven't even washed my hair yet."

"We can do it in the shower later and I'll wash your hair for you after. Was that all?" His hands are shaking and the muscles in his forearms are flexing rhythmically.

"You don't care that I look like a vagrant?" I ask with my heart in my hand.

"Sadie, baby, rest assured that even if I knew what a vagrant was I still wouldn't care that you apparently look like one."

I laugh. "A hobo, vagabond, drifter. You know?"

"Cutest hobo I've ever seen. I especially dig your fluffy socks."

"Thanks."

"We good now?"

I grin. "Oh. We're so damn good."

"Thank fuck for that!" He growls, pulling my body against his much larger one. My toes are barely touching the ground when he sinks his face against the crook of my neck and hugs me.

Not what I expected, but somehow *better*.

His body is shaking and then I realize it's *me*. I'm trembling in his arms.

He runs his hands up and down my back while he holds me. Kisses the side of my neck in featherlight presses of lips to skin.

"Relax, baby. Let me hold you."

I let out the breath I didn't realize I was holding and sink further into his embrace. He's warm and smells of mint, Irish Spring soap, and something unique and manly. I soak in the scent and sigh deeply, feeling his chest against mine, his heart pounding. I expected to be nervous and ever so slightly freaked out in this moment. And I sort of am. But mostly, this feels natural and right. Like I've finally found home in human form and it's Evan.

Life. Altered. Forever.

For what feels like seconds and eternity at the same time, our labored breaths and heartbeats synchronize. His hands rub up and down my back and sides in soothing sweeping caresses that lull me into a dreamy haze that's filled with nothing but him, this moment. The first time we get to hold one another.

"You are the most perfect creature," he says. "I feel honored to be holding you close, feeling your breath against my neck. I don't know how to explain it…"

"Meant to be." I squeeze him tighter and run my fingers through his hair, allowing the now longer layers to slide through my fingers like water over river rocks in the heat of summer. Good God, this man gets me poetic. Scratch that. He just gets me in general. And that knowledge, that acceptance, moves me like nothing that's ever come before. My eyes are watery, my throat tight. But I will not cry and make this weird. I won't. Probably.

He leans back and cups my face. His blue eyes are shining and magically, filled with a rawness I've always craved in a man but never had. It's awe. He's in awe of this moment. In awe of me.

With deft movements, he walks us back into the apartment, shutting and locking the door behind us. This is it.

"Kiss me, Evan." I swallow down the anticipation and anxiety of such an important moment. We only get one first kiss.

"It feels like I've been waiting a lifetime to kiss you." His thumbs trace the apple of my cheeks and that's when I realize I'm crying. Big fat wet tears slide down my face. He dips forward and kisses first one tear-stained cheek and then the other before he closes his eyes and presses his nose to mine.

"I'm in love with you, and I haven't even kissed you," he murmurs against my mouth. A secret and a revelation.

My entire body quivers, words I've never felt before battering at my heart, filling my soul with all that is him. Us. What we are to one another. So much emotion I don't even know what to do with it all. Tears pour down my cheeks and over his fingers. "I'm in love with you too, and it's crazy, wild, and better than anything I've ever known."

"Baby." His lips barely touch mine, but I feel that word race through my body in ribbons of electricity.

"I never even believed in the insta-love stories. This is so completely unexpected," I whisper.

"But good."

"Amazingly so. Kiss me." I nudge his nose with mine, wanting—*needing*—to have him make the first move.

"My pleasure. My Sadie." He murmurs against my lips until his fingers sift into my hair and grip the back of my head while he takes my mouth in a searing kiss.

I open immediately, wanting to taste the man I love more than I need to inhale my next breath. Mint pierces my taste buds pleasantly as the combined warmth of our tongues dance. Spiraling around one another in a carnal display of the heat between us.

One of his hands leaves my hair, glides down my body, and

goes straight for my ass. His large hand grips and squeezes the globe until I'm pressed higher and more firmly against his body. I can feel his cock hard against my belly and moan in delight knowing I did that to him.

He's ravenous in his pursuit of my mouth. Nipping and licking deep, sucking my tongue, nibbling on first my top then my bottom lip until my flesh feels deliciously bruised and swollen, but I don't stop. I can't. I want him too much. I'm obsessed with his tongue, his lips, his *taste*.

We kiss for so long, I didn't even realize we were becoming oxygen starved until he pulls away to take a breath. I'm pressed against the nearest wall gasping for air, dizzy with desire and lust.

"Jesus, I had no idea it could be this good. Fuck, my woman can kiss." He rests his forehead to mine while breathing deep, his hands sliding up and down my waist, ribs, and then back down to my hips.

I cheese out by his compliment, smiling wide and grinning like a woman in love. Because I am a woman in love.

In love with Evan Sparks.

Holy shit.

The thought ravages my soul and shoots me into action. With deft fingers I lift my tee up and over my head. Evan follows suit. A game of Simon Says without words is being instructed and he's an apt student. Curling my fingers around the waistband of my yoga pants I shimmy them off. He drops his gym shorts and we're both left in our underwear. His being a pair of black boxer briefs with an impressive hard-on straining the front. Nice.

Without further ado, I wrap my arms around his neck, shift my weight, and hop into the air. He catches me easily at the ass as I wrap my legs around his waist and take his mouth.

He gets the hint and moves us to the bedroom. Which is basically a series of movements pressing me harder against random walls, his erection firm against my center. I'm moaning and groaning and disoriented with a hunger so intense I start to rock my hips against his length. Luckily, one of us is thinking of the practicalities. He closes the bedroom door so sweet Gloria can't decide to pay us a visit mid-sex. Right now, I want to be the only pussy in Evan's life.

"Christ!" He pulls his mouth off mine once I feel him stumble against the bed. He lowers me down and I open my legs. Ready and willing. He falls between them and cups my head. "Everything is so much more with you." He shakes his head as if he can't believe it.

I smile and gaze into his lust-filled eyes. They're so dark blue they're the sky at midnight. Magical, life-altering, earth-shattering.

"Evan...I...I..." I honestly don't know what to say to him. To solidify what this means to me. How he makes me feel. How very much I'm gone for him. Lost to this man I barely know and yet I know almost better than I know myself. More than anything, however, I feel safe.

He lifts his body up, and shifts down the mattress, his gaze stretching all over my body and then back up to my face.

Evan smiles and it lights up my fucking world. The way he sees me. How beautiful I feel lying under him. He makes me feel special, priceless.

He presses a finger to my mouth. "I know. I feel it too."

I swallow and nod, my heart ripped open and bleeding for this man.

Evan purses his lips, his features changing from soft and adoring to cute and teasing. "Sadie, my love, this is the best moment of my fucking life." I chuckle and he bites into his bottom lip. "I think it's only fair that we start this very special act with one thing and one thing only."

I narrow my eyes and grin, kicking my feet under him where he's straddling my thighs.

"Oh, and what pray tell is that very special act?"

He waggles his brows and runs his hand down the front of his impressively tented boxer briefs. "It's time you finally show me your tits, princess. I want those beauties offered up to me."

Aw, thank God, teasing Evan is back. One moment we're so intertwined and intense I can hardly breathe, the next easygoing and comfortable. I can definitely handle a lifetime of this.

♡

## EVAN

Finally having her in my hands is sending my brain straight into overload. I can't think beyond her and me and now. The building could be burning down and I wouldn't even notice. With a shimmy and a grin, Sadie drags up the sports bra, baring her chest to me. Best breasts ever.

"Hello, new best friends," I say solemnly, placing a gentle kiss on each pink nipple. They're already hard little peaks, making my mouth water.

Sadie's laughter turns into moaning as I give in to temptation and suck on one. Licking and gently biting at the sweet tip. Her hips churn, rubbing her thong-covered pussy against me. And Christ, I can smell her. Her arousal. It scents the room and makes my already rock-hard dick weep with need.

I may as well just tattoo the girl's name on my forehead now and be done with it. Because I haven't gotten inside her yet and she already owns me. The fact that I told a woman I loved her for the first time stays in the back of my mind, just waiting for a what-the-fuck with a dash of fear. Every single male instinct in me is on high alert. Like belonging with someone, having them in my face day in and day out is some shitty fate I should be running from as fast I can. Only it isn't happening. I meant what I said and I'm exactly where I want to be. As Sadie said, we're meant to be.

"Evan," she says, concern in her voice. Which is not what I want to hear at all. A little line is embedded between her brows. "What if we don't have chemistry?"

"What?" Now I'm just confused. With no blood left in my brain, it happens easy enough. Still the words and their insane meaning break through eventually. "Sadie. Baby. Does it feel like we don't have chemistry?"

"Well, no. But what if we don't fit?"

I grin.

She rolls her eyes. "I'm not talking about the size of your cock. I mean, what if we don't gel in bed?"

I rest my forehead against her chest, getting my thoughts in order. "You're right to have this concern, my love. In fact, I think we need to assume that you and I are going to need some time to figure out how best to sexually please one another. And we should commit to this side of our relationship here and now and plan for lots of fucking."

"I'm being silly, aren't I?"

I grin wide. "You're wet. I'm hard. We're both very excited and the signs are all good. There's no need to assume we're not going to be rockin' in bed, darling."

"Sorry. I'll try to stop worrying."

"No problem." Heavy sigh. "Okay. Where was I?"

"Tits."

"Right. Let's move this along, shall we? Put your worries to bed, so to speak." I lick my lips and slide my hands down her sides. Over the curve of her waist and the flare of her hips and ass. Juicy like a peach, just as I thought. Definitely going to bite that later. Then I hook my fingers in either side of her thong and drag it down her legs. She helpfully curls them up, allowing me to get rid of the offending item of lingerie faster. "You have such cute little feet. Look at those toes."

"I like my feet. My hands are kind of weirdly big though."

"That's all right. I have something big for them to wrap around later. Your apparently weirdly large hands are going to come in good use, baby. Trust me."

She giggles. "Funny. Okay, get rid of your underwear too. And make it quick."

I do as ordered. My unwieldy dick bounces around, slapping against the slight round of her stomach, as I reach over to grab a condom out of the collection of open and waiting boxes on the bedside table. Just a straightforward wrapper for the first time. We don't need any distractions or enhancements. Not this go-around.

"I can do that," she offers.

"Next time. I'm so wired right now I'd probably come if you touched me." On it goes and yes. Thank God for that. I drag the bulbous head of my cock up and down her drenched slit. "And, baby girl, you have a particularly pretty pussy. Jesus. Look at it all swollen, pink, and so wet. Fucking beautiful, Sadie. So much more gorgeous in real life."

She gasps, her eyes rolling back into her head, as I rub my crown against her hot spot. All women are lovely, but Sadie's cunt is particularly breathtaking. And so delightfully sensitive. I massage her clit, ramping her need up higher. She sure as shit isn't worrying about anything right now. Breasts rising and falling at a frantic pace with each labored breath, she's well on her way to coming.

"Hell, Evan."

Meanwhile, my blood is beating like a drum. Pounding through me, demanding I get a move on. The sight of her, smell of her, every damn thing about her just turns me on. My cock pulses and my breath catches. As much as I'd love to wow her with my foreplay abilities, that's going to have to wait for later.

"Stop fooling around and put it in me," she says.

"Yes, ma'am." I chuckle, desperate for her.

I line up my dick with her entrance and push in nice and slow. Savoring the sensation of filling her for the first time. Of feeling her hot body encase me. Now my mind is really blown. The whole damn world is reduced down to her skin against mine, her legs wrapped around my hips, urging me on. Despite having done this many times before, I'm a new man when it comes to sex with my woman. My heart is aching inside my chest at the perfection of being inside her for the first time.

It's as if I'm going to cry. Or come. Possibly both.

A fine sheen of perspiration dots her face and the dazed yet loving look in her eyes is nirvana. I want to remember everything. Every single moment. But even more than that, I want to move. The thrill of feeling her nipples dragging against my chest as I surge in and out. Slow at first, then building up speed. Her ankles dig into my ass cheeks, urging me on. Deeper. Harder.

My grip on her wrists tightens, and I hold them down above her head. Because something in her writing tells me she likes a dash of kinky shit with her loving. Good with me. Her arms flex, as she tries to break free. But the sly sexy smile on her face says it's definitely her thing.

"Let me touch you?" she asks in a breathy voice.

"Just feel."

"Fuck." Her head tips back, gifting the long slender column of her neck to run my lips against as her hips grind against mine. "Evan, it's so good."

I lick a bead of sweat off her jawline and give her my most feral grin. So the girl's got me wild and worked up. Not surprised. I'd like to say something clever to her, but my mind is wiped. All I can think about is those delicate little muscles in her pussy quivering around my cock. The pink in her cheeks deepening to a scarlet red as she gets closer and closer to coming.

Heaven has nothing on sex with Sadie. I grind the base of my dick against her clit and her mouth falls open. The sweetest little gasps falling out of her mouth. Each one of them sending a bolt of electricity straight through my chest and swirling hot at the base of my spine.

Truth be told, I'm beyond ready. My balls are drawn up tight against my body. Every ounce of pent-up tension, this heady burning desire for this woman is ready to blow, spill hotly inside the woman I love. Then it happens. Her back bows and every inch of her delicious body tightens. The muscles of her sex squeeze my dick until I'm ready to explode.

Her eyelids close and a gorgeous, serene beauty takes over the features of her face as Sadie comes. Her body milks my shaft for all its worth, pushing me straight over the edge with her.

Fuck me. My hips crash against hers. I want to get as deep inside of her as I can. Hell. I'd meld us together permanently if I was able. White hot light blinds me, my body shaking. Nothing's ever been this good. No touchdown or perfect pass. No trophy or win. Nothing.

I just manage to roll off of her as opposed to crushing her with my weight. Because I'm done. Drained. Side by side, we lie on the mattress, both working at catching our breath. I manage to roll my head to the side, all the better to watch her post-orgasm. Still gorgeous. She lies limp and sated on my bed. Damned if she doesn't belong there. I want to look at this sight every night of my fucking life.

Once my heart has stopped hammering, I say, "You're right. We're hopeless together. That was awful. Worst sex of my life."

Sadie laughs softly.

"Might as well just break up now. I'll help you move your shit back into your apartment, 'cause I'm a gentleman like that."

She swats me in the chest. But really, it's more like her hand just kind of flops onto me. "That'd be great, thanks. I got what I came for."

"Hmm. On second thought, we've put a lot into this relationship. We should probably work hard at the fucking in order to make a real go of it. You know, practice makes perfect and all that jazz. You sure you don't want to stick around for round two?"

She opens one eyelid and gives me an assessing look. "I don't know, Evan. Think you got it in you?"

My smile is all sharp teeth and leering. "I don't know, my love," I say, rolling back onto my side to reach out and delicately pinch one of her pretty pink nipples.

She moans and stretches her long body, almost as if she's put herself on display just for my viewing pleasure. Immediately, my dick starts to stir back to life. What can I say? She inspires me. "Let's find out, shall we?" I pinch the other nipple while leaning over and sucking the bruised one into my mouth.

"Oh my, yes. Let's find out."

# Chapter
## FIFTEEN

## QUARANTINE: DAY 15

EVAN

A RAY OF SUNLIGHT STREAKS ACROSS MY EYES WITH pinpoint accuracy as I roll over and press my face into the pillow. Reaching out my arm, I search for Sadie's warmth and only find the empty sheet. Not only empty—the sheet is cold, which tells me that she's been out of bed for a long time.

Opening my eyes and pressing up onto a forearm, I rub the sleep out of my eyes and scan the room. The bathroom light is off, so she's not there. There is a head-sized dent in the pillow. Okay, I didn't dream the night of amazing sex and coming together for the first, second, and third time.

I frown and push back the covers. Naked, I pad to the dresser and grab a pair of plaid pajama bottoms and tug them on commando. Still bare chested, I hear clicking. A rhythmic cadence coming from the living room.

Frowning, I head to investigate.

Jake's desk and computer are off as I approach the living room.

And aw, there's my girl. Sitting on the love seat, legs stretched out and resting on the coffee table, her laptop is on her legs and she is typing away. Her golden hair is down around her face and falling in wild waves over her shoulders and back. I'm surprised to see a pair of bright teal glasses perched on her nose.

Her fingers are flying on the keyboard so fast I swear they blur a little.

I watch her work. She's stunning. Her focus on the story is so intense that she doesn't even realize I'm there. I could probably do jumping jacks behind her and she wouldn't notice.

Allowing myself this quiet moment, I study her. Sadie is every man's dream come true. Long toned legs with some heft at the hips and upper thighs. Smooth, naturally tan skin. A plump ass that's made for fucking. A tiny waist—though she doesn't think so. My large hands and body practically dwarf the woman, which I know amuses her beyond reason. Her tits are magical. I'm a man obsessed with her breasts. A perfect handful yet small enough I can get a nice amount in my mouth. The woman is beauty from tip to toe. My mouth waters and my dick punches against my lounge pants with the desire to take her again.

I wasn't wrong when I said we need to fuck this intense situation out. Maybe Jake's right. When you love someone, it's pleasure and pain in equal measures. Pain from the wanting, the endless desire that seems to bubble just under the surface when I'm near her or when the thought of her enters my mind. Then the pleasure when she looks at me with hope and love shining in her eyes. The way it feels when we finally merged, when I made love to her. Christ, there is nothing better.

Nothing.

And I thought I was married to the game—that that would be the only obsession in my life, the only thing I was committed to. However, what I feel for Sadie far surpasses those feelings.

Football is my true passion. And while I really hope the situation with work comes out on the positive side, now I've got Sadie. If I lose my job, I've still got her—and she's worth more. I can make money doing a lot of things. Probably many things I'll genuinely enjoy and possibly even love, but I don't think anything in my future will ever hold a candle to what I feel for this woman.

The clacking sound suddenly stops. She lifts a finger in the air and brings it down on a key before sighing happily and smiling. She removes her glasses and sets them on the end table next to her.

"What's my girl smiling about?" I come around the love seat and sit at her side.

Her eyes are glittering with joy. "I wrote three chapters! And they're good. Really good."

"Oh?" I dip my face close to hers and kiss her softly.

"Apparently a lot of sex makes my muse super productive."

My cock agrees, hardening with every ounce of her face and body I soak in. Her happiness is like an aphrodisiac. She's wearing my T-shirt from yesterday and it's ridden up her thighs, gifting me a seductive expanse of skin to caress.

I place my hand on the thigh closest to me. "Did you save it?"

Her gaze hasn't left mine, but I can tell the second her eyes heat as I toy with the hem of my shirt against her leg.

"Mmm-hmm."

"Good," I say softly, closing the lid and moving the laptop off her thighs before setting it on the coffee table. I push the table back with my foot and then slide to the floor on my knees, maneuvering my body in front of hers.

"You look super sexy in your glasses, baby."

She licks her lips and her cheeks pinken. I wonder what else gets flushed and dark pink.

The one thing she never let me do last night was to taste her. To make her come with my mouth. Every time I trailed down her body, she begged me to fuck her. What was I supposed to do? My woman wants my cock, I'm giving it to her.

Every. Single. Time.

"Everything about you is sexy." I spread her legs and shift them until they cage me between them.

"Is that right?" she smirks.

"Yep." I cup both and circle my thumbs around her kneecaps lightly.

"My knees?" She laughs, sounding a little ticklish.

I lean forward and kiss the right one and drag my tongue around the kneecap before doing the same on the other.

"Oh, wow. That's um, sensitive."

I grin a Cheshire cat smile. As I slide my hands up the outsides of her thighs, I hum and curl my fingers so I can tug her body down the seat until her thighs open wider.

She gasps and her legs tremble.

I'm incredibly delighted to find her bare pussy greeting me when the shirt rides up. Her arousal and unique scent coil in the air between us. It's like the sweetest smelling flower just after a heavy rain.

Intoxicating. Exotic. Mind-melting.

"No panties? Naughty girl."

"Evan…" She sighs and fists her hands at her sides.

"Hmm… what should I do to naughty girls who tease their men?"

She swallows and I watch the movement in her neck as her mouth falls open subtly to allow her labored breaths. "I don't know. Fuck me?" That has her grinning. My sassy girl taking over.

I tsk and shake my head reaching my hands around to her round ass and bringing her closer to the edge. I back up and press her knees wide open, revealing her to my greedy gaze.

"Fuck. There is so much I want to do to you. Lick you. Suck you. Finger you. Fuck you." I swallow down the desire coating my tongue imagining what she tastes like, teasing my senses before gorging on what we both want.

"Okay. Yes. I want all of those things." She attempts naturally to close her legs, maybe hide herself a little, but I hold them wide open looking my fill of her flushed sex. The way the heart of her glistens and convulses with every breath.

"I'm going to make you come over and over until you beg me to stop," I say, holding her legs open, my eyes zeroed in and hyper-focused on my prize. Her hips thrust, humping the air, her pussy clenching before my eyes.

It's graphic, hot as sin, and tempting me like a snake-charming seductress.

My dick punches hard against my loose pants. I shove them down and hear her groan at the site of my erect cock, my palm encircling the base and stroking up just once. A tease. I've never been harder in my life.

"Evan, baby, please..." Her hips churn in invitation and I'm gone.

I lay my mouth over her sex and take one long, luxurious lick. Her honey-coated taste explodes on my tongue the same way biting into a ripe watermelon does, juice flowing down my throat, coating my lips and chin with her flavor. I swirl my tongue all over her, savoring every inch of her until her fingers are twisted in my hair and her hips are thrusting wildly.

Doubling my effort, I dip my tongue into her heat, licking and learning every inch. What makes her clench her thighs. What makes her sigh. What makes her mewl. I suck each lip and nibble first, then pet each one with long laps of my tongue, avoiding the tight kernel of nerves I know she's dying to have me touch. Being as attentive as I know how, I work at her, taking her higher and higher.

"Baby..."

"You taste so fucking good. I could eat you every day and never get enough."

Finally, I twirl my tongue in a tight circle around her clit and she cries out, her fingers fisting my roots as wave after wave of her orgasm rush through her.

Once her convulsions slow, I grin before plunging two thick fingers deep, searching her front wall for that elusive spot that will make my woman lose her mind. I curl my digits up and she jerks her hips as I find exactly what I'm searching for.

Her eyes widen. "I can't twice in a row." She looks almost panicked—as though if she isn't able, she'll let me down somehow. But one thing my girl is going to find out about me is that I'm relentless when in pursuit of something I want. And I want this. Bad.

"Oh yes you can," I state. And it's a promise.

Sliding my fingers against the wall of her sex, I focus my attention on her tight little clit. It's so swollen and red. Like a firm little cherry just picked off the tree, I suck on that piece of fruit, tugging up and down on her cunt, finger-fucking her hard and deep.

Her body shudders under my efforts.

"You're so wet, you're dripping down my chin," I say while licking up and down, glancing at her angelic face.

"I don't know…I don't understand." She watches as I kiss then suck her clit into my mouth.

She closes her eyes, her head falling back as she surrenders. Simply lets her arms fall to her sides, her body going languid as I physically work her. Controlling every ounce of her pleasure. This orgasm seems far stronger as it rolls over her body. Her chest jerks toward the ceiling, arching magnificently. She locks her legs around my body and digs her heels in, using her hands to grip the back of the couch.

She's brilliant in her pursuit. Hungry for more, for something she doesn't even know to expect.

I finger her hard, almost brutally as her body wrenches back and forth under the power of my hold on her.

"Jesus, Evan, no, I can't. It's too much." She gasps, her breath coming in and out in quick bursts.

I hold firm, suck harder, and bite lightly down on her juicy little clit.

She screams, an avalanche of ecstasy pouring through her veins.

Wanting it to be the best she's ever had, I stay on her, sucking, licking, eating until orgasms rolls over her, one after another. Tears shimmer in her eyes as she gasps, those salt-filled drops falling down the sides of her cheeks in beautiful rivers I want to kiss. Her hips are still thrusting, greedy for every last speck of pleasure she can take in, and I hold on, giving her all the love and desire I have inside me.

Eventually she tries to push my head away. "No more. *Please*, no more. Too sensitive," she says. But when I don't stop because I'm an animal, mindless in my pursuit of her pleasure, she grips my hair by the roots and yanks me off.

I know I've lost my mind. The haze of lust threads through my blood, every muscle in my body throbbing, aching to meld with her, to take, to rut, to fuck.

"Need you," I snarl through clenched teeth, my body strung so tight I could break like an overextended rubber band at any moment.

"I'm right here." She reaches for me as I stand and push my pants completely off. My dick is velvet-wrapped titanium, the crown swollen and purple, leaking at the tip.

Sadie shifts forward and takes my cock into the heat of her mouth, moaning around the sensitive flesh. I almost come right then but she wraps a vice-like fist around the base of me and goes to town.

"Fuck!" I roar, feeling like a king, as the woman I love pleasures me with her mouth.

And she's talented. Goes straight for the deep-throating like a damn expert, dragging her slippery tongue all over my length then taking me to the back of her throat.

"Damn it, woman." My balls draw up feeling like five-pound weights between my straining thighs as I try not to fuck her face. "Need to come," I grit out.

She smiles around my dick and looks up at me with the prettiest blue eyes, her red mouth looking obscene around my girth. I trace my thumb around her lips stretched over around my cock. I tease her mouth while stroking my skin, drenched from her licking and sucking.

One of her hands cups my sac and caresses the tender jewels between her fingers. My eyes roll back in my head and I can't help but thrust in and out of her mouth. She takes every plunge willingly, excitedly, going deeper with every movement.

She eases back down my length, prodding the little slit at the top with just the tip of her heavenly tongue. It's filthy and exactly what I need.

"Your mouth... Jesus... I'm gonna blow, Sadie." I grunt and breathe through the spears of bliss bursting throughout my body. My cock aches, my balls throb, and my heart pounds as Sadie takes me deep, running her hands around my hips to dig her fingers nails right into the meat of my ass cheeks.

I roar and fuck her face, losing control. I grip the back of her head and fist her silky hair at the roots, my hand flexing against her scalp as she takes every thrust, bouncing eagerly with the effort until the pleasure rises up inside me to the pinnacle of euphoria. The rapture of her warm hot mouth, the endless suction, the tease of her tongue has me expending jolt after jolt of my essence into her waiting throat. She mewls and moans, swallowing me down until I'm a shivering mess of raw emotions and liquid bones and muscle.

Sadie pulls me onto the love seat. The second I'm sitting, she straddles my lap and removes her T-shirt. I can't even think straight enough to comment on seeing her spectacular tits because she reaches behind me for the afghan and wraps it around her naked back. Then she leans forward against my chest.

Skin to skin.

She presses her forehead to my neck and kisses my chest. I wrap my arms around her, allowing her warmth to sooth my ravaged body and soul.

"I love you, Sadie. I'm not sure I'll ever be able to express how much, but this feels close," I murmur, kissing the top of her hair and resting my lips there, inhaling her lavender scent along with the combined smell of us.

She sighs against my chest and snuggles deeper.

"Now I know what real love and happiness feels like. And it's scary, Evan."

"Why?" I hold her tight.

"Because now that I know how good it is, I never want to lose it."

♡

## SADIE

Gloria gives herself a long and luxurious bath on Jake's living room rug while Evan and I sit side by side on the couch with our laptops. She is a glorious creature, but I've restrained myself from smooching on her so far. Turning all swollen red and itchy is less fun than you'd think. So far, the allergy medications are working, thank God. And Evan ran around the apartment with the vacuum cleaner earlier to try and keep fur to a minimum. The floofy baby was horrified at the noise and bravely hid in a cupboard the entire time.

All in all, the three of us are a picture of domestic bliss. Chicken breasts are marinating for dinner, and I've also been threatened with a salad. I honestly don't mind Evan trying to improve my general health through better food choices. Especially with the threat of illness hanging over all of our heads. So long as he doesn't mess with my snacks, we're fine.

I'm working on my social media presence, posting in my fan group, asking how everyone is doing. A couple of nurses and other people who have family working in health care are having a hard time. They're scared and frustrated, and I don't blame them one bit. My group instantly rallies around the women, posting messages of love and support. The romance community really is a beautiful thing.

On my author page I ask what everyone is reading, a question that always gets good interaction. Some people are too worried and distracted to be able to concentrate on anything. Others are escaping into books to ease the anxiety. And there's no right answer. No one best strategy for dealing with these horrible and scary times. Some people are stress-baking or getting into crafts while others are binging Netflix.

Parents mention the many challenges of homeschooling. Lord knows, I doubt I could explain anything above fifth grade math. Then there was how best to keep some sort of routine for kids while managing their stress levels. Other people are in quarantine alone, starved for fresh air and human touch but too afraid to go out. We're all worried about the elderly in the community and furious at those who aren't taking social distancing seriously. One COVID denier pipes up to tell us we're all fools who are overreacting. I shut that down fast. Moron.

I hate feeling helpless. When you get down to it, I'm fortunate and privileged. Right here and now, I donate to a local food bank and give away a couple of gift cards to readers in my group. I don't spend huge amounts, but it's something at least.

Suddenly, Evan jerks besides me and says, "Fuck me."

"I told you we need to take a short break on that front," I mumble, still focused on watching a book trailer for one of my peers. It's awesome. I make a note to contact her and ask who designed the video and also to score me an advanced reader copy. The books look incredible.

"No. It's her. It's fucking *her*. The girl who drugged me at the party. Mindy." He stabs a finger at the screen of his computer. A blonde-haired woman is raising a glass of wine in the picture alongside several others. "I was starting to think I was going crazy and had invented her or something. But there she is!"

"Evan, that's fantastic."

"This was posted by an ex-cheerleader a while back. She quit to have a baby, if I'm remembering right." He shoves a hand through his hair all aggravated-like. "Drinks with friends. That's all it says."

"She didn't tag the people in the picture?"

"No. Shit."

"And no one by the name of Mindy liked or commented?" I ask, setting my laptop aside and pushing closer to him.

"Doesn't look like it. I've spent the last hour going through the cheerleaders' pages and this is the first time I've caught sight of the woman. No mention of a Mindy or Melinda or anything even close to it. Dammit!"

"Calm down and give me that." I confiscate the laptop from him and get busy saving the picture in question. "I have an idea."

"What?"

"Reverse image search. Sometimes I see a random picture of a male model floating around the Internet. And I'd like to use them for a cover, but their name isn't mentioned, right? So I do a reverse image search to track down other photos of them to find out who they are." My fingers dance across the keyboard. It's a simple enough matter really, putting the photo into a search engine. I just hope it works.

He stops his freak out and stares at me. "Baby, that's genius."

"Thank you. Though to be fair, I didn't actually invent it. I just happen to know about it. Which possibly means I spend way too much dicking around on the computer, but oh well." I smile. "Did you know if you send the words pew pew from your iPhone to another iPhone it does this little laser light show for you? I saw that on Twitter last night."

"Focus, sweetheart."

"Right. Sorry." I inspect the screen. "Not her. Not her. Bingo! Yes. Here's a shot of her on Instagram. Okay, here we go."

I enlarge the picture and Evan scowls. "That's Levi with her at some party."

"Who's Levi?"

"One of the guys on my team." His jaw is clenched so hard I worry his teeth might crack. A dental visit is not in our near future.

"Okay. Well, the account belongs to one @mindybegood. I'm guessing that's not her real surname, but some made up saucy cutesy nonsense. She's apparently a dancer and dog owner. Nothing about where she lives or her place of work. And she's a little careless with her online security and hasn't locked down her account. Which works for us." I slide the cursor up the screen, bringing more of her pictures into her view. "What can we see here?"

"Throwback to her school's cheerleading outfit." I point to the picture in question. The girl is really pretty. Blonde like me but that's where the similarities end.

"Is that worth searching?" he grumbles.

"Eh. Hard to say. It would show where she came from, but not necessarily tell us where she is now," I offer.

A grunt from Evan.

"Family BBQ. A selfie with her French Bulldog named Button. Button actually features quite prominently. What else have we got?" I scroll through the screen. "A shot of her in a bikini. What a hot bod. I can see why you followed her into that bedroom."

"Your body's better and those days are long behind me." He huffs, clearly unhappy looking at pictures of a woman who screwed him over big time.

"Oh yeah?"

And then he goes and does it. Gives me the softest, warmest look with love-filled eyes. "Got everything I need sitting right here beside me."

"Evan," I whisper.

"Not going to lie to you. I was a player, Sadie. Those days are over."

I don't want to give into the unwelcome anxiety swirling in my gut. But then I'd rather not have to lie and smother my concerns either. Doesn't seem like that would make for a healthy relationship. So here we go. "You really think once we're out of lockdown and all of this is cleared up you're not going to want to go to those team parties and run wild again?"

"Only if by run wild you mean have a beer or two before getting home to you. Spending time with the team is important. I'm not going to lie to you or build any false expectations. Being a baller is more than a job. It's a lifestyle to a certain degree. And we've got to build that brotherhood between us, nurture it. But that doesn't mean I'll be doing anything that would hurt you, baby. Besides, most of the time I'd hope you'd be by my side."

Him wanting me around with his friends makes me feel a tiny bit better but not enough for the worry and fear that's bubbling up inside of me.

"You really think you can be happy with just this? With us?" I ask, my heart once again on my sleeve. Sheesh. The emotional maturity and shows of trust necessary for going forward with this man are huge. Big giant leaps of faith that could easily wind up with me being crushed or hurt. But here we are. "This isn't going to alter my lifestyle all that much. I'm pretty much a shut-in by nature. But you're giving up a certain amount of your social life by being with me."

His gaze narrows on my face, his jaw set. "Sweetheart, I'm not giving up shit. I'm gaining you and that is everything. Trust that I know what I want for me. And baby, that's you. Okay?"

"Okay." Ugh. My eyes are watery. Again. "Um. Here's an interesting photo. Scantily clad and posing with feathery fans. I wonder if she does burlesque? Though that won't necessarily help us since the nightclubs are shut down and I doubt we'll be able to find anyone to talk to even if we could locate where she performs. Pity she doesn't tag her pics with locations."

"Yeah." I can feel the hope leaching out of him and I hate it. I hate that this is messing with his life and I wish I could do more.

"Night out with the girls. Do you recognize any of these faces from your cheerleading team?"

Lines furrow his forehead. "No."

"There's that shot with your friend. Does the background look familiar to you at all?"

He sighs. "Looks like a sports bar near home that we've been to a few times. The owners are pretty cool about us being there, don't make a fuss or anything and don't let anyone bother us."

"That's nice, but unfortunately it still doesn't help us. What the hecking heck is going to help us track her down during a pandemic? That's the question."

"We need her home address. Her phone number or something concrete like that. We need to talk to her and find out what the hell went down."

I nod, lips pursed in concentration. "Despite the number of romantic suspense and detective books that I've read, I'm not being much use here. Sorry."

"That's not true. You've gotten me way further than I'd have managed on my own." He slumps back against the couch and stares at the ceiling. "Maybe I'll give Polly my publicist a ring. Update her on what we've found and ask her if she's got any ideas."

"Worth a try." Which is when my cell, sitting on the coffee table, starts buzzing like crazy. I pass Evan back the laptop and reach for the phone. Messages from Zahra. A constantly updating line of them. I unlock the screen and open up Messenger. And that's when I see it. "Holy shit."

He tenses. "What is it?"

"Photos of us. From when we went to the pharmacy the other day." An endless parade of screen grabs march past my gaze. I don't think my eyes could get any wider. And all the while, a yawning pit opens in my stomach. Because this can't be good. It just can't be. "Sparky gets smutty. A modern fairy tale for troubled football star. This is…Jesus, it's everywhere."

# Chapter
## SIXTEEN

### QUARANTINE: DAY 16

SADIE

WHEN YOU GET RIGHT DOWN TO IT, I'D KIND OF been in denial about the whole dating a famous person thing. Ignoring the fact that Evan was a public figure was entirely possible due to the current situation with the whole world on pause. Or at least, that's what it feels like. And it's not like I have no experience with this sort of thing. People at book signings want my autograph and to have their photo taken with me. Within Romancelandia, I'm relatively well known. But my fame is nowhere near this level.

"My high school boyfriend wants to know if I can get him a signed jersey." I pace up and down the living room with my cell in hand. Gloria is not happy with me. I know that much. She sits on the kitchen bench, giving me a most aggravated glare. "We only went out for three weeks before he dumped me."

Evan sits on the couch, watching me with a deliberately blank face. "Just delete the message."

"Also, a lovely lady by the name of Karen who blew you in a hot tub in Seattle a few years back says hi. She also says she's still available when you're ready to kick my fat ass to the curb.

Charming, Karen. So much for the sisterhood." My anger isn't entirely rational. But I don't care. "Sex in a hot tub? That is not hygienic. Though I'm sort of impressed the woman is able to hold her breath that long under water."

"I love your ass."

"A random dude from Oakland says he'd totally do me. That's nice. I really appreciate the vote of confidence." I pace all the way to the windows and then turn back towards the kitchen.

"Random dude from Oakland can keep dreaming. You're mine."

I keep scrolling. Like a mad woman. "This person wants to know what Tarah thinks of me. Who's Tarah, Evan?"

"You really didn't look me up at all, huh?" he asks, stuffing a cushion behind his head. There's a vaguely pained expression on his face now. This should be interesting.

"No. I was respecting your privacy. Waiting for you to tell me about your past or anything I needed to know."

He prods at his teeth with the tip of his tongue. "Um. Yeah. Tarah was a swimsuit model I took to a Valentine's Day charity event thing. Nice girl. A one-off. We had fun. Once."

"You dated the model Tarah Moore?"

"I wouldn't call it dating." He sighs.

I flop onto the couch with a dramatic sigh. "Holy cow. She's gorgeous."

"You're gorgeous," he says.

"And you went out with her this year?" My voice wobbles and I hate it. Hate every second of the burn of insecurity that comes with dating not only a celebrity but someone who's so incredibly good looking.

"Yes."

"I see." My heart plummets. Tarah Moore is a goddess. I'm a weirdo introvert novelist.

A frustrated-sounding groan spills from my man. "Sadie. Baby. We're together now. None of this matters. Let's just pretend we both came to this relationship virgins. Both of us pure and untouched. I never knew any swimsuit models or girls named Karen. You didn't date pencil-dick Sean and your idiot high school boyfriend sure as hell doesn't exist. Deal?"

"Ha. I'll think about it." Think about how perfect Tarah is. I pout.

"Everyone out there has an opinion. Doesn't mean we need to give them head space." He smooths down my hair with a hand, leans over, and kisses the crown of my head. "You're going to drive yourself crazy reading the comments on all of these dumb-ass articles. None of these people know us. None of them have a fucking clue who we are or what we mean to each other. Our lives are our own."

"I know." And I do know what it's like. "Hell, I don't even read my own reviews. Constructive criticism from a source I trust, absolutely. Let me hear it. I want to learn and do better. But a random person on the Internet who wants to blast me because there was too much sex, too little sex, too much profanity, too little profanity. The plot was weak. Book wasn't funny. The bad guy was hotter. You name it, I've heard it. I just thank them for buying my book and taking the time to read it but am usually able to let it go and focus on the fact that I finished it. I put my heart and soul into it and then set it free. People are going to like it or not. I have no control over it."

"Then why are you beating yourself up about this?"

I roll my head to the side, all the better to see his handsome face. "I love you. This just kind of took me by surprise. I'm going to try and calm down now. Let go of the fact that everyone in the world seems to want a piece of our happiness. It's none of their business and it sucks that they even care."

"I'm sorry you have to put up with it, darling. It's the biggest downside of the job."

"But it's a job you love so it's worth putting up with. I'll get my bearings. Bitch, moan and groan about this today because it's new, then I'll move on."

Evan's phone rings on his lap. He ignores it completely, focused solely on me. God, he's so good to me.

"Baby, your phone." I glance at the screen and my heart starts pounding. "It's Levi!" I shriek and grab the phone, my hand shaking as I press it into his.

"Fucking finally, he calls me back!" He accepts the call. "Yo, Levi."

I curl into Evan's side. "Put it on speaker," I whisper. I have no right to ask him to share his call but I'm dying with anticipation. Last night we sent the image of him with Mindy via text and Evan tried to call his friend but got no answer.

Evan doesn't even comment when he puts the phone on speaker and holds it on his lap.

"Man, I'm sorry I couldn't call last night. Been held up with my parents. Mom's got the virus and she isn't doing well. Dad was losing it but this afternoon she seems to be in brighter spirits."

"Fuck bro, I had no idea. I'm sorry man," Evan sympathizes.

"Sucks. She's on day five and it seems to go up and down. The doctors are hopeful she'll come through it fine but of course now Dad, me, and Brent are at high risk. We're all quarantined and taking our temperatures daily but it's only a matter of time."

Jesus. That has to be the scariest thing in the world. To not only have your mother be down with a virus we know very little about, one that has no vaccine or well-known method for treatment, but to also be almost assured that you are going to get it. I curl my body even closer to Evan and rest my forehead on his mighty shoulder.

"I'm sorry. I wouldn't have texted if I'd known, but that woman in the picture is the woman who drugged me that night of the party."

"The one who dragged you to bed?"

I can't help the full-body stiffness that comes over me. Evan sighs and wraps his arm around my back, forcing me to put my head against his chest. Hearing his heartbeat instantly soothes the ugly green monster slithering around my mind.

He sighs. "Yeah, man. Do you know her?"

"I do. Kinda. Seeing this picture, I just put the two together. When I met her the first time, she was more of a brunette. And I was trashed. It was sometime last year...I think after we won against The Bolts in LA. Met her at a club. Took her to my hotel. Spent a fun night with her. Shit, can't remember her name." He sounds as though he's trying.

"Mindy," Evan states flatly.

"Yeah, yeah, that was it. I think I have her number. Hold up."

I sit straight up and scramble for my notepad and a pen.

"Yeah Mindy Goode with an E on the end."

Guess the Mindy Be Good Insta was closer than I originally thought. Levi reads off the number and I write it down.

"She the one that set you up?" he asks. His voice sounds a little tortured. Why, I don't know.

Evan lets out a long breath. "I think so, yeah."

"Shit, brother. I'm sorry I didn't put two and two together until you sent this pic. Honestly, I didn't really remember much of what happened that night myself. I've got to lay off the sauce. It's doing me no favors. After being here, helping Mom fight, watching my Dad eaten up as though his whole world is crumbling down with every coughing fit she has, I've come to realize I need a change. A big one."

Evan cups my cheek and smiles softly. "Yeah, I've made a few changes in my own. Life-altering ones."

224

"Does it have anything to do with the spectacular blonde I saw you with plastered all over the rag sites? Sadie Walsh the romance writer?"

"Yep. She's my world, man. Fell ass-over-tit in love with the woman. During quarantine, no less. She's Jake's neighbor."

Laughter rings through the phone. "Leave it to you to find the woman of your dreams during a pandemic."

That has Evan chuckling too. "Fate, I guess."

"You never so much as thought twice about keeping a woman. What's so special about this one?"

Evan licks his lip and stares into my eyes. "Besides the fact that she's so damn beautiful it's like looking into the sun. Almost hurts. She's also incredibly witty, makes me laugh all day every day."

"Someone who can do that during this shit. Fucking priceless."

"Yeah and she's talented. I've read her books."

"You? Read a romance novel? Shut the fuck up!"

His surprise has Evan laughing hard and I enjoy watching his face change from worried to happy. "I was hard up to know about her. Thought it could teach me more. All it taught me was she can tell a story and has a filthy mind!" He waggles his eyebrows at me in that silly manner that makes me giggle.

"Hell, yeah. That's a bonus, buddy."

Evan grins wickedly. "That it is. Well thanks for getting back to me. Having a full name and a number helps tremendously."

"Hey, I hope you find her and get the deets on what went down."

"Me too." Evan rubs at his forehead. "Keep me posted on your Mom and how the rest of you are doing, yeah?"

"Got it. Thanks, brother. Hope this all gets worked out, this virus disappears, and we can all go back to normal."

"God willing," he agrees.

"Definitely. Later," Levi says.

"Later. Be safe." Evan hangs up the phone, tosses it on the table, leans his elbows on his knees, and puts his head in his hands.

The weight of the world is back on my man's shoulders and I hate every godforsaken second of it.

"Baby, this is good news. One more step forward. Let's consider this a win." I run my hand up and down his back in soothing sweeps, hoping to ease the tension.

He nods. "I'm worried about his mom and the fact that the four of them are in the same house together. Since one of them has the virus, it's most certainly going to get them all."

Aw. My guy is worried about his friend, not his career. I curve my arm around his strong back. "Honey, you don't know that. You have to think positive."

"Yeah, but it's hard with everything going to shit across the world. My career is at risk. Fuck, none of it matters more than everyone's safety."

I place my forehead against his back. "You're right. None of the rest of it matters right now. In the grand scheme of things. Doesn't mean it's not important. We'll deal with it all."

"Together?" He almost sounds wistful.

I smile. "Absolutely."

He turns and places a soft kiss to my lips. "Thank you, baby."

"For what?"

"For being you. For being here. For loving me, warts and all."

I grin wide. "Evan, I've seen every inch of you completely naked. You have no warts. Just smooth, sexy skin."

He reaches for me and pulls me into his lap. I wrap my arms around him and hold on. He dips his head to my neck and just breathes. Holding me close.

Right then I decide no matter what happens, I'm going to be there for him. Protect him from whatever I can. And hold him when I can't.

♡

## EVAN

"Sweetheart, you look at the phone one more time and I'm turning you over my knee," I warn in a light tone while rolling the lean ground beef into perfect two-inch meatballs.

Sadie scrunches up her nose. "She should have called by now." She's frustrated and antsy. Every few minutes she checks my phone and then glares at it as though she were willing it to ring, then getting pissed when it doesn't. "And we've already discussed that threat. Non-consensual spanking is a no go."

"Understood. But it's only been a few hours since I left a message and texted. Relax. Besides, she may not reach out. I know she was involved in something nefarious against me. Helped to set me up. I honestly don't think she'll call. It's more likely she'll avoid me and block me from calling."

Sadie huffs while filling a pot with water for the spaghetti noodles. "It's rude not to return someone's call."

"It's far ruder to drag an unsuspected man into a viper's den, feed him to the media, and try to ruin his career. This woman obviously has no qualms about hurting someone. I'm just trying to understand why me? I mean, she could have given me the picture and tried to get millions for it."

She gasps. "You have millions?"

I grin and chuckle. "Baby, how much do you think pro ballers make?"

She shrugs. "Guess I never thought about it. Is it a lot?"

"Depends on how good you are, your past record, how long you've been in the business and such. My last contract was a cool fourteen million."

"For how many years?"

"Honey, that's for one year."

Her eyes practically bug out of her head. "Wow. My boyfriend is super rich! That insane. I'm gonna use that information in my next call with Mom and Dad. Money talks and bullshit walks, as they say. I'm going to woo them to your favor with the mighty buck!"

I shake my head. "Whatever it takes. Though I'm sure when they meet me, I can do all the wooing myself."

"Once Mom sees how good looking you are, she's immediately going to start dreaming of little towheaded grandbabies. Tell her how much you like children and that will do it." She winks.

I'm just about to respond with how I'd like to show her exactly how I plan to give her my babies when my phone rings again.

Sadie reacts as though a bomb went off, flinging the wooden sauce spoon in the air, sauce flying across the cupboard on the opposite wall.

"Jesus, woman! Calm down!" I laugh.

"Who is it?" she gasps, holding the dripping spoon over the small sauce puddle pooling on the floor.

I point to the mess on the wall and cupboards. "Baby, could ya maybe deal with that while I get the phone?"

She frowns and then reacts to what she's done. "Crap!" She tosses the spoon onto the holder and then dashes to grab a towel.

I pick up the phone. "It's Trina, baby, not Mindy. Chill."

Her entire body seems to slump. My girl, so ready to take care of her man.

"Hey, Trina. How's it goin', lady?" I answer.

"Evan. Hello, sweetie." Her voice sounds trashed.

"Trina, what the heck? Your voice is shit. What's going on?" I ask.

A huge coughing fit can be heard and my heart plummets to my stomach.

"Trina, are you okay?"

More coughing. "F-f-found some…" She retches and I swear it's as though she's hacking up a lung.

Gooseflesh appears all down my arms and a shiver races down my spine.

"You said the cough was nothing!" I respond angrily. "Have you been to the doctor? The hospital?"

"Sweetie, I got the virus. It's taking its course but I'm working through." She hacks for another solid minute.

My heart pounds and sweat prickles against my brow. I hold a shaking hand hard to my ear as I listen to the woman who has been the closest thing to a mother I've had, since losing mine at fourteen, sound worse every second that passes.

"Evan, listen to me. I found Mindy," she claims through a rasp I can barely hear.

"What do you mean you found her? I got her name and phone number from Levi tonight. What did you find?"

Another coughing fit.

Fuck. I pace the room and watch as Sadie turns all the burners to low. She crosses her arms over her chest and rubs her biceps up and down. Her gaze radiates pure love and compassion as I freak the fuck out.

"Got a copy of an approved ch-cheer application t-today. Fr-from Coach Bates." Who is the football coach, *my coach*, and not the head of the cheerleading division. "For M-mindy Goode. Set to st-start this sp-sp-spring. B-big pay and n-not through t-the normal ch-cha-channels." She sputters and wheezes deeply.

"What? Why the heck would Coach send over a cheerleading app? And why would he be the one approving it unless…fuck!" I'm seething as the pieces of the puzzle start to come together.

"S-sent you a c-opy, boy," Trina rasps and then goes silent.

"Trina?" I say but get no response. "Trina!" I scream into my cell but get nothing in return. "Trina, please, please, honey, pick up the phone!!" I yell.

After twenty seconds of listening to dead air and my heartbeat, I hear Tom's voice as if far away. "Trin sweetheart, Trinny, wake up. Wake up! Oh my God, no! Help, I need help!" he cries, and my heart is ready to burst.

Eventually he picks up the phone. "Hello, hello?"

"Tom! What's happening? It's Evan." I pace into the living room.

"She's passed out. She's not breathing. She's been so sick, oh my God. I gotta call for help," he says and then hangs up on me.

Dead air.

I stand there with Sadie at my back, both her hands pressed to my shoulder blades. "Evan…" she whispers, her tone filled to the brim with sadness.

The reality of what I just experienced spears into my heart and rips it into tiny little pieces. I drop to my knees right there in the center of the living room. Tears fill my eyes and pour over my cheeks. I slump as the pain of what I heard invades my form. Trina. My beloved adopted mom. The only woman who has cared about me since my own mother.

Visions of her swim across my mind.

Her barely able to speak. Trying to help me.

Endless coughing.

The silence over the line as I waited to hear anything.

Tom's cry, as I imagine her lying there lifeless and not breathing.

"Please, God. No, don't take Trina. Let her be okay. Please God, let her be okay." I press my fists to my eye sockets and let the waves of sorrow take their course.

Sadie's arms cover my waist as her body brackets me from behind. "Let it out. Let it all out. I'm right here. I'll take care of you."

I hold her arms and bring her hands up to my lips and kiss each of her fingers. "Don't leave me, Sadie. Promise you'll never leave me."

Her head rests against my neck as I feel her tears sliding down my neck. My sadness is hers. And hers is mine.

"I won't ever leave you. I promise. We're in this together."

# Chapter
## SEVENTEEN

### QUARANTINE: DAY 17

EVAN

WARMTH. THAT'S ALL I FEEL WHEN I BLINK OPEN MY scratchy, tired eyes and come face-to-face with a sleeping angel. Sadie's golden hair is all over her face and neck, but I swear she's never been more beautiful. Her arms are wrapped around me, as mine are around her. Our legs are intertwined comfortably.

Flashes of last night come back. Her letting me cry a river like a lame ass. I simply broke the fuck down. Hearing about Trina. Finding out about Mindy. Coach. It all hit me at once and I cracked. Shattered into a million shards all over the living room. But my girl was there.

Sadie held me until I couldn't cry anymore. Wiped my tears, cleaned my face, and cuddled up with me on the couch until my stomach rumbled loudly. Without a word, she brought me three fingers of whiskey neat just as I like it and finished up dinner while I stared out at the empty night.

Once dinner was done, she plated me a huge helping, turned on some mindless reality TV show, and ate by my side. When we finished, she took my plate, refilled my glass, and brought along one of her own. We sat and drowned our sorrows in togetherness, booze, and boring TV.

Until I got the call from Tom, just shy of midnight.

Trina didn't make it.

She died from complications. The virus had taken over. Trina's lungs couldn't withstand the fight.

Gone.

One minute she was on the phone with me, the next, not breathing.

Sadie held me through the news, brought me to bed, and wrapped me in her arms while I cried myself to sleep. The last time I did that I was fourteen years old. I'd just found out my mother had died.

The news made me raw. The loss and the reality of how close it was felt intense and devasting to us both. Sadie cried with me. Our tears mingled until they turned to kisses and light touches. Then she made love to me. Removed our clothes and set about making her man feel something that was beautiful.

The experience cemented this woman in my soul in a way I would never forget.

Fuck everything else. I live for her. To make Sadie happy. To make myself happy with Sadie. To build a life. A life worth living.

Now fully awake, I reach out a hand and trace her curved cheekbone and run my fingertips along her hairline until her lashes flutter like butterfly wings against her face and her eyes open.

"Mmm, hey handsome. How are you feeling this morning?"

I continue to trace her skin because I love it and I can. Touching her is a luxury I don't think I'll ever get used to. Nor would I want to.

"Better. Still hurt. Brokenhearted over Trina."

She reaches out a hand and cups my scruffy jaw. "It's normal to feel that way and you likely will for a long time. She was important to you."

I nod and take a deep breath, trying to let the sadness go if even for a moment. Turning flat on my back I remember what she said. "Right before…" I rub my hand over my face not wanting to think about what happened. "Uh, during the call. She said she received a cheerleading application with Mindy's name on it."

"Huh. Interesting timing, but why is that a big deal?"

"Because it was sent and stamped approved by Coach Bates and not the cheerleading coach."

She frowns. "So that means the coach did a dirty and slid the application through improper channels?"

"Yeah. But why? Unless it was payment for something?"

"Something like drugging a player and setting him up for a crash and burn of his career in order to get herself the job she wants as a cheerleader with the team?" She sits up and her bare breasts come into view.

I grin, reach out, and pinch a pretty, pink tip.

She smacks my hand away. "Don't get frisky. We need to figure this out."

I sigh. "What does it matter anymore? The world is ending and Trina is dead. I've got you. Fuck everything else."

Sadie narrows her eyes into little slits. "Are you kidding me? You've been trying to figure this out for three weeks and you're going to give up now? When you're right on the edge of finding out the truth?"

"Like I said, who cares anymore?"

"You care. Trust me on that. It might not feel like it right now, but you do, Evan." Sadie jumps out of bed beautifully naked. Gloria, who was resting on the foot of the bed, hops down with her ass in the air and prances towards the kitchen, likely thinking Sadie was going to feed her breakfast.

My girl grabs my T-shirt from yesterday and slips it on sans panties. Nice.

"I'm calling that lying little skank! Right now. I'm going to get the proof you need."

Then something Trina said right before she collapsed blazes through my memory bank. "Baby." I shuffle out of bed, grab my lounge pants, and tug them on. "Honey, Trina said she'd send me a copy of the application. That would be the proof we need."

At least for that part. Doesn't fix the planted steroids which is still a hard point with the legal team. As far as I knew, they were still undecided about the outcome of that particular issue.

I make my way into the living room and find Sadie on my laptop.

"Password," she demands.

"Football2015. Capital F."

She taps in my code rapidly.

"She said she'd send the e-mail?" she asks, bringing up my Gmail account.

"Yeah."

She has her sexy glasses on, and her entire body screams that she's serious and in investigative mode. Over the last couple days, I've watched my woman do her research and she's a master.

I come around the loveseat and sit on the couch next to her. She's nodding at something she's reading before she points at the screen. "Right here. This section. Offer signed by Coach Bates. Application approved by Coach Bates. Is this enough to clear you with the team?"

I shake my head. "No. Without her confession that she drugged me and set me up I'm still in trouble. The only thing this does is prove that she had motive."

"Unless you call her and leave a message stating that you know the truth and have a copy of her dirty application all signed and approved by Coach Bates. And that you'll be taking it to the people over his head and her bright and shiny future is all over unless she talks to you. You might also mention that your publicist is looking at releasing this highly incriminating evidence to the press. Then leave it open for her to call back or you'll also be notifying the police and they can come and investigate. A nice solid triple threat to set her pretty little head to spinning."

"Damn, baby. You're good."

She gifts me a beaming smile and smacks her bare thighs. "I write this shit for a living. Get her freaking out. But tell her only what she needs to believe in order to give her enough rope to hang herself on." She gets up, finds my phone, and brings it to me.

I don't waste any time ringing Mindy's phone.

Shockingly, she picks up. "Hello?"

"Mindy, this is Evan Sparks."

"I have nothing to say to you, stop calling."

I put the phone on speaker and Sadie clicks record on her phone to capture the entire conversation. My woman is so smart.

"Oh, I think you have plenty to say and more to hear. I've got a copy of your approved cheerleading application right in front of me."

"You lie!" She is practically shrieking.

"Nope. And right on the section toward the bottom there's Coach Bates's signature on the offer and on the part where he approved the application. I know Coach put you up to this and I have your payment right here. A full three-year contract on the Oakland Marauders' Cheerleading Squad. Worth tons of cash in the future—modeling gigs, corporate appearances, swag, calendars, and the like... Not to mention you'll become a celebrity overnight."

"How did you get a copy of that! Coach Bates assured me you'd never find out!" Her voice rises in anger.

"Yeah. Well, I did. And if you don't tell me everything about that night, and how you came about those drugs or the ones in my locker..." I throw those in for good measure to see if she bites. "... then I'm taking all of this to the press and the authorities."

"No! You can't do that. I'll be ruined! I just wanted to be a cheerleader and he promised no one would get hurt!" she yells and then sobs into the phone like a child.

"Tell me everything. From beginning to end. What happened?"

Sadie smiles, gets up and I watch her body shimmy to the kitchen and pop in a coffee pod. Then she coos at Gloria and gets her food ready.

"Coach Bates reached out to me about three months ago. Saw my application and asked if I wanted a sure way onto the team."

I grind down on my molars but otherwise stay silent.

"He paid me five thousand dollars to find a guy who would sell me steroids off the street. Told me I could keep whatever was left. I bought several vials that had approximately thirty milliliters. Which was actually really cheap, so I got to bank most of the money. God, I shouldn't have done it," she whimpers.

"So, you bought the dope. Then what?" I glance at Sadie's phone to make sure it is still recording.

"Um, Coach met me at a park and picked the stuff up. Then he gave me a few pills. I was supposed to put two of the pills in your drink later that week at a party he told me to attend. Then he handed me a bunch of other drugs and told me to set the scene."

"And you did?" I want her to confirm loud and clear.

"I'm sorry, Evan. I really am. I just...I wanted to be a cheerleader since I was a child and I could never get in and..."

"And did you drug my drink that night of the party?" I bring her back to the matter at hand, not giving two shits what she wants. She fucked up my life.

She's in full tears, her breath hitching every so often. "Yes. I came on to you and after I made sure you were super drunk, I got you a new drink and put the two pills in it. He said it would just make you sleep and promised it wouldn't hurt you."

My nostrils flare at the anger seeping into every single one of my pores at a sickening fast speed. "Then what?"

"I-I uh, got you on the bed, we kissed for a while, and then you passed out."

"Mmm-hmm…and?"

"Evan, really. I didn't mean to hurt you."

"And then what, Mindy? What did you do?" I roar into the phone, no longer capable of keeping the lid on my control. My muscles are straining, my throat is dry, and electricity is running through my blood with the need to run, just run, and never stop.

"I planted the coke he'd given me and the joints. Messed up the room some more with a couple of bottles of beer. Tossed my bra on the bed then took some pictures with my camera."

I close my eyes. Before I can plow my fist through the wall, I feel a calming presence near. I know it's Sadie in all her beauty simply standing in front of me. An expression of concern mars her pretty face. She reaches out and puts her palm flat against my heart. Instantly I clamp my hand over hers and hold it there, needing her to ground me so I don't fly off the handle.

"Then, uh, I sent the pictures to Coach as proof I'd done what he asked. He gave me the e-mail to log into that he'd created and the newspaper contacts I was supposed to forward the image to."

I take a deep breath and it all falls into place.

"Thank you, Mindy. For finally telling the truth. I wouldn't hold your breath for that cheerleading position, and I don't know what this means, but I personally will not be pressing charges against you. I can't promise that the team lawyers won't."

"But you said you wouldn't tell the authorities!"

"And I won't. But I will be clearing my name. Goodbye, Mindy." I let go of Sadie and disconnect the call. Sadie picks up her cell and stops the recording.

"It's almost done." She smiles.

"Yeah. There's only one more thing I can't figure out?"

Her brows come together in an expression of confusion. "And that would be?"

"Why? Why would Coach Bates try to burn his best running back? It makes no sense."

♡

## SADIE

Things happen fast after that. Polly, Evan's publicist, isn't taking any chances. She releases the recording and documentation to the press, while also sending them to the team's owner and the police. Under normal circumstances, I guess the paparazzi would be all over us. But the best they can do in a lockdown is buy a picture of me pacing while Evan sits on the couch taken by someone in a nearby building. The quality isn't that great, but still. My hair is a mess. Lucky I wasn't wearing the leggings that have a big-ass hole beneath my left butt cheek. That would have been truly special.

And what a douche move, invading our privacy like that. I'm fast getting the feeling that celebrities aren't seen as being real people. More of a commodity to keep the masses amused. An object built to entertain. Their pain and angst is used to feed the hungry. After that, we keep the curtains closed from there on out and don't go out on the balcony.

Meanwhile, the coach is photographed racing to his car, head down, trying to cover his face with a hand. No pictures of Mindy. I guess she went underground or is currently very busy helping the police with their investigation. Suck it, girl. I don't have an ounce of pity for her. She brought all of this on herself.

Evan is on one phone call after another. Giving statements to various people, being interviewed, and preparing what to say to the press with Polly. He also updates his brother and father, which is lovely. I'm glad he has good people at his back. It's all one hell of an involved process, clearing his name, and it won't happen overnight. But it is happening and I couldn't be happier. I keep a steady supply of drinks and snacks flowing to my man. Though he mostly just eats the carrot and celery sticks and doesn't attack the Reece's Pieces with the gusto they deserve, so I help him out a little. That's what partners are for.

When my cell buzzes and Mom's name pops up on screen, I sigh and pick it up.

"Sadie," she says in a rush. "Don't hang up. Are you okay?"

"Yes, Mom. We're fine. You saw the news, huh?"

She sighs in relief. Maybe I was a little harsh on her, cutting off all communication like that. Then I remember Sean with all his bullshit expectations standing outside my front door. Nope. My parents bought their spell in time out on themselves. "What's going on? Your picture is everywhere! Some reporters even called here asking for a comment. As if I'd comment on your private life!"

"You didn't talk to them?"

"Of course not, sweetheart."

Phew. "Thanks, Mom. I appreciate it."

"So he was set up by his awful coach and some dreadful woman? That's terrible. That poor man. Thank goodness he has you to help get him through all of this," she says. "You tell Evan we're thinking of him during this difficult time and he has our support too."

I think I just got whiplash. "Ah…thanks. I'll do that."

"Maybe I'll send him my German coffee cake. Though I'm not sure how well it'll go in the mail."

"Yeah. I'm not sure that would work. How about some of your peanut butter cookies instead?" Because Evan will eat like one to be polite and then I'll have the rest of the box to myself. Awesome.

"Good idea. Martha's niece from next door will take them to the post office for me. She's been wonderful, helping out with our groceries and everything."

"I'm glad, Mom." My heart hurts a little that I'm not the one there to help my parents get what they need during a time like this.

"She's a fan or yours, did you know?"

"Really?" I grin. "I'll have to send her some signed books. I really am grateful that she's helping you and Dad stay indoors."

"Yes. Well. Hopefully this silly stay-at-home nonsense will be over soon and we'll get back to our regular lives. We're old, Sadie. We don't want to spend our last years stuck at home staring at each other bored stupid."

"Do you want to spend your last days fighting for breath, dying alone in a hospital?" I ask in my best fake sweet voice. "A friend of Evan's passed away just last night, Mom. This couldn't get any more real."

Silence from her. "I'm sorry he lost a friend. And I already told you we're staying put. There's no need to use that tone on me."

"Okay, Mom. Thank you for being so reasonable." I am mostly sincere. Mostly.

She huffs. "Your father says hello. He says he never believed what they were saying about Evan. Too much raw talent, apparently."

Give me strength. "Right."

"It's wonderful that you've found a man who can look after you. Those football players earn quite a lot of money at his level."

"We look after each other, Mom. And I'm not interested in his money."

"Of course not, dear," she says soothingly. "But a wealthy

husband would certainly make life easier for you. No more worrying about rent in between payments from your books and so on. Of course, he'll need to hire a housekeeper or cook for himself. That was never one of your strong points."

"I can cook," I grouse.

Dad's laughter comes through clear and Mom has a smile in her voice. "No, you can't, dear. Lord knows I tried to teach you, but you were always happier with your nose in a book."

"I'll have you two know I cooked dinner last night and hardly burnt it at all. Just a little around the edges. But Evan didn't care. He ate it anyway. So there."

"Good for you, sweetie. I don't suppose you two have talked about the future yet?"

"Right now we're just concentrating on clearing his name and getting through lockdown. It was nice to talk to you, but I have to go, Mom."

"All right. We love you. Take care."

"I love you both too. Bye." I set down my cell and ever so subtly bang my head against the table.

"That was your folks, I take it?" Evan asks with a grin.

"They always believed in you and they're very happy you're rich."

He laughs. "Excellent. Good to know they're on our side now."

"Are you sure you want to take on the crazy that is my life?" I offer him my most pitiful pout.

"Yep."

"You didn't even hesitate."

"Nope." He tips his chin at the laptop in front of me. "Getting any work done? This must be damn distracting for you."

"It's all fine and good. We deserve this win. You deserve it." I smile. "And yeah, I'm working on the blurb. Reducing a story you're in love with down to a couple of short punchy paragraphs sucks. However, it must be done. On the plus side, all of this exposure in the press has given my book sales a bump."

"That's fantastic. Nice to see a silver lining."

"Yeah."

He rises from the couch and starts doing a series of stretches. With everything going on, he hasn't done his full regular workout today. And for a gym junkie like him, that's got to be doing his head in. Not only being stuck indoors, but not being able to exert his usual amount of energy on sports, etc. He's dealing with so much right now, but my gaze still glues to his ass when he touches his toes then drops into a series of squats. A good girlfriend would volunteer to sacrifice herself on the altar of his lust. Or my lust. Whatever. You can't say sex isn't a decent workout when done right. And boy does Evan know how to do it right.

"You're ogling me," he says.

"Sure am."

"Take a picture, it'll last longer."

"Would you mind if it was video because there's a lot of muscle flexing going on here which would come in use later. When you're like playing an away game and I'm on my own and lonesome."

He chuckles. "You won't need it. We've already proven our proficiency at phone and FaceTime sex. Besides, you could always travel with me. Think about it."

"I'll do that. In the meantime, let me make you some food."

A look passes across his face. Fear, possibly. "You don't want some help with that? What were you thinking of?"

"Oh my God. You don't think I can cook either."

"I didn't say that."

"I feel so betrayed." All dramatic like, I clutch at my chest. Honestly, I could have been an actress.

"Baby—"

I give him a wink. "Relax, Sparky. The kitchen is not my natural habitat and I'm well aware of this. I was going to order in carryout. We need to support small businesses."

"Nice idea. Be a good opportunity to tip their kitchen workers and all. Want to help me give away some of my money?"

"I'd love to." I pick up my cell and get to my feet. Watching him stretch has got me wanting to move around some too. Not that I didn't get my steps up recently with all of the stress-pacing. This time I do more of a relaxed leisurely stroll around the living room. "Let me see. Are you in the mood for Chinese, Thai, Indian, or pizza?"

"Surprise me."

"What? No fat content stipulations? No grilled meat and salad on the side requirements? Who are you and what have you done with pro athlete and all around super healthy guy Evan Sparks?"

He just gives me an amused glance.

"My mom is making cookies for you, by the way."

"Yeah? You going to let me have any?"

I draw my lips up on one side. "Look, I'm not saying it's out of the question. But let's not commit to anything just yet. My mom is a mad good baker. Let's go with pizza for dinner. I'm so ready for a serving of carbs covered in melted cheese."

"Sure, baby."

"Garlic bread? Hells to the yes." I dance where I stand flipping through the coupons to see if there are any good ones.

"Sadie?" His voice is sharp and on edge. "What the fuck is this?"

"Huh?" I look up to find him sitting in front of my laptop, reading my work. "Oh. It's the blurb for my new book. Like I told you."

His gaze narrows on the screen. "Oh no, darling. You did not tell me about this. The girl falls for the pro athlete living next door during a quarantine? And that athlete is going through a scandal having been falsely accused? What the hell else did you borrow from my life?"

"It's not about doping. I told you about some of that."

"It's fucking close enough." His tone is direct and drop-dead serious. What gives?

"Evan, you're overreacting." I wave my hand in the air. "These people are not us. They're just characters on the page. So I was a little inspired by our situation. Even the press compared us to a fairy tale. Doesn't change the fact that the book is fiction."

"You didn't base any other parts of this story on things that happened between me and you?"

"Well…I mean…"

"I don't believe this shit." He slams the laptop shut and tosses it to the couch. "You really think after weeks of being torn apart online I'm interested in having any more of my private life up for public consumption?" His face takes on a mottled shade of red. "I trusted you, Sadie!"

"Please don't yell at me. I can explain." I hold up my hands in surrender.

His face turns to absolute stone right before my eyes. "Save it." He bites out. "I've heard enough bullshit lately to last me a lifetime. Never expected to get used and betrayed by you, though. The one person in this entire world I fall in love with screws me over." He shakes his head.

I just gape. "You-you don't mean that. Evan, I would never—"

"You already did," he sneers.

"Baby, no. You're not getting it. You're seeing this all wrong!" My eyes fill with tears and I can't help but let them fall. My heart pounds out a staccato rhythm against my chest and I feel like I'm at the start of a panic attack.

"Keys!" He holds out his hand.

I frown. "Keys?"

"Your keys. Where the fuck are they?" he growls through his teeth.

"Um, in my purse. Did you," I choke out the words, "w-want me to leave?" I wipe my now runny nose against my sleeve.

I watch as he pilfers through my purse and pulls out my keys. Without a word, he goes to the front door and slams it shut. I follow and stop at the closed door until I hear him cursing in the hall, opening my apartment door, and then slamming that one shut too.

He escaped me, and went to my house.

What the hell just happened?

# Chapter
## EIGHTEEN

### QUARANTINE: DAY 18

SADIE

I't's well after midnight and I can't sleep. The memories of pain and betrayal on Evan's face run circles in my mind. And he hasn't come back home. Well, technically he's at my home, likely sleeping in my bed. I sit up in Jake's bed and pull my knees against my chest.

How can I fix this?

I've thought about his anger and why he got so mad. At first, I didn't understand. What I wrote has always been one hundred percent up to me and the only people my choices affected were my readers. Maybe they wanted a book about a different character. Maybe they didn't want me to switch lanes and write romantic suspense for a change. I don't know. But this time, with this book... Hell. Hours of pouring through every possible scenario have brought me to one clear, concise, reason.

I screwed up.

Huge.

By taking from our lives, I betrayed his trust. Everyone wants a piece of him, especially since the scandal. People will be clamoring for this book knowing it is based on our love story. Which would be awesome for book sales but detrimental to my relationship. And do I really want the public at large to know how we met and fell in love? No. My family, sure. His family, definitely. Our friends? Maybe. The media…absolutely not!

Jesus, I ruined everything. What was I thinking? Was I even thinking?

I wasn't. Just like my mother complains all the time. My head is in the clouds, having private conversations with fictional characters.

Looking at it now, I have so much to be sorry for.

Tears prick the backs of my eyes, but I've cried enough. Now is not the time for wallowing in my pity party for one. No, I need to take action. Grovel on my knees if I have to and win back my man. No matter what it takes.

Slipping out of bed, I take his robe from behind the bathroom door and put it on, covering my thin tank and panties. Finding his keys is easy. They hang on a hook by the door. I take the keys, then grab the flash drive I made for him. Mission driven, I go out into the empty hallway and lock the door to Jake's apartment. Then I send up a little prayer that in his anger, Evan didn't lock my apartment door.

Eureka! I turn the knob and push it open, being as quiet as possible. I keep my movements small as I shut and lock it behind me.

I tiptoe through my apartment, noticing nothing has changed since I left it a few days ago. God, that seems like a lifetime ago. How can so much happen in such a short space of time? A pang of sadness punches at my heart at the thought that I may end up here alone again if this doesn't go well.

Swallowing down my sadness and fear, I make it to my bedroom. Evan is sleeping on his back on what I consider his side of the bed. His chest is bare, hair mussed, and lips just barely open.

Still, I notice the furrow of his brow as though even in sleep he can't find true rest.

My heart pics up a battering ram's beat against my chest as I remove the robe and set it over my chair. Slinking to the other side of the bed, I pull back the covers and slide in.

Evan doesn't stir. Not until I shimmy over to him and hook a leg over his and an arm over his belly.

"Mmm, done writing, baby?" Evan murmurs obviously not remembering what happened earlier this evening.

I sigh and snuggle in. "I love you, and I'm so sorry, Evan," I whisper, needing him to not only know it but to feel it straight through to his bones the way I do.

His form stiffens in my arms, and my heart clenches and my throat goes dry.

He removes my arm, nudges my leg away, and sits up, pushing himself back against the headboard. Within a few seconds, my nightstand light is on and I can truly see the effect of my betrayal.

His eyes are tired and red-rimmed, dark circles underneath that weren't there before. His expression is one of agony.

Those pesky tears come back with a vengeance as I sit up cross-legged. "I need you to let me talk."

He shakes his head and his jaw tightens. "Sadie."

I reach out a hand and grab onto his thigh. "Please. When you screwed up, I let you speak. If you don't like what I'm about to say, you can kick me out of my own house."

That has his lips twitching, but he stays silent.

I swallow, firm my spine, and look straight into his eyes. "You're right. I messed up. Big time. At first, I didn't even realize what I was doing. Authors take inspiration from their lives all the time."

He moves to speak, but I press two fingers against his lips lightly and shake my head.

"It's not an excuse and it doesn't change the fact that I was wrong." I sniff as twin tears fall down my cheeks. "So wrong. When you left, my heart left with you because you own it now. I gave it to you, and I don't ever want it back."

"Sadie, baby…" he whispers, sounding emotionally ravaged.

"No! I need you to know that I didn't do it on purpose. I told you that I was having a long battle with writer's block. Then this hot football player moves in next door during a pandemic and whammo! The muse is back. Honestly, I had no idea our own love story would play out through this, but it flowed so well I just kept going. And you're right, it's almost a retelling of our story and I don't want random people to know how we met and fell in love. People that matter to us knowing, yeah. Not the world. It's too private, too special. Like handing them a piece of our hearts. I didn't see that until you painted that picture for me."

More tears fall as he reaches out, but I back away, get off the bed, and pick up his robe.

"Don't leave, sweetheart." His voice is battered and filled with need.

"I'm not. I brought you something." I pull the memory drive out of the pocket and walk over to his side of the bed and hold out my hand, palm open. "I want you to have this. It's the only remaining copy of the book. I deleted all the others. I'm giving it to you. I'll never publish it. Not ever," I choke. "Please." I get down on my knees prepared to beg and plead for my man. "Just don't let this be the end of us, because I don't think I could survive it. Not after having the love of a lifetime."

"Get up here." Evan reaches for me and drags me onto his lap.

I straddle him and burst into tears against his neck. "I love you so much. I can't lose you. I don't ever want to lose you."

He holds me against his form so tight we may have melded together. "You're not going to lose me. Never, Sadie. You're mine and I'm yours. After being without you this evening, I don't ever want to experience that again. You've become a part of me."

"I'm so so sorry," I sob against his skin, my tears wetting his neck and chest. "I hate myself for what I did. Risking our love like that."

He tunnels his fingers into the long waves of my hair and cups my head forcing me to back away from my perfect hidey hole against his neck.

"You didn't do it on purpose and our love story is special. I can see wanting to share something so beautiful, but I agree. It's ours and you giving up the only copy of your book, coming here, crying a river? It says it all. It proves I'm more important to you than anything. And Sadie, I feel the same. I'd give up everything for you. To have you in my life, in my bed, as my other half. I plan on marrying you when all this is over, sweetheart. Nothing between us ever again."

He wants to marry me.

I explode into another bout of wracking sobs.

"Come here." He cuddles me against his chest until the tears and sorrow abate and my breathing starts to normalize. "You done? Can I kiss you now?"

I smile, lift my head, and nod.

He takes my mouth in the sweetest touch of lips to lips. I sigh into his kiss and he takes it deeper, his tongue sliding tantalizingly against mine in a series of long then short licks.

"You know what the best part of fighting is?" he whispers, sliding his tongue along the column of my neck before nipping the lobe of my ear.

I gasp. "What?"

"Make up sex. Lots and lots of makeup sex." He thrusts his hard cock against my center.

"Oh, hell yeah!" I grind down against his erection as he dips both hands into the back of my panties and palms and squeezes my ass.

"Top off, now! Give me my pretty tits," he demands, and I'm quick to oblige.

I rip my top off, lift one of my breasts, and feed it to my man. He sucks on the tip with gusto, growling with the effort.

"Other one," he barks.

He sucks and twirls his tongue over to my other breast while I grind along with his thrusts, ramping up my desire a hundred-fold.

"Both at once," he insists.

Wanting to give him everything, and wanting his mouth on both my breasts, I press my globes together and watch in awe as his tongue sucks at each erect nipple, making them bright red with the effort.

"These tits. I can't get enough of them." He pushes my hands away and palms them both, watching avidly as he pinches each tip.

He keeps going until I feel small bites of pain. I arch into the sensation and dry hump his length. My panties are soaked and I'm ready to be fucked.

"Evan, need you, honey," I say before it turns into a cry of pleasure under his skilled ministrations.

"Sit up."

Mindless, I do as he asks and ease up to my knees. The sides of my panties are small strips of elastic which he takes no time at all ripping and shredding with his bare hands.

Arousal flares inside me so intense my pussy clenches and my clit throbs.

"Saw your pills in the bathroom this week. Got tested when the team did their other tests. You know I'm clean and I trust you."

"I'm clean." I lick my lips and look down at his lap. The tip of his dick is visible at the band of his boxer briefs as though it's trying to escape on its own.

He shifts his underwear down, and I reach back and yank them the rest of the way past his legs and feet.

"Hop on, want just you and me."

God, how I want that too. Taking no time at all, I straddle him, lining up his rounded crown with my slit, and ease him inside. It's a tight fit in this position but I wouldn't stop for a million dollars. I work my hips in a circle, wetting his cock with my essence which makes it a much easier slide home.

A series of words flutter across my mind.

Full.

Home.

Love.

Us.

"Jesus, Sadie, you feel good. Never had better, baby. Not ever." He wraps his arms around my back, gliding his fingers through my hair before taking my mouth.

The kiss turns into a marathon that ends up with me riding his cock fast and hard.

When I come the first time, he takes me through it, pulls me off, and turns me onto my hands and knees. Then he notches his cock at my entrance and slams home.

I cry out and drop my head forward moving with the power of him taking me from behind. He's absolutely massive in this position. He fucks me so hard my tits bounce and my teeth rattle, but I keep rearing back against him, wanting more.

"My girl wants a brutal fucking, huh?"

"Yes!" I scream out. "Harder," I beg, wanting him to merge with me so completely we can't figure out where one person starts and the other ends.

"Your wish, my command, princess." He growls, cups my shoulder, and pounds into me.

I see stars. Beautiful lights flickering magical colors as the pleasure spirals into a vortex of nothing but ecstasy.

My entire body is misted in sweat as he fucks me. This is

not lovemaking but then again, it still is because it's us. Sadie and Evan. Finding what makes us both happy.

A bliss so intense shoots through my bent form forcing me to arc powerfully into each wave of desire. My second orgasm soars through my system, heating my blood, sending sizzling electricity through every neuron and pore until I'm utterly lost to the sensations.

"Fuck, yeah! You can take more!" he growls. Then he reaches a beefy hand around my body to cover a breast and hauls me up until my back is plastered against his front. Evan jackhammers into my body with his thick cock from behind destroying me all over again with unbelievable pleasure. Not like anything I've ever known.

For a long time, he takes me as though he can't stop, won't stop. His body shakes and trembles with the effort to continue fucking me.

I reach an arm around his body to cup the back of his head. I ease a shoulder back so I can move my head to the side. "Kiss me," I demand.

His mouth crashes over mine. I take his tongue, suck it hard, and then his entire body jerks and convulses, his cock shooting hotly inside me. He keeps going until his body finally slows, and he gently slides in and out of me as though he doesn't want to leave.

"Evan, honey, you can't fuck me forever…as much as I'd like you to."

His response is a grunt.

Apparently intense sex turns my man into a Neanderthal. Good to know.

Finally, he stops moving his hips. The space where our bodies meet is now just a messy playland of our combined releases.

"Shower?" I suggest, and his eyes light up.

Instead of an answer, I get another grunt, and he sweeps me into his arms and heads toward my bathroom.

Once we get there, he sets me down. His eyes are dark and wild with love and lust.

I wrap my arms around his neck and focus on his handsome face, wanting to pour everything that's in my soul into this moment.

"You forgive me?"

He nods.

"You still love me?"

He smiles.

"You want to marry me one day?"

"Would marry you tomorrow if I could, Sadie."

I grin wide. "I love you so much. I'll never forsake what we have again. I promise."

He dips his face so close our noses touch. "I believe you and I love you too."

♡

## EVAN

Later that day I'm plating up lunch. A sandwich and salad for me, a sandwich and chips for Sadie, when my phone rings from where I left it in the living room. We're back in Jake's apartment because that's where all the food is. And Gloria the fat cat.

Sadie comes around the counter and looks at our plates. "Why you would willingly eat a salad instead of chips is beyond me." She hands me my ringing phone.

I glance at the display and it says Unknown Number. I've been avoiding them because most of them are going to be people I don't want to talk to. Sadie enjoys those calls. My woman loses her mind every time a press call comes through. I've taken to handing her those calls. She uses her vast vocabulary to make every last one of them feel like total slime. Because that's what they are. Slime-coated vultures wanting a piece of our story. I've already made my formal statements. Did all the interviews I'm going to do. Now it's time to live my life.

Against my better judgement, I click accept and put the damn thing to my ear.

"Yeah?" I answer because this isn't a 'hello, how are you' type situation.

"Um, Mr. Sparks, I assume?"

"Yeah, you got him. What do you want?"

"This is Lieutenant Browne from the Oakland Police Department. I wanted to follow up with you."

"Already gave my statement, man. Got nothing more to say."

"Actually I just wanted to let you know that we've charged Donald Bates and Mindy Goode."

"No shit?"

Sadie frowns while holding a chip in front of her and mouths, "What?"

I shake my head and hold a finger up to her.

"Ms. Goode confessed. Mr. Bates has taken a plea deal to avoid a maximum sentence."

"What does that mean for me?"

"Well, first and foremost, I wanted to tell you they can't hurt you and they will serve time, although it likely won't be much. Since Mindy gave us everything and came clean first, she will get three months in jail and have to do a year of community service."

I grin. "Nice. And Coach Bates?"

"Up to a year in jail with the possibility of release in six months for good behavior. He will have three years of community service and can't ever hold a position in a sports-related field again. Not that he'd be able to get one."

"Did, uh, did he happen to mention why he did what he did? I'm still unclear as to why I was targeted."

"Oh yeah. He said you were up for renewal of a fourteen-million-dollar contract."

"So?"

"Well, turns out the investors told him that if he could cut several million, he'd get a million in bonus. Apparently, that wife of his is bleeding him dry. With you out of the picture, the next running back was worth far less. Multi-millions less without a solid record and history under his belt. However, Bates also didn't want you being picked up by a competing team."

"You're kidding? He wanted to ruin me and my reputation so he'd score a million-dollar payout? He tried to destroy my entire life for cash?"

A hammer slamming against my chest would have hurt less. I rub at the sore spot I feel at my heart. A man I cared about, thought cared about me, willingly fucked me over for money. Before I know it, my woman's arms wrap around me from behind, her forehead to my back, soaking me with her love and comfort.

"That's whack," I mumble, trying not to let my extreme anger out.

"It is. And between me and you, and on behalf of the entire Oakland PD who are all huge fans of the Marauders and yours, as well as being a member of a brotherhood, he deserves more than he got."

I smile. "Yeah, well, he lost his reputation, his career, and his freedom. The exact things he tried to steal from me. So, I guess when it's all said and done, I won."

Sadie's arms tighten around my body.

I finish the call and drop the phone to the counter. I spin around and look into Sadie's beautiful face.

"If all of this hadn't happened, I would never have met you."

"Now that's a silver lining." She smiles prettily. A smile I want to look at for the rest of my life.

"Yeah, it is. Because in all of this, I not only won against him, I won the girl too."

She grins, her arms wrapped around me, her chin resting on my chest. "Can we eat now?"

I dip my head and take her mouth in a soft kiss.

"Yeah, baby, we can eat."

She attempts to let me go but I grip her tighter. Her brow furrows. "What is it?"

I chuckle and just look at her. "Who could have imagined through all of this, the scandal, your writer's block, me hiding out in Jake's place, that I'd find the woman of my dreams and fall in love under quarantine."

"Love Under Quarantine?"

"Yeah." I run my hands down to her spectacular ass and give it a little squeeze.

"That would have been an awesome book title." She winks and then stands up on her toes and takes my mouth in a sweet kiss.

"Nah, nobody would read it anyway," I tease, half-joking.

She giggles and I walk her back over to our lunch.

Yep. A lifetime of being quarantined with Sadie...won't be enough.

I'll always want more.

*The End*

# KYLIE SCOTT
## Titles

**Stage Dive Series**

*Lick*

*Play*

*Lead*

*Deep*

*Strong*

*Closer*

**Dive Bar Series**

*Dirty*

*Twist*

*Chaser*

*Trust*

**Flesh Series**

*Flesh*

*Skin*

*Flesh Series Shorts*

# AUDREY CARLAN

## Titles

### Biker Beauties
*Biker Babe*
*Biker Beloved*
*Biker Brit*
*Biker Boss*

### International Guy Series
*Paris*
*New York*
*Copenhagen*
*Milan*
*San Francisco*
*Montreal*
*London*
*Berlin*
*Washington, D.C.*
*Madrid*
*Rio*
*Los Angeles*

### Lotus House Series
*Resisting Roots*
*Sacred Serenity*
*Divine Desire*
*Limitless Love*
*Silent Sins*
*Intimate Intuition*
*Enlightened End*

**Trinity Trilogy**

*Body*

*Mind*

*Soul*

*Life*

*Fate*

**Calendar Girl**

*January*

*February*

*March*

*April*

*May*

*June*

*July*

*August*

*September*

*October*

*November*

*December*

**Falling Series**

*Angel Falling*

*London Falling*

*Justice Falling*

# ACKNOWLEDGEMENTS

We'd like to thank the amazing team of people who helped us make this book happen so quickly!

First and foremost our thanks go to our extraordinarily considerate and supremely talented editor **Jeanne De Vita**. You took on this project not knowing what you were going to get and stuck by us chapter by chapter. We are humbled by your commitment and support.

To **Jena Brignola** our graphics designer for knocking out an incredible cover with zero time allotted for messing around. You blow us away with your ability and craft.

To **Amy Tannenbaum** for being the most awesome and incredibly accepting agent in the world. You found out two of your authors were working together and championed the pairing from the beginning and got right to work the minute we notified you. Simply astounding what you're capable of.

To **Jeananna Goodall** for not only introducing Kylie & Audrey but for also planting the seed that the two of us should work together.

To our beta team **Tracey Wilson-Vuolo, Tammy Hamilton-Green, and Gabriela McEachern** for being the most incredible cheerleaders and support system two women a world apart could ever have. We can't thank you enough for reading every chapter and giving your feedback daily. It was above and beyond the call of duty and we are so grateful.

To our photographer **Brian Kaminski** for the utterly perfect image that graces this cover, you are magic with a lens.

To the **Readers**, we couldn't do what we do and provide for our families with you. Your support is everything. Thank you from

From AUDREY to **KYLIE**

I'm feeling very schmoopy about you right now. Thank you for considering me when you came up with this grand idea of a couple falling in love during the pandemic. It really gave me something beautiful to focus on during such an ordeal in real life. On top of that, I feared writing with a partner but have always wanted to try it. I can't believe how easy and exciting it was, especially in light of the fact that we are on different continents! I look forward to writing more books with you in the future. The possibilities are endless lady! Madlove. AC

# *About*
# KYLIE SCOTT

Kylie is a *New York Times* and *USA Today* best-selling author. She was voted Australian Romance Writer of the year, 2013, 2014, 2018 & 2019, by the Australian Romance Writer's Association and her books have been translated into twelve different languages. She is a long time fan of romance, rock music, and B-grade horror films. Based in Queensland, Australia with her two children and husband, she reads, writes and never dithers around on the Internet.

Facebook: www.facebook.com/kyliescottwriter

Instagram: www.instagram.com/authorkyliescott

Twitter: twitter.com/KylieScottbooks

Bookbub: www.bookbub.com/authors/kylie-scott

Website: www.kyliescott.com

Reader Group: www.facebook.com/groups/599197093487040

Goodreads: www.goodreads.com/author/show/6476625.Kylie_ Scott

Bookbub: www.bookbub.com/authors/kylie-scott

Amazon: www.amazon.com/Kylie-Scott/e/B009CJ8188

# *About*
# AUDREY CARLAN

Audrey Carlan is a #1 *New York Times*, *USA Today*, and *Wall Street Journal* bestselling author. She writes wicked hot love stories that are designed to give the reader a romantic experience that's sexy, sweet, and so hot your ereader might melt. Some of her works include the worldwide phenomenon Calendar Girl Serial, Trinity Series and the International Guy Series. Her books have been translated into over 30 languages across the globe.

## NEWSLETTER
For new release updates and giveaway news, sign up for Audrey's newsletter: audreycarlan.com/sign-up

## SOCIAL MEDIA
Audrey loves communicating with her readers. You can follow or contact her on any of the following:

Website: www.audreycarlan.com
E-mail: audrey.carlanpa@gmail.com
Facebook: www.facebook.com/AudreyCarlan
Twitter: twitter.com/AudreyCarlan
Pinterest: www.pinterest.com/audreycarlan1
Instagram: www.instagram.com/audreycarlan
Readers Group: www.facebook.com/groups/
AudreyCarlanWickedHotReaders
BookBub: www.bookbub.com/authors/audrey-carlan
Goodreads: www.goodreads.com/author/show/7831156.
Audrey_Carlan
Amazon: www.amazon.com/Audrey-Carlan/e/B00JAVVG8U

Lightning Source UK Ltd.
Milton Keynes UK
UKHW011030260720
367199UK00001B/182